P9-DKD-957

A vision of Pete naked, with warm water glazing his skin, flashed into her mind.

Mary Rose shook her head hard and sat down on the sofa, sifting through the magazines on Pete's coffee table, mostly law enforcement publications and racing rags. The summer they were together, she recalled, he'd read all the golf journals...and the racing rags. Some things never changed.

But some things did. Ten years ago—July 7, to be exact—she'd married Pete Mitchell. They'd lived together for a little over a month in the one-room apartment he'd rented, sharing the cheap furniture that came with the place, subsistence groceries and the red Mustang her parents had given her as a graduation present. Not to mention the fantastic sex.

After ten years they were obviously different people, at different points in their lives, not the kids they'd been long ago. Mary Rose didn't act on impulse anymore. She considered options, made plans, evaluated results. Yet after ten years, here she was again... in Pete Mitchell's place.

The Third Mrs. Mitchell

Lynnette Kent

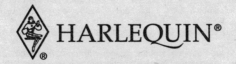

TORONTO • NEW YORK • LONDON
AMSTERDAM • PARIS • SYDNEY • HAMBURG
STOCKHOLM • ATHENS • TOKYO • MILAN • MADRID
PRAGUE • WARSAW • BUDAPEST • AUCKLAND

If you purchased this book without a cover you should be aware
that this book is stolen property. It was reported as "unsold and
destroyed" to the publisher, and neither the author nor the
publisher has received any payment for this "stripped book."

For Kathy, Barbara and Julie,
my sisters…in law and so much more.

ISBN 0-373-71080-1

THE THIRD MRS. MITCHELL

Copyright © 2002 by Cheryl Bacon.

All rights reserved. Except for use in any review, the reproduction or
utilization of this work in whole or in part in any form by any electronic,
mechanical or other means, now known or hereafter invented, including
xerography, photocopying and recording, or in any information storage
or retrieval system, is forbidden without the written permission of the
publisher, Harlequin Enterprises Limited, 225 Duncan Mill Road,
Don Mills, Ontario, Canada M3B 3K9.

All characters in this book have no existence outside the imagination of
the author and have no relation whatsoever to anyone bearing the same
name or names. They are not even distantly inspired by any individual
known or unknown to the author, and all incidents are pure invention.

This edition published by arrangement with Harlequin Books S.A.

® and TM are trademarks of the publisher. Trademarks indicated with
® are registered in the United States Patent and Trademark Office, the
Canadian Trade Marks Office and in other countries.

Visit us at www.eHarlequin.com

Printed in U.S.A.

Dear Reader,

As a navy wife, I appreciated the opportunity to travel
across the United States and see firsthand the amazing
diversity and beauty of this country. When the time came
for my husband to retire, however, the choice of where to
go was never in doubt…we couldn't imagine settling down
outside the South. Neighborhoods where all the children
play together and treat each other's houses, and parents,
as their own, backyard vegetable gardens and lazy, sun-
soaked summers, honeysuckle vines and moss-draped
live oak trees—these are our childhood memories, this
the lifestyle we wanted our daughters to experience.
We've come close to our ideal in North Carolina, although
the bustle of the modern world now penetrates all but the
remotest country retreats. These days, even rural backwaters
have their Internet cafés, rush-hour traffic and crime
statistics.

Still, I have a deep affection for the real South and the
people who live here. And so I'm offering Superromance
readers a series of books set in a small Southern town,
stories about folks who stayed nearby after high school or
who have come back to make a home in the place where
they were born. There's plenty of material to draw from,
since life gets complicated when you know everybody and
they all know you, when your smallest transgression is the
main topic of conversation the next morning over breakfast
at the local diner!

Sometimes, though, the place that's all too familiar
is the best place to make a brand-new start. In
The Third Mrs. Mitchell, Mary Rose Bowdrey discovers
that coming home means dealing with the mistakes and
misjudgments of the past… not to mention Pete Mitchell,
the man she's never quite managed to forget. Pete's got his
life all planned out; after two failed marriages, he's taken

himself out of the relationship game permanently. But when these ex-lovers keep running into each other, their best intentions aren't enough to keep love from having its own way.

I hope you enjoy the first book in my AT THE CAROLINA DINER series. I love to hear from readers—feel free to write me at my new address: PMB 304, Westwood Shopping Center, Fayetteville, NC 28314.

All the best,

Lynnette Kent

Books by Lynnette Kent

HARLEQUIN SUPERROMANCE

Watch for the next book in Lynnette Kent's AT THE CAROLINA DINER series, *The Ballad of Dixon Bell*, coming in March 2003.

Don't miss any of our special offers. Write to us at the following address for information on our newest releases.

Harlequin Reader Service
U.S.: 3010 Walden Ave., P.O. Box 1325, Buffalo, NY 14269
Canadian: P.O. Box 609, Fort Erie, Ont. L2A 5X3

CHAPTER ONE

THE RED PORSCHE flashed by at an impressive 84.7 miles per hour.

Parked within the deep shade of the pine trees in the median, Pete Mitchell sighed, pushed his shades up on his nose, then flipped the switch for the siren and the lights and eased his patrol car into the northbound lane of Interstate 95. Another day, another speeder, another hundred dollars for the county.

Traffic was light at 3:00 p.m. on a Thursday and he caught up with the Porsche before five miles had passed, noting the South Carolina license plate. The driver glanced in the rearview mirror as he moved over behind her in the right lane. Her fist hit the steering wheel in frustration.

"Gotcha," Pete told her with a grin, staying close as she slowed to a stop on the shoulder of the highway. After checking for oncoming traffic, he eased out of the car and set his hat straight on his head, then took his time getting to the driver's window.

The windowpane slid down as he came close. A long slender arm stretched out with a driver's license and registration sheet clipped between two pink-frosted fingertips. The diamond tennis bracelet weighing down that elegant left hand could easily have doubled as a handcuff.

"Trying out for a NASCAR berth, ma'am?" Pete slid the papers free. "I think you've confused Interstate 95 with Darlington Speedway.'' He turned on his toe to head back to the cruiser, but one glance at the license stopped him cold. Taking off his shades, he checked out the name again. Looked at the face in the picture. Swore under his breath.

Mary Rose Bowdrey. Born May 1, 1974. Height, five-eight; weight, one-thirty. That hadn't changed in ten years. Eyes, blue—the color, as he remembered, of the Atlantic Ocean at noon on a sunny day. Hair, blond—a rich gold shot through with streaks of silver which didn't show up in the lousy license photo. Pete hadn't known her long enough or well enough to be sure whether all that color was natural or not.

After all, they'd only been married thirty-six days.

He pivoted back to the window, automatically taking off his hat. ''Mary Rose?''

The red door swung open. The best legs on Hilton Head Island during the summer of 1992—and probably every year since—unfolded into the sunlight. In one smooth move, Ms. Bowdrey stood up out of the car and faced him, pushing up the sleeves of her navy-blue sweater, tucking strands of shiny, shoulder-length hair behind her ears. ''I don't believe this. Pete?''

''That's right.'' He needed a second to remember the next line. ''Uh…how are you?'' His mama always said good manners could salvage even the most bizarre situations. ''It's been a long time.'' Not that he could tell by looking at the woman in front of him. Still sleek as a cat, this Mary Rose could be the eighteen-year-old girl he'd spent that summer with. Married.

Worked so damn hard to forget.

His first ex-wife gave him a beauty-queen smile. ''That it has. I'm fine. How about you?'' With a faint clink of diamonds and gold, her hands slipped into the pockets of her short white skirt, heading off any impulse he might have felt to give her a hug. She kept her dark sunglasses on, so he couldn't read the expression in those marine-blue eyes.

Pete didn't need an interpreter for this message: *Keep your distance* was as clear as the nearby billboard for fast food and gas. "I'm good. Where're you headed?"

"New Skye. I'll be visiting my sister for a little while."

"That so?" He'd have felt better if she'd said the sky was falling. The possibility of Mary Rose spending more than an afternoon in the same county he lived in, let alone the same town, was big-time bad news.

Why couldn't he have been asleep when the Porsche passed through?

Pete shook off the feeling of dread creeping up his spine. "Well, it looks to me like you're in kind of a hurry to get there. Speed limit's sixty on this stretch of road, you know."

Mary Rose bit her bottom lip, which was frosted with the same pink as her fingernails. "I guess I wasn't watching the speedometer. I'll slow down from now on. I promise."

"I hope so." Pete turned toward the cruiser again. "You get back in the car. I'll be with you in a couple of minutes."

Standard procedure didn't use up much brain space, which was good because Pete registered a definite lack of available cells at the moment. Working on autopilot, he wrote up the ticket, logged in the information and ran a check on Mary Rose's license. There were no outstanding violations on her record, which probably meant she'd talked the other suckers who pulled her over out of writing her up. Maybe she took off her sunglasses for them.

When he handed the citation through the Porsche's window, Mary Rose gazed up at him, her mouth open in surprise. "You're giving me a ticket?"

"You can contest the charge in court. There's a trial date on the sheet. If you fail to appear, your plea of guilty will be assumed and you'll be expected to pay the full fine."

"But…" She pressed her lips together for a second, then relaxed them into a sweet, coaxing curve he remembered all too well. "Come on, Pete. There's no traffic. I wasn't hurting anybody. Can't you let this one go?"

He wasn't even tempted. "Sorry. You keep it under the speed limit from now on, all right?" Tipping his hat, he stepped back, needing to get away. Fast. "Good seeing you again, Mary Rose. Take care."

Mary Rose watched through the rearview mirror as Pete Mitchell returned to his car. The man was still seriously gorgeous, being possessed of wide shoulders, narrow hips and a tight butt, plus those light gray, dark lashed eyes gleaming like polished pewter in his tanned face. When they were together all those years ago, he'd worn his black hair pulled back in a short ponytail, but the regulation highway-patrol buzz cut wasn't bad at all. A little austere, maybe, but Pete had always been a straight-arrow kind of guy at heart.

That was why he'd married her in the first place, right? You got a girl in trouble, you took responsibility. If you were lucky, she lost the baby and set you free.

Her ex-husband had been nothing but lucky.

Blowing an irritated breath off her lower lip, Mary Rose put the car in gear, checked for traffic and eased into the sparse flow. Pete followed in his cruiser; while she kept the needle carefully set at sixty, he breezed past her with a wave.

"Oh, of course." She hit the heel of her hand on the steering wheel. "Mr. Big Shot doesn't have to obey the speed limit." She threw him a furious glance as he took the next exit, once again vanishing from her life.

Or maybe not. He had grown up in New Skye, graduated in the same class with her older sister, Kate. Did he still live there? What were the chances she might see him again while she was in town?

Mary Rose shuddered at the thought, tempted to turn around and head straight back to Charleston, damn the speed limit.

But running away was not an option. Kate was in deep trouble. She sounded more desperate with every phone call.

And not even the possibility of another encounter with the man she'd never quite managed to forget was going to keep Mary Rose from standing by her sister during the worst days of her life.

Fifteen minutes after leaving her ex-husband behind, Mary Rose took the interstate exit for the town of New Skye, North Carolina. She hadn't been home for at least six years; her final Christmas in college had been her last visit, despite her parents' repeated invitations. Nobody climbed the ladder of success in the business world by indulging themselves with extended vacations. This was the first time since graduate school she'd taken off more than five business days in a row.

Anyway, it wasn't as if she never saw her family. They all spent a week together in the condo at the beach every summer and a week skiing in Colorado every January. She talked to her parents once a week and chatted with Kate and her kids whenever either of them had a spare hour or so. That was as much family togetherness as Mary Rose, personally, could stand.

So now she studied her hometown with interest as she drove through. The outskirts of New Skye—with its service stations and fast-food restaurants, the water-treatment plant, the police academy, the firefighters' training tower—could have been any small town in the Southeast. Plenty of asphalt, few trees and the flat Sandhills landscape did little to invite a traveler to linger longer than it took to get a tank of gas.

But then she turned off the commercial strip to drive slowly along Main Street, toward Courthouse Circle. This wasn't the dead downtown scene she remembered from her high-school years. On each side of the newly bricked street, antique shops, coffee bars and cafés inhabited what had once been empty storefronts, or worse, bars and pick-up joints. The old movie house had been renovated and was showing an art film she'd seen advertised recently in New York. Huge pots of pansies and daffodils punctuated the sidewalks underneath newly-leafing pear trees.

Mary Rose clicked her tongue in amazement. New Skye had certainly changed for the better in her absence.

She was glad to see that some things remained the same, like the Victorian elegance of the county courthouse, standing tall on its island of bright green grass. Traffic circled around the red brick, white-columned building, one of the oldest in town—the fire of 1876 had destroyed all of the business district except the Presbyterian and Methodist churches, the courthouse and the Velvet Rose Tavern. Thankfully, the Velvet Rose had succumbed to its own fire only a couple of decades later. The downtown branch of the public library—still functioning, still imposing with its white marble—had been built in its place.

On the far side of Courthouse Circle, Main Street followed a single hill rising up out of the flat terrain. On top were some of New Skye's finest residences, built mostly in the early 1900s, though a few dated back to before "The War." Mary Rose doubted that the folks in Charleston, where an old building might claim construction in 1725, would be terribly impressed with New Skye's "historic district." Looking at the area with a fresh perspective, though, she thought the wide porches, fancy columns and wrought-iron fences were charming.

Kate's home was one of the largest and grandest on The Hill. A semicircular porch graced the front of the three-story white house; the magnolias flanking either side of the brick walk must have been fifty feet tall and a hundred years old. Thankful to be done with driving, Mary Rose parked at the curb and got out, stretching her arms above her head.

As she started across the grass, the front door opened and her sister stepped onto the porch, looking for all the world like a Southern belle from the distant past. A cloud of soft dark curls framed her oval face and graceful neck. She was tall and slender...alarmingly so.

"Have you forgotten how to fry chicken and cook gravy?" Mary Rose took hold of her sister with a tight hug. "You're skinny as a rail."

Kate pulled back to laugh at her. "Says the woman who weighs all of a hundred pounds."

"One thirty-five, as a matter of fact. I've developed a passion for frappuccino with my morning bagel."

"Then it's a good thing we've got a café here on The Hill that makes them perfectly. Come into the house." They stepped out of warm spring sunlight into the cool, gleaming perfection of Kate's home.

"This is beautiful." Mary Rose surveyed the parlor's rich combination of purple and gold fabric with mahogany antiques. "You do know how to dress a room."

Kate waved her into a chair on one side of the fireplace. "How was your drive? You must have left early to be here so soon."

"I drive fast," Mary Rose said, and then frowned as she remembered.

"What's wrong?"

"I, um, got stopped by a state trooper just a little ways south of town."

"Did he give you a ticket?" Mary Rose nodded soberly, but her sister just smiled. "Don't worry, honey. The D.A.'s wife is a member of my Sunday-school class at church. I'll get her to talk to him about dismissing the fine."

"That's not the worst part." She took a deep breath. "The trooper was Pete Mitchell."

Kate gave her a blank stare. "Mitchell? Who…? Oh." She pressed her fingertips against her lips. "*That* Pete Mitchell? Did he remember you?"

"He definitely remembered." And the distance in those cool gray eyes had warned her that the memory wasn't a pleasant one. "It's kind of hard to forget being married, even for only a month."

Kate shook her head. "I haven't seen him in years. I guess I thought he'd moved away." She faced the mantel and made unnecessary adjustments to the perfect placement of the Wedgwood teacups arranged there. "Do you suppose you'll run into him again? I'd hate to have you uncomfortable while you're here, worrying about meeting up with your ex-husband. That's so…difficult." The last word trembled with despair.

Mary Rose came up behind her sister, putting her arms around the thin shoulders. "I'm not worried about it one way or the other. It's not like I've been moping over him for ten years."

Kate's head rested heavily on her shoulder. "And then there's your job. I can't believe you just up and left, during tax season, no less. Are you sure they'll let you go back? What about all your clients?"

"All my clients got their taxes filed before the first of April because I pushed and prodded and nagged them to. I filed mine in February. And if the bank doesn't want me back…well, too bad. I've accrued enough leave that I'd have to be here a couple of months before they could legitimately fire me. And they won't. I make them too much money. So stop worrying about that." She turned Kate around to face her. "What I'm worried about is you. You look so tired."

Kate's smile failed to dispel her very real air of exhaustion. "There's a lot of yard work to be done, now that it's spring. Plus the auction at the children's school, which we just finished up, and the Azalea Festival, not to mention all the usual driving to lessons and practices and such. I've been…busy."

She obviously didn't want to go into any more detail right this minute, or explain why her husband, even after moving out of the house, couldn't assume some responsibility for his children.

Mary Rose tapped the pads of her fingers gently on her sister's pale cheeks. "That's why I'm here, to take over some of the routine stuff. I can handle the driving, and help you with the garden, and do some cooking, too, though you might be sorry you let me in the kitchen. Just tell me what's on the list."

"Well…" Kate bit her lip, hesitating.

"Seriously. What can I do for you right this minute?"

With a sigh, her sister gave in. "If you brought Kelsey and Trace home from the soccer game at school, I could get the laundry caught up. Mama and Daddy are coming for dinner for your first night here and I need to put the roast in—''

''Consider it done. Just give me your keys. I can't fit two other people in the Porsche.'' Jingling Kate's key chain, Mary Rose headed for the front door. ''New Skye High, right? They haven't moved it or anything?''

''You could drive there blindfolded,'' Kate called across the front lawn. ''Nothing has changed out that way in the last twenty years!''

''MY TURN.'' Kelsey held out her hand for the soda can. Beside her, Lisa took a quick slurp before passing the drink.

''No fair! I bought it, didn't I? You didn't even leave me half.'' Tipping her head back, Kelsey chugged the rest of the contents, feeling the whiskey burn as it slid down her throat.

''You got the first drink. Anyway, there's more soda in the machine.'' Her friend leaned close, lowered her voice. ''And half a bottle of Jack Black in the car.''

''True.'' The smoky liquor swirled in her head, and Kelsey smiled. ''What's the score now, anyway?'' Out on the soccer field, red and gold New Skye jerseys chased across the grass, blurred into green Clinton High uniforms, separated out again. She couldn't see clearly enough to make out the numbers.

Lisa squinted into the distance. ''Score's tied one to one.'' She hiccuped loudly and then started to laugh. Helplessly, Kelsey laughed with her, leaning against Lisa's shoulder until they both tilted back on the bleacher bench into the knees of the girls behind them.

''Kelsey? Is that you?''

Oh shit. A teacher. Kelsey straightened up and tried to stop giggling as she turned toward the person standing on the ground, staring up. She blinked hard, bringing the face into focus. It wasn't a teacher. For a second, she didn't recognize the woman at all. Blond and thin and tan and...

"Aunt M!" She never knew how she made it to the ground, just that she was there with her arms thrown around her favorite relative in the world. "I didn't realize you were coming today."

"Obviously." Pulling back, Mary Rose looked her sternly in the eye. "Are you all right?"

"Sure. Of course." Kelsey smoothed her hair back, wished she'd had time to pop a piece of gum. "What are you doing here?"

"Your mother asked me to pick you and Trace up after the game. It looks like that will be a while yet."

"Um..." Gazing toward the scoreboard, Kelsey couldn't read the numbers. The ground tilted under her feet and she put a hand on the nearby bleacher support to stay steady. "A few minutes, anyway."

When she looked at Mary Rose, her aunt's soft, pretty mouth had tightened and her eyes had narrowed. In that second, Kelsey knew she was doomed.

"What are you—"

"Mary Rose Bowdrey!" Mrs. Gates, the chemistry teacher, sailed toward them. "I don't believe my eyes. When did you get into town?" Very tall and very pregnant, Mrs. Gates took Mary Rose in a hug that all but swallowed her whole.

Kelsey closed her eyes. *Shit.* Mrs. Gates had graduated in the same class with Aunt Mary Rose. Judging by their enthusiasm, they must still be pretty good friends. As soon as they came up for air, they'd be sniffing her breath and treating her like a delinquent.

"Uh...Aunt Mary Rose?" She tugged at the sleeve of

a gorgeous navy sweater that had to have come from New York. "I promised my friend Lisa we'd go to the diner for a few minutes. The team always gets a milk shake after a home game." Like she didn't know that, like the kids at this school hadn't been doing the same thing for nearly forever. "Can you pick me and Trace up there?" She tried on a suck-up smile. "Would that be okay?"

Mary Rose looked as if she wanted to say no, but then she glanced at Mrs. Gates, still holding her arm. "Sure, Kelsey. That'll be fine. I'll meet you at the diner about thirty minutes after the game ends." Her expression promised there would be hell to pay afterward.

But for the time being, Kelsey was free. "Thanks!" She didn't lean in for another hug. "See ya!" Grabbing Lisa by the hand, she scurried and stumbled to the other side of the bleachers, out of the line of sight of any nosy adults.

"Here." She dug in her purse, brought up a dollar and thrust it at Lisa. "Go get two more ginger ales and meet me by your car."

But Lisa shook her head. "Game's almost over, Kelse, and I can't go home smelling like whiskey. One whiff and my mom would take away the car and the license and ground me for the rest of my life. We need to sober up."

"Screw sober." Kelsey started for the drink machine.

"I'm leaving," her friend called. "See you tomorrow."

With Lisa went the whiskey. Kelsey stopped in her tracks, shoulders slumped. She could buy her own booze—she had the fake ID Trace had made in her wallet. But she couldn't get to the liquor store without a car.

So she drifted back to the soccer field, to watch without enthusiasm as New Skye won the game. Wearily,

Kelsey followed the crowd to the diner, listened to the same stories she'd heard all day at school, ordering a cup of coffee to mask the smell of liquor on her breath.

And wondered how her life had come to be such a mess.

As far back as Pete could remember, Charlie's Carolina Diner had been the place for New Skye High kids to hang out after ball games, and tonight was no exception. Judging by the noise pouring out when he opened the door, the home team had won. Teenagers crowded into the green vinyl-covered booths along the walls, shared chairs at the tables, rotated and rocked on the silver pedestal stools at the counter that usually marked adult territory. Working his way through the chaos, Pete took the one empty stool in the back corner, under a framed poster of Elvis.

"Hey, Trooper Pete." A thick-wristed hand with a Semper Fi tattoo on the back slid a white mug of coffee his way.

"Hey yourself, Mr. B. Standing room only tonight."

Charlie Brannon nodded. "Soccer game went into double overtime, had to finish with a kickoff. NSH beat 'em three-two. What'll you have?"

After fifteen years of eating at Charlie's, Pete didn't need a menu. "Meat loaf sounds good."

"You got it." A broad man with iron-gray hair and a permanent tan, Charlie headed toward the kitchen door, his stiff-legged stride the result of an encounter with a land mine in Southeast Asia in the sixties. He still wore his hair Marine Corps short and held his shoulders as straight as if he were standing at attention. He could bark orders with the best drill sergeants, which was why incidents of actual trouble occurred less frequently at the diner than at the public library.

Pete sipped his coffee, one ear tuned to the talk around him while his brain replayed the sight of Mary Rose standing out there on the interstate in the afternoon sunshine, close enough to touch. With a single smile, the woman had cast a spell over him ten years ago.

And damned if she hadn't gone and done it again today. He'd been a basket case all afternoon, thinking about Mary Rose Bowdrey. What was his problem that he couldn't get her out of his mind?

"Hey, Pete. How's it going?"

He looked up to see Abby Brannon standing on the other side of the counter with his dinner plate in her hands. "Good enough. How about you?"

"Just fine." She slid his plate in front of him, put out a ketchup bottle and moved the salt and pepper shakers closer. "You want something to drink besides coffee?"

"Tea would be great. Your dad's looking good today. Is he sticking to his diet?"

Abby didn't ask if he wanted his iced tea sweet or unsweet. She'd been pouring for customers in this town since she was twelve, and she knew everybody's preference. "As long as I stand over him like a hawk and watch every bite he puts in his mouth." Setting down his glass, she blew out a frustrated breath that lifted her light brown bangs off her forehead. "I haven't been able to bake coconut pies for a month now. He steals a piece— or two or three!—in the middle of the night when I'm asleep."

Pete grinned. "Too bad. I could go for a piece of coconut cream pie."

She nodded. "You and me both. But the doctor said he needs to lose at least twenty pounds. So until he does,

I guess we're out of luck. With coconut, anyway. How about lemon meringue? Dad doesn't like lemon meringue.''

''That's a close second.''

''I'll bring you a piece when you're done.'' Pete watched as she moved down the counter, checking on drink refills, laughing with the kids as she handed over checks written out on an old-fashioned notepad. Abby wore the same uniform every day from March through October—a white T-shirt, khaki slacks and running shoes. In the cooler months she wore a white button-down shirt and a dark blue sweater.

Year-round, though, she had nice, full curves that fired a guy's imagination and got him thinking about something besides frozen pizza dinners eaten in front of the TV, or even the great food she served up at her dad's diner. Assuming the guy had options in the relationship department, of course. Some did, some didn't. After striking out at marriage—not once, but twice—Pete put himself very definitely into the second category. And so he and Abby stayed just friends.

She came back with the lemon pie. ''Did you hear that Rhonda Harding has moved home from Raleigh?''

''Yeah? I thought she had a good job with one of the research companies up there.''

''She used to, but she and her husband got divorced and her mother's sick.'' Abby glanced at him, her green eyes crinkled in a smile. ''Y'all were hot and heavy senior year.''

He shrugged and looked down at the soft peak of lemon filling on his fork. ''I had to take somebody to the prom.''

''Maybe you can pick up where you left off. You've

been living like a monk for a couple of years now, Pete. Time to explore the possibilities.''

''I am not a monk.'' His cheeks had gotten warm. ''I go out now and then.''

''With women like me—the ones you've known since kindergarten and think of as sisters. Not exactly high romantic adventure.''

''I do not think of you as a sister. And anyway, when was your last date, dear Abby?''

She took his teasing with a grin. ''I just dish it out. You have to take it.''

''Yeah, right.'' As he rolled his eyes, Pete caught sight of the clock over the counter. ''Besides which, I don't have time for—what was it?—'high romantic adventure.' I race on the weekends and weeknights I'm at school with the REWARDS program. Can you put this pie in a box for me? I need to get set up before the kids start coming in at seven.''

''No problem.''

He was on his feet and thumbing through the bills in his wallet when the bell on the front door jingled. A single glance at the new arrival set him to swearing under his breath.

Her again. How bad could his luck get?

She'd pushed the sunglasses up on top of her head. Now he could see the deep blue of her eyes as she surveyed the crowded room, obviously searching for somebody. Not him, of course. Pete gave a second's thought to the idea that he might escape out the back of the diner before he got caught.

Not a chance. Before he could move, she looked his way. And frowned. Mary Rose wasn't any happier to see him than he was to see her.

That made him mad…and made him determined to

talk to her. He put the cash for dinner down on the counter, stowed his wallet in his back pocket and headed across the room.

"Hello, there." He had to stand fairly close to her to be heard over the noise, close enough to note the softness of her skin, the cute curves of her eyebrows. "Taking a tour of the old stomping grounds?"

The frown smoothed out into a tolerant smile. "Looking for my niece and nephew, actually. They were at the soccer game and said they were coming here afterward. I was talking to Lydia Gates and didn't realize how much time had passed. But I'm supposed to get Kelsey and Trace home for dinner."

"Hard to find anybody in this mob." Was it his imagination that she smelled like honeysuckle?

"Especially with you standing right in front of me." Mary Rose kept her smile steady, but she fully intended the insult. Having Pete Mitchell this close was interfering with breath and thought, with sanity itself. Damn the man, anyway. Why hadn't he eaten at home tonight? Seeing him twice in one day was simply two times too many.

His dark eyebrows lowered as he stepped to the side. "Sorry. I'll leave you to your search."

"Thanks." The tension eased a little as he moved toward the door. She turned around, pretending to look for the kids, but all she could really see was Pete's face in her mind's eye—the strongly set jaw, the well-shaped mouth, those serious silver eyes.

"Pete!" Abby Brannon held out a box from behind the counter. "You forgot your pie!" Her voice carried easily over all the noise.

Without seeing him at all, Mary Rose felt Pete hesitate, felt him appraise the necessity of brushing past her to get the box, then having to turn around to face her where she stood in front of the door.

"Keep it for me," he shouted, his voice deep, a little rough. "I'll pick it up tomorrow morning." The bell on the handle jingled harshly as the glass door was opened, then swung closed.

Mary Rose drew a deep breath. *Score one for our side.* She'd managed to drive Pete Mitchell completely off the premises...a trick she'd never quite managed when it came to her heart.

AS USUAL, Pete got home late. Running the REWARDS program meant that he spent four nights a week at the high school. He rarely had a chance to relax before 10:00 or 11:00 p.m.

Even on a bad day, though, he didn't begrudge the effort. Respect, Education, Work, Ambition, Responsibility, Dedication and Success—REWARDS—were the watchwords of his rehabilitation classes for juvenile offenders. He'd realized a long time ago that these at-risk kids needed somebody to draw the line between them and the life that would destroy them. A good group of volunteers in the police, sheriff and highway patrol offices joined him in standing that line.

He hadn't exaggerated when he told Abby he didn't have time for romance. Besides, he did have female companionship—Miss Dixie was sitting on the back of the couch, staring out the window with her tongue dangling, when he pulled up in front of the house. She disappeared when he hopped out of the Jeep and started down the walk, but as he reached the front steps he could hear the frantic squeals and pants and barks she used as a greeting.

As soon as he had the door open, the little beagle was

leaping at his legs, almost as high as his waist. Grinning, he caught her up against his chest.

"Yeah, yeah, I hear you, Dixie, darlin'." She licked his face up one side and down the other, with a couple of swipes at his mouth for good measure. "Yeah, I know it's been a long time. I got off work late, couldn't get home before class. But I'm here now, so you get yourself outside while I make you a little snack."

At the back door, she wiggled out of his hold and headed with obvious relief for the far corner of the yard. In just minutes she was back inside, though, licking up the small scoop of food that was her reward for a day spent all alone, slurping at her refilled water bowl. Business taken care of, Pete pulled a bottle of beer from the fridge and went out onto the back deck, leaving the door open so Dixie could join him when she finished.

Slouching down on the forty-year-old glider that was the only thing he'd asked for from his grandmother's house when she passed away a few years back, he twisted the top off the beer and took a generous swig.

Man, what an afternoon. Seeing Mary Rose *twice* in the space of four hours had done a number on his brain. What if it happened again? Was he going to have to sneak around town like a burglar for fear of running into his first ex-wife?

Most of the time, Pete tended not to worry too much about the future. With his job, the future could come to a screeching halt at any minute; that was the reason his second marriage bit the dust. His second wife hadn't wanted to open the door one day to the news that her husband had died in the line of duty. Pete had accepted Sherrill's need to escape that uncertainty in the same way he accepted the uncertainty itself. *Que sera, sera.*

But tonight, the idea of turning a corner in the grocery

store and facing down Mary Rose Bowdrey had him breaking out in a cold sweat.

"Really dumb," he told Miss Dixie when she hopped up beside him on the glider. "She's just a girl I knew a long time ago."

Dixie stretched out beside him, inviting a rub on her very full stomach.

"Okay, so I knew her really well." Pete stroked his knuckles along the beagle's midline. "I couldn't get enough of her. She was like royalty—I never expected to be with somebody so...so perfect. Totally blew my mind when she walked up that day on the golf course and asked me for a lesson." He chuckled as he thought about it. "We both knew she didn't mean golf."

But then he sighed. "Major mistake, Dixie, darlin', getting involved with somebody that different." He finished the last of the beer, set the bottle on the deck and stretched out on the glider with Dixie on his chest. "Major mistake getting involved at all. I'm sticking with you, girl."

The dog closed her eyes in bliss as Pete wrinkled her ears, massaged the special spot under her chin, scratched along her back. "You're just glad to see me when I get here, aren't you, Dix? You don't spend your time worrying about me, and your only requirements are a full tummy and a soft place to sleep." He let her settle against his shoulder and propped his chin on the top of her head. "No expectations, no regrets. You're the only kind of female a man like me needs, Miss Dixie."

Pete closed his eyes and got a vision of Mary Rose's pink lips and blue gaze, the defiant lift of her chin as she stared him down in the diner.

He sighed again. "Let's just hope I can remember that little piece of wisdom when the time comes."

CHAPTER TWO

As FAR AS Mary Rose was concerned, dinner with her parents was an exercise in holding her tongue. And her temper. And her breath.

"The roast is delicious," she told Kate after a bite.

"A bit rare, I think," their mother commented. "Your father likes his meat well-done."

Judging from his focused assault with knife and fork, Mary Rose thought John Bowdrey probably liked his roast just as he'd found it. Time for a change of subject. "The game looked pretty intense, Trace. Were you playing a particularly good team?"

Without taking his eyes off his plate, Kate's son shrugged one shoulder. "I guess." He was a handsome boy, tall and rangy, with his father's blond hair cropped close. When Mary Rose had seen him last winter, he'd been the bright, enthusiastic kid she'd always known.

Then, the week after the annual family ski trip in January, Trace's dad had moved out of the house and announced his intention to divorce Kate. Mary Rose would never have guessed, witnessing L. T. LaRue's behavior in Colorado, that he had desertion on his mind.

In the months since, Trace had become sullen and uncooperative. His grades had plummeted from high A's to barely passing. Worry over him, and over Kelsey's rebellious attitude, had worn Kate to the bone. Mary Rose wasn't sure her sister even realized the full extent of the problem. There had been a distinct tang of alcohol in the air around Kelsey at the soccer game this afternoon. The girl hadn't been obviously drunk, and Mary Rose hoped that whiff of liquor had drifted from the friend trailing Kelsey. That would be the easy way out.

But she'd learned long ago that the easy way out rarely was. "It must be getting close to prom time. Are you going this year, Kelsey?"

Across the table, her niece shook her head, her blond hair gleaming with gold under the soft light of the chandelier. "It's just a stupid dance."

"It's the most important dance of the year." Frances Bowdrey pressed her napkin carefully to her lips, then gave her granddaughter a bright smile. "I can't imagine why you wouldn't want to go."

When Kelsey didn't answer, Kate did. "She's only a sophomore, Mama. She'll go next year."

Their mother rarely took no for an answer. "Oh, I'm sure some nice junior boy would be happy to take such a pretty girl to the prom."

Kelsey stared at her grandmother for a moment, her brown eyes wide and wild, her cheeks flushing deep red. Then she pushed sharply away from the table and, without a word, stalked out of the dining room. Her footsteps pounded up the staircase and along the upstairs hall, ending with the slam of her bedroom door.

Eyes round, eyebrows arched high, Frances looked at her older daughter. "What was that all about? Are you going to allow her to leave the table without being excused?"

"Mama…" Kate pressed her fingers to her lips for a second. "Surely you remember…Kelsey's boyfriend Ryan broke up with her last week. He's a junior. They would have gone to the prom together."

Frances pursed her lips. "That's no reason to be rude."

"Of course it is." Ice clanked on crystal as Mary Rose set her glass down a little too hard. "Being dumped is the world's greatest tragedy for a fifteen-year-old." She hadn't liked the experience as an eighteen-year-old, with Pete Mitchell, either. And then there was Kate's situation. "I should never have brought the subject up. I'm sorry, Katie."

Her sister shook her head. "You didn't know. I think I'd better try to talk to her. Please go on with your meal."

Neither Trace nor his grandfather needed those instructions—judging from their unswerving attention to their plates, they hadn't even heard the conversation. Mary Rose played with her mashed potatoes and listened as Kate climbed the stairs and walked down the hall. She heard a knock, but there was no sound of Kelsey's door opening.

"Well." Her mother buttered a small piece of biscuit and put it delicately in her mouth. After a sip of tea, she looked at Mary Rose. "Wouldn't you rather come home with your father and me? I'm sure our house is more restful."

Mary Rose had lost her appetite completely; she pushed her plate away and laid her napkin beside it. "I didn't come to rest, Mother. I came to give Kate some help. That will be easier if I stay here."

Trace put his fork down. "I'm going up to my room."

Beside him, his grandmother put her hand on his arm. "The appropriate way to leave the table is to ask if you can be excused."

The boy rolled his eyes. "Yeah. Whatever."

But when he tried to stand, Frances kept hold of his wrist. "Trace LaRue. You will ask politely to be excused." Watching resentment and temper flood into

Trace's brown gaze, Mary Rose wondered if her mother had pushed too far.

Then John Bowdrey looked up from his dinner. "Do as your grandmother says, Trace." His stern tone would not be argued with.

Trace's shoulders slumped. "Can I be excused? Please?"

Frances smiled and patted the back of his hand. "Of course, dear. Run and do your homework."

Mary Rose wondered if her mother heard the boy's snort as he left the dining room. "This might not be the best time for etiquette lessons, Mother. Trace and Kelsey have enough problems just handling their lives these days."

"Etiquette makes even the worst situation easier." Frances got to her feet. "Shall we clear the table?"

"Sure." Mary Rose wasn't surprised when her father simply got to his feet and left the dining room without offering to help. Her mother had him well trained—domestic responsibilities were strictly female territory.

Kate had used her fine china for dinner, which meant hand washing all the plates and the sterling silverware that went with them. Trapped at the sink in Kate's ivy-and-white kitchen, up to her wrists in suds, Mary Rose was held hostage to her mother's commentary on the state of Kate's life.

"I can't imagine what she was thinking, letting L.T. leave like that."

"He didn't give her a choice, Mother. From what Kate says, I gather he announced he was moving out, picked up his bags and did just that."

"She should have stopped him, for the children's sake."

Mary Rose blew her bangs off her forehead and

scrubbed at a spot of gravy. "How would she have stopped him? Thrown herself in front of his car? Grabbed hold of his knees, weeping and pleading? Kate has some pride, for heaven's sake."

"There are ways to hold on to a man who wants to stray." Frances Bowdrey's voice was tight, low.

When Mary Rose turned to stare, all she could see was her mother's straight back. "Mother? What—?"

Trace came into the kitchen. "Didn't Mom say there was cake?"

His grandmother turned. "I believe she made a German chocolate cake. Have a seat in the dining room and we'll bring in dessert and coffee."

He shook his head. "I'll just take a piece to my room." Despite her repeated protests, he got a plate, cut a two-inch-thick slice and poured a glass of milk, then disappeared again.

Mary Rose followed her nephew down the hall. "Trace, is your mom still talking to Kelsey?"

"Never did. Kelse wouldn't open the door. Kate's in her own room." Taking the stairs two at a time, he left her standing at the bottom.

"What a mess this is." Frances spoke from just behind Mary Rose. "I think I'd better talk to Kate. She's got to do something."

"Mother…" Mary Rose put a hand on Frances's arm to keep her from climbing the steps. "Dad's waiting on his cake. Why don't you fix his coffee and the two of you have dessert? I'll talk to Kate."

Obviously torn, the older woman glanced upstairs and then toward the living room, where her husband sat with the newspaper, his foot crossed over his knee, jiggling in a way they all knew well. "You're right. But be sure to tell Kate I'll call her tomorrow. There are things she needs to hear."

I doubt that. But Mary Rose kept her skepticism to herself as she climbed the stairs.

WITH RELIEF, Kelsey heard Kate's door open and shut, and the murmur of voices behind it. She'd been afraid Aunt Mary Rose was coming up to talk to *her* about this afternoon. About booze and teenagers and the evils thereof.

And she would really hate to have to tell her favorite aunt to go to hell, especially on her first night in the house.

She glanced at her backpack on the floor at the foot of her bed. She had two tests tomorrow, and a boatload of homework waited for her attention.

Tough shit. Rolling off the bed, Kelsey grabbed a pack of cigarettes from the bottom of her sweater drawer and stuck her head out into the hallway to be sure the coast was clear. A second later, she was closing Trace's door quietly behind her.

"Ooh, cake." She tossed him the cigarettes and snatched up the remains of his dessert. "You ate all the icing, jerk."

"That's the best part." He lit a cigarette for each of them, passing hers over as he went to open the windows. "Was that Auntie M coming upstairs?"

Kelsey drew in a deep lungful of smoke. "Had to be. Grandmother wouldn't be so quiet."

"I wish she'd stay out of our business."

"M?"

"Gran. Drives me crazy, the way she's always giving me orders. How'd we get such a witch for a grandmother, anyway?"

"I take great comfort from the fact that she's not really ours." Kate had married their dad when Trace was a baby, after their real mother had disappeared. So the Bowdreys weren't actually their grandparents at all, not by blood anyway.

"That's right. We turn eighteen, we never have to see her again."

"Hell of a long time to wait."

"Tell me about it."

They smoked together in peace for a few minutes. Trace's room was at the back corner of the house above the screened porch, with windows on two walls and big trees blocking the outside view. Kate had let him paint the walls and ceiling black and put up wildly colored posters—not rock groups, but totally weird computer-generated artwork. Some of the posters glowed in the dark; Trace's room was an eerie place to be with the lights out.

"I got Janine's ID finished," he said, rummaging through the papers piled deep beside his computer desk. "Looks good to me."

He handed over a North Carolina driver's license with a picture of her friend Janine Belks, currently a sophomore in high school, but recorded on the license as age twenty-two. Kelsey nodded. "You've got those holograms down cold. I don't think the guys at the license bureau could tell the difference."

"Just be sure you get the money before you give it to her, okay? I don't like getting ripped off."

"No problem." Another long silence flowed past. "There's a party Saturday night. Gray Hamilton's folks are going up to Chapel Hill for the soccer game. He's got the house to himself." She blew a smoke ring, then grinned. "And a hundred of his closest friends."

Trace shook his head. "Boring."

"I suppose you can do better? Like playing computer games with Ren and Stimpy?"

He gave her the finger for calling his best friends by the names of cartoon freaks. "Beats getting trashed and passing out on the floor with a bunch of drunks tripping over you."

"Gray's house has twelve bedrooms. I plan on passing out on a bed in one of those." Taking one last, long drag, Kelsey dropped the butt of her cigarette into a soda can on the windowsill. A tiny sizzle and a wisp of smoke proclaimed its demise. "Dad's supposed to pick us up Saturday morning for breakfast."

Her brother's response was vulgar and totally appropriate.

"He'll be pissed if you don't show up again."

"Am I supposed to care?"

"No." Kelsey sighed. "But I have no intention of enduring another meal with him and the Bimbo by myself. And if neither of us goes, he'll stand downstairs and yell at Kate for an hour. She doesn't deserve that."

Trace stared at the poster plastered on the ceiling above his bed, the landscape on some planet out of a heroin addict's nightmare. "I hate her." Kelsey knew he meant the Bimbo, the secretary their dad would bring to breakfast. Not Kate. Kate was all the mother he'd ever had.

She gave him the only reason that might work. "If we cooperate, maybe he'll think about coming home."

He cocked an eye in her direction. "Bullshit."

"Maybe not."

"I'll think about it."

That would have to do. "'Night." She crossed to the door, listening for sounds of someone out in the hallway.

"Kelse?"

"Yeah?"

"What's wrong with us? What else does he want?"

Kelsey rested her head against the panel and closed her eyes. "God only knows." With a deep breath, she opened the door, stepped out and closed it behind her. "And She's not telling."

ON FRIDAY AFTERNOON, Mary Rose nosed Kate's Volvo into a long line of equally sensible, passenger-safe vehicles and waited her turn to pick up Kelsey and Trace from school. She had to smile, thinking of herself as a car-pool driver. If she and Pete had stayed married—if their baby had been born—this might have been a daily routine in her life. That little boy would have been ten this year. There might have been brothers and sisters…

She shook her head, squeezing her eyes shut against the futile, irrational urge to cry. What in the world was she thinking? Why had that long-ago tragedy suddenly reared its head?

Because of Pete, of course. Seeing him again had undone ten years' worth of forgetting and resurrected a pain she really couldn't afford to relive. Except for Trace and Kelsey, children played no part in her present and future plans. There were real advantages to a life without kids, and she enjoyed as many as came her way.

The car behind her beeped its horn, and she realized the line had moved up. Easing closer to the van ahead of her, she scanned the groups of kids hanging around outside the school building, hoping to spot Trace and Kelsey among them. Even after she reached the head of the queue, though, the LaRue kids were nowhere to be seen. When minutes passed and her passengers didn't show, the security guard told her to move on. Mary Rose tried to protest, but the woman in the bright orange vest simply shook her head and waved with both arms in a gesture that said, clearly, "Get out of the way."

Two additional trips through the line later, Trace and Kelsey still hadn't appeared. Muttering a few choice words, Mary Rose drove to the student parking lot— nearly empty now—and left the Volvo there. She had no idea where in the building Trace and Kelsey might be. But when she found them…

The nearest entrance was one of the doors on the back of the gymnasium. Rounding the corner, Mary Rose stopped short at the sight of what looked to be battle lines drawn up in the narrow asphalt alley between the high gym walls and the chain-link fence marking the edge of school property. Seven or eight Hispanic boys on one side taunted the three white kids who stood backed up against that fence. The gibes were in English, but there were extra comments in Spanish, with mocking laughter and lewd gestures. After a moment, she realized that one of the outnumbered boys wore the brilliant yellow, long-sleeved T-shirt she'd seen just this morning in the car on the way to school. Trace.

She started to call out, just as the fight exploded. One of Trace's friends charged the other group and was sent sprawling on his back on the asphalt. When Trace bent to give him a hand up, he got a kick in the backside that sent him down on his face. And then there was a jumble of bodies, the sick sound of fists pounding against flesh, curses in English and Spanish.

Mary Rose headed back the way she had come, intending to summon help, but found the principal already running toward her, with Kelsey and another girl behind him. The sound of a siren in the distance heralded the approach of more assistance. For a dreadful second, she wondered if Pete would respond to the call, then decided with relief that the highway patrol would let the local police handle this kind of incident.

"Break it up! You hear me? Get back!" A big, heavy man, Mr. Floyd waded into the fight without any apparent concern for his own safety, jerking kids apart by the shirt collars. In another minute the police car arrived; between them, the three men separated the combatants and ended the fight.

"What's this all about?" Mr. Floyd stared down at Trace and each of the other boys. "Who started it?"

But no matter how many times he asked the question, none of the kids would give an answer. Even after they were marched like a string of prisoners to the principal's office and written up for violence on school grounds, no one offered an explanation.

"It wasn't Trace's fault," Kelsey told Kate and Mary Rose later, after they got home. "Eric Hasty made a comment in class about a wrong answer Johnny Vasques gave. They've been sniping at each other all year long. And when Trace and Bo and Eric went outside at the end of gym class, Johnny and his friends were waiting for them. Trace was trapped. He didn't have a choice."

"You could have walked away," Kate told her son as he sat at the kitchen table with an ice pack on the side of his face. "You didn't have to fight."

"And left Bo and Eric there by themselves? I don't think so." Dropping the ice pack in the sink, he stalked out of the kitchen, then pounded up the stairs to the refuge of his room.

"Men and their honor code." Mary Rose shook her head. "Not a tradition I understand very well."

"It's like something out of the Middle Ages." Kelsey folded her arms on the table. "Eric's sister is a year younger than him, and when he caught her talking to Johnny at lunch last fall, he threw a fit. His family doesn't think Mexicans and Americans should mix. So there's been this running feud going all year, and today I guess it just erupted.''

Kate took her coffee cup to the sink. ''I guess I'll have to put Trace on restriction. Honor code or not, I can't have him fighting in school.''

''Oh, come on, Kate. It's not his fault.'' Kelsey got to her feet. ''He was just backing up a friend. It's not like he started the fight.''

''The two of you should have been out front, waiting for Mary Rose to pick you up.''

''I told you, this thing started before school got out. I went to find Trace and they were already fighting. Please, Kate. Don't punish him like that. I know he'll stay out of trouble from now on. I promise.''

''How can you make a promise like that for your brother?''

''I'll talk to him. Make him see he has to behave. You know he listens to me.''

''Does that include getting him to be polite when you go out with your dad tomorrow morning?''

Kelsey swallowed hard. ''Sure. We'll be good as gold. Cross my heart.'' She suited action to words.

With a deep breath, Kate gave in. ''Okay. No restriction this time. But if it happens again…''

''No more fighting. Guaranteed.'' She gave her stepmother a quick hug and started out of the kitchen. At the doorway, though, she turned. ''Does that mean he can come to Gray Hamilton's party with me tomorrow night?''

Mary Rose's first impulse would have been to say no. Kate hesitated. ''They just live around the block, right?''

"Yes, ma'am."

"And you'll be back by eleven-thirty?"

"Yes, ma'am."

"I suppose that will be all right, then."

"Thanks!"

Alone with her sister in the kitchen, Mary Rose shook her head. "They're a real handful, aren't they?"

Kate nodded. "Since they got out of elementary school, I haven't had much practice at discipline. L.T. was always the one in control, and he made the decisions pretty much by himself. Maybe I took the easy way out, but fighting with him was just more than I could bear." She sighed. "Now I'm making the decisions. I'm not sure things are going very well."

"You know what's good for them and what's right." Mary Rose placed her empty cup in the dishwasher. "Trace and Kelsey will settle down as you get more practice and they get used to listening to what you have to say. Give yourself, and them, some time. Everything will work out just fine."

She hoped.

SWEAT DRIPPED into Pete's eyes as he swayed from side to side, breathing fast, dribbling the ball and looking for a way around the opponent crowding him. He feinted left; Tommy Crawford moved with him, arms spread wide, ready to steal. "Screw that," Pete muttered, pivoting on his right foot to turn his back to Tommy.

"Mitchell!" Twenty feet farther away from the basket, Adam DeVries held up his hands. Pete sent the ball like a bullet straight toward his teammate's face, watched in satisfaction as Adam caught and immediately redirected it in a soaring arch over the length of the court. *Swish...*

the ball dropped straight through the net. Two points, and the game.

Adam came across the court. "G-good pass, Pete."

"No thanks to Tommy, here." He punched Crawford in the shoulder. "I thought you were coming down my throat."

"Us short guys gotta be aggressive." Tommy shook his head as Rob Warren joined them. "Sorry, man. The guy must be wearing Super Glue. I couldn't shake the ball loose."

Rob gave them all his slow grin. "We have to let them win sometimes, right? Anybody else ready for breakfast?"

Without debate they jogged off the outdoor basketball court of New Skye High School and headed across the street to the Carolina Diner. When he wasn't working, Pete's Saturday morning schedule never changed—two-on-two b-ball with DeVries, Crawford and Warren from 7:00 to 9:00 a.m., followed by the biggest breakfast Charlie and Abby could dish up.

"Three scrambled, double bacon, grits, biscuits and stewed apples," he ordered a few minutes later. "And tea."

"That's a no-brainer." Abby grinned at him. "You ever consider trying something different? Oatmeal's good for your heart."

Pete let his jaw hang loose as he stared at her. "My heart is doing just fine, thanks all the same."

"Oh, really?" She raised an eyebrow. "Is that why you ran out of here the other night like the place was on fire? Without taking your pie?"

He snapped his mouth closed, feeling his cheeks heat up. "I had to get to the school."

"It looked to me like you had to get away from Mary Rose Bowdrey. Fast."

Three pairs of eyes lifted from the menus to his face. "M-Mary Rose B-Bowdrey is in town?" Adam sat back in his chair and linked his hands behind his head. "Isn't she…?"

"Yeah, yeah." Pete rearranged the salt and pepper shakers, started in on the sugar packets. "No big deal."

Rob took a swallow of coffee. "You were married… what? A month?" Having done her worst, Abby sashayed back to the kitchen.

Pete shrugged. "Something like that."

"Her sister's in the middle of a divorce." Like the Bowdreys and Adam, Tommy was part of the Old Town crowd—the families who traced their names back for a century or more in New Skye history, who mostly lived in big, elegant houses on The Hill, and who pretty much ran the town. "I hear the kids are really messed up over it."

"If he ran his family the way he runs LaRue Construction, I'm not surprised the family got b-busted up. And speak of the d-devil." Adam sat facing the door. "Here they are now."

Pete heard the bell jingle, but he had his back to the entrance. There was no way he could ask who had just come in, so he sat there with a rock in his stomach, certain that Mary Rose had arrived with her family for breakfast. Certain that he could not eat a single bite with her on the premises.

But then the newcomers moved to a booth in his line of sight. He let his shoulders slump in relief. It wasn't Mary Rose—just the kids, Kelsey and Trace, with their dad and his girlfriend.

Rob shook his head. "That is one unhappy bunch.

Does L.T. really think his kids are going to warm up to the woman he left their mother for?''

''L. T. LaRue th-th-th-thinks he can g-g-get a-away with any damn thing he p-p-pleases.'' Although usually barely noticeable, Adam's stutter worsened when his temper flared. ''I'm f-f-f-fixing one of his m-m-m-messes right now. He underbid me on the Whispering Pines n-n-nursing home job a few years ago, but the…the s-s-s-s-second-rate air-conditioning s-system already needs replacing, there's n-no adequate insulation anywhere in the complex, and the 'new' stove and refrigerator in the k-k-kitchen were seconds bought at a scratch-and-dent sale.'' He shook his head and muttered a word under his breath—without stuttering—that described L. T. LaRue perfectly.

Pete kept an eye on the LaRue kids while he ate. The epitome of sulky teenagers, they avoided looking at their dad when they spoke to him, which wasn't often and only in response to a question. They appeared to be pretending that the woman sitting beside L.T. didn't exist at all. Melanie Stewart, LaRue's office receptionist and the focus of his midlife crisis, was barely a half a decade older than the man's daughter. She wore her honey-blond hair piled high, put on her makeup with gusto and wore her clothes tight, displaying a set of curves that explained LaRue's infatuation to any man with eyes in his head.

A hand fell on his shoulder. ''Hi, guys. Who won?''

Another Saturday-morning ritual—Jacquie Archer came in for breakfast before starting her workday as a farrier. Thanks to mild weather and good terrain, the counties around New Skye were known as prime horse country, and Jacquie had a full-time job visiting stables and farms to shoe their horses.

Pete looked up at the woman beside him. "Hey, Jacquie. The best team, of course."

She rolled her eyes. "There's no 'of course' about it, Mitchell. You've been running this little tournament since tenth grade and I've decided the outcome just depends on who got to bed later on Friday night." Arms crossed, she stared at them with one eyebrow raised. "Considering the four of you are bachelors with the social lives of slugs, that makes the odds practically even." While they were still protesting, she turned on one booted heel and went to join her daughter, Erin, in the booth next to L. T. LaRue and his kids.

"'The social lives of slugs.' Man, I'd call her bluff on that one." Tommy finished his toast, then shook his head. "If it weren't the truth."

"I've got a construction b-b-business to run. This is all the time I can s-spare." Adam poured syrup on his pancakes. "Besides, who's she to talk? When's the last time we s-saw Jacquie with a d-d-d-date?"

Pete gave it some thought. "That would be the senior prom. Remember, she left right after graduation to go up north so she could train with that Olympic rider. When she came back a couple of years later, she'd been married and widowed and had Erin." The girl must have heard her name amidst the din, because she looked at Pete and grinned. Even wearing jeans and a T-shirt, she made him think of an elf, with her pointed chin, dark eyes and short dark curls, so different from her mother's corn-silk blond braid.

And so different from Kelsey LaRue in the seat behind her, who was dressed like some jailbait rock singer all the kids idolized—tight jeans, belly-baring tank top and too much makeup. As Pete let his gaze wander, he noticed L.T. pointing a finger at his kids, talking hard and getting red in the face. Before he finished, Kelsey jerked herself out of the booth.

"I don't give a damn about what you planned or how much money you spent." Her voice shut down all the other noises in the diner. "If you wanted to be with me and Trace, you should've stayed at home. I'll go to hell before I go anywhere with you and your...your... concubine!"

She stomped through absolute silence to the door, flung it open with a hysterical jingle of the bell and stormed outside. Before the door could close again, Trace caught the handle and followed his sister.

Another mute moment passed, then folks at the tables and the counter started up their conversations again, throwing a few sidelong glances at L.T. and Melanie in the process. Pete looked at his basketball buddies. "Do you suppose those kids are walking home?"

Rob sat facing the streetside window. "Looks like it. They're at the corner, waiting for the light."

"That's no good. It's a five-mile walk through some of the worst parts of town." And the girl was dressed like a hooker ready for work. In those neighborhoods, there would be guys ready to take the offer, even at ten on a Saturday morning. Pete put cash for his share of the breakfast bill on the table and got to his feet. "Thanks for the game, guys. See you next week."

Just as he reached the door, he felt a tug on his sleeve. Abby stood behind him, holding the box with his lemon meringue pie slice. "You're always rushing out these days. Take it easy, okay?"

He took the box and gave her a one-armed hug. "I'll do my best. You keep Charlie on his diet."

Then he went out to make sure Mary Rose Bowdrey's niece and nephew got home safe and sound.

CHAPTER THREE

KELSEY DISCOVERED almost immediately that two-inch platform sandals were not designed for walking. The kind of walking she was doing, anyway—jogging across the four-lane highway outside the diner, or striding uphill on the shoulder of the road with pieces of gravel slipping underneath her arch, her toes, her heel.

The third time her ankle turned on a rock, she kicked the damn shoe as far as it would go…across the road and into the ditch on the opposite side.

"That was stupid." Trace finally caught up with her. "How are you gonna walk home with one shoe?"

She couldn't answer, because that would mean loosening her jaw and taking her teeth out of her upper lip, which was the only thing keeping her from breaking into tears at this point. And she wouldn't cry over *him*. She wouldn't.

Heaving a sigh, Trace crossed the road and sidled down into the ditch. As he bent to pick up her shoe, a car roared up the hill in their direction. Instead of passing by, though, the dusty red Jeep stopped right beside her, blocking Trace on the other side.

Was she about to be abducted? In broad daylight at ten o'clock on a Saturday morning?

She braced herself as the door opened. The guy who got out didn't look like a pervert—he was actually pretty cute, for being so old. His hair was too short, but he had great shoulders, visible under a sleeveless navy sweat-shirt, and fantastic legs. He looked familiar, but she couldn't quite place him.

Then he flashed a badge. "Pete Mitchell, with the highway patrol."

Had her dad sent the cops after them? Typical. "Was I speeding or something?"

The state trooper frowned at her. "I don't think it's a good idea for you to be walking home on this road. Get in, I'll give you a ride."

Trace came around the front of the Jeep. "Who's this?"

Another flash of the badge. "I'm taking you and your sister home."

"Yeah, right." Kelsey took her shoe back from Trace and braced herself with a hand on his shoulder while she put it on. Thank God the ditch wasn't filled with water. "Like we haven't heard the drill since we were babies. 'Don't ride with strangers,'" she mimicked in a falsetto tone.

The man rolled his eyes. "I'm glad to know the message stuck. Too bad you didn't hear about staying out of the wrong neighborhoods. This road takes you right into the worst part of town."

"We'll be okay."

"Sure you will, 'cause you're riding with me."

Kelsey crossed her arms and stared at him, hard. "No way."

Hands propped on his hips, Pete Mitchell shook his head. "Look, I'm a...a friend of your aunt Mary Rose. We've known each other a long time." He cleared his throat. "She wouldn't like it if I let you wander around town on foot. It's an hour's walk, easy, from here to your house. Just get in the car, and I'll have you home in ten minutes.''

A friend of Aunt M's? Oh, yeah…this was the guy who had stopped Mary Rose in the diner Thursday after the game. They'd talked for a second, then he'd left, and Mary Rose had stared around with a dazed look in her eyes and her cheeks blazing bright pink.

Just *friends?* Sure they were. This might be interesting, after all.

Kelsey let her hands drop to her sides. ''I guess maybe we would be smart to get a ride. It's a long way home.'' She gave Pete Mitchell a friendly smile.

Trace's eyes widened. ''Kelsey? What the hell—''

The trooper relaxed and grinned back at her, and suddenly she realized how sexy he was.

''I'm glad to hear you've got good sense. Let's go.''

Kelsey got into the front seat of the Jeep while Trace, muttering under his breath, climbed in back. The engine started with a rumble but Pete Mitchell waited until both she and Trace had buckled their seat belts before shifting into first gear and starting up the hill.

''Manual transmissions are so cool,'' Kelsey commented, watching the trooper change smoothly from second to third.

He let the engine noise build to a roar, then flashed another one of those grins before easing into fourth. ''Makes the driving a lot more fun. But working a clutch takes practice. You're not old enough for a license yet, are you?''

''I've got my learner's permit. But all I get to drive is my mom's Volvo. It's automatic. Boooorring.''

''I notice your aunt's Porsche is a six-speed. Maybe you should bug her to let you drive.'' His smile looked…wicked?

"Hey, good idea." She glanced out the window at the neighborhood they were going through, at houses with sagging porches and yards littered with tires and trash. A gang of boys stood on one street corner, smoking and jiving each other over gangsta rap from a boom box on the sidewalk.

Kelsey shivered. Walking past that group would have been scary. No question.

She felt more than saw Pete Mitchell glance across at her. "That was some argument, back at Charlie's."

So much for polite conversation. "I don't want to talk about it."

"No problem." He nodded and glanced at Trace through the rearview mirror. "I hear you played a good game Thursday. Leading scorer on the JV?"

"Yeah." Trace was at his most uncommunicative.

"Bet you can't wait to get on to the varsity squad. You're in—what?—eighth grade? I guess you've got a couple of years yet. Think you'll play football, too?"

"Don't know. Maybe."

Pete gave up on coaxing the boy into saying something on his own. Forcing a kid to talk was the quickest way to kill any chance for communication. The best results came from letting them know the option was there and then backing off until they decided to take it.

Sure looked as though the LaRue kids could use somebody to listen, though. The air around the two of them practically boiled with what they weren't saying. A divorce in the family was toughest on the kids—all this bad stuff happening around them over which they had no control.

The rest of the drive passed in silence. Without comment, Pete braked for the stop sign at Boundary Street— the unofficial border between the poorest section of town, with its public-housing projects and broken-down rentals, and the historic, luxurious homes on The Hill. On the south side of Boundary, kids lived with a whole different scale of troubles. Troubles that made Kelsey and Trace look as if they'd landed in Oz by comparison.

"Here you go," he said as he pulled up to the curb in front of a house probably worth more than all the buildings south of Boundary Street put together. The announcement wasn't necessary—Kelsey and Trace were scrambling out of their seat belts as fast as the latches would release. "Have a good day."

Trace stalked off without so much as a nod. Kelsey got out, then leaned back into the car with a smile that flirted a little too much for Pete's comfort. "Thanks."

He gave her a discouraging lift of his eyebrow; her immediate pout told him he'd made his point. "You're welcome."

"Kelsey?" The girl straightened up and looked over her shoulder at the woman coming around the side of the house. Pete followed Kelsey's gaze and groaned silently. If the blond curls piled on top of her head hadn't advertised who this was, the honeyed voice would have.

Damn. His plan was to drop the kids off without running into their aunt. Wasn't it? No ulterior motive here, right?

Fighting a sensation of imminent doom, he eased out of the Jeep and propped his arms on the roof. "Hey, Mary Rose. You're out early."

She held up a pair of garden clippers, as if that explained everything. "What's going on? Kelsey, where's your dad?"

Kelsey imitated her brother's indifferent shrug. "Who knows?"

"He was supposed to bring y'all home."

"Well, he didn't." Before her aunt could say another word, Kelsey stomped up the walk and slammed the front door behind her.

That left Pete to face the question in Mary Rose's blue eyes. "They, uh, had an argument. At the diner."

"And how did you get involved?" The suspicion in her tone suggested the ulterior purpose he hadn't acknowledged.

"The kids left on their own, intending to walk home. I didn't think that was such a good idea, so I caught up and gave them a lift."

"Oh." Her cheeks turned a deep pink under her tan. "Thanks. They should know better than to walk here from Charlie's."

"Kelsey was too mad to be thinking about much of anything."

"Did you hear the argument?" She held up a hand before he could answer. "What am I saying? No doubt everybody in the diner heard."

"Well, yeah. L.T. had some trip planned, but Kelsey told him she wasn't going and then stomped out."

Fists propped on her hips, Mary Rose stared down at the sidewalk, shaking her head. She wore a pink knit shirt, which clung close to her breasts, and pale jeans, which hugged her hips and thighs. The sight stirred something hot inside him that Pete knew he had no business paying attention to. After all these years, after two failed marriages, he could leave well enough alone. Right?

"Well, thanks again." Throwing off her preoccupation, Mary Rose sent him an impersonal smile. "We appreciate your taking care of the kids."

Wrong answer. Every time she put him at a distance, Pete got an irresistible urge to close the gap. He walked around the front of the Jeep, braced his feet on the curb and leaned back against the passenger door. "Did you come into town to take care of your sister's garden?"

Mary Rose glanced at the clippers in her hand. "I'll do whatever Kate needs. She's pretty overwhelmed right now."

"Why don't you let the yard service take care of things?"

Her mouth tightened and her eyes blazed. "Because when L.T. moved out, he stopped sending his landscaping crew to do the work. And the allowance he gives her doesn't exactly cover a lawn service."

Pete muttered the word Adam DeVries had used earlier to describe LaRue. "She should sic her lawyer on him."

"Easier said than done." She fiddled with the clippers, opening and closing the blades. "Daddy wants to keep the situation low-key, attract as little publicity as possible."

"Your dad is acting as her lawyer? But he does business with LaRue, doesn't he?" Pete thought for a second, then shook his head. Her father had, after all, engineered *their* divorce. "Why am I not surprised?"

"Don't make it sound so…so selfish. Daddy wants L.T. and Kate back together. He thinks that by making as few demands as possible, L.T. will…will feel less resistance to coming home."

"Seems to me he's interfering the same way he did ten years ago. Telling your sister what's best for her instead of letting her decide for herself."

"That's ancient history."

"More like history repeating itself, I'd say."

Mary Rose took a breath to protest, but the words wouldn't come. Not when she was standing here face-to-face with Pete Mitchell, remembering how her parents had badgered her into getting a divorce. She recalled her dad's calm, rational arguments, delivered nonstop until she couldn't seem to think on her own.

"I'm sorry for your sister," Pete said, breaking into her thoughts. "Sounds like she could use at least one person on her side. And not," he said, with a pointed look at the clippers, "just to do the yard work."

"I am on her side!"

He tilted his head. "Are you? Better be sure, Mary Rose. Looks like the stakes are pretty high. There are two kids involved."

"I'm aware of that. Kate and Kelsey and Trace are the only people who matter in this situation." Who was she trying to convince? Why did it matter what Pete Mitchell thought, anyway? "Have a good Saturday."

"You, too." He straightened up away from the Jeep and walked back to the driver's side, giving her a chance to stare at his tight butt and the long length of tan legs left bare by his gray cotton-knit shorts.

Mary Rose swallowed hard. Falling in lust with a gorgeous guy—*this* gorgeous guy—had caused her enough trouble for one lifetime. She did not intend to make the same mistake twice. Besides, there were enough people in this family making mistakes already. Somebody needed to think straight. To stay in control.

Over the last ten years, Mary Rose had made staying in control her specialty.

When she stepped into the house through the front door, Kate was coming down the stairs. "What happened? They've locked themselves in their rooms and won't talk to me."

Mary Rose told her what Pete had said. "L.T. is behaving like an idiot."

Kate sat on a step, folded her arms on her knees and

curled over until her face was hidden. "I don't know how to make things better."

"I don't think that's your responsibility." Sitting beside her, Mary Rose put an arm around Kate's thin shoulders. "You're not the one who messed them up to begin with."

"Mama says—" Kate took a deep breath, but didn't continue.

"I know what she says. But she wasn't there, Kate, and she doesn't know everything. You did the best you could, and L.T. left anyway. So now we just have to figure out how to help Trace and Kelsey get past this."

"How can I, if they won't talk to me?"

"That's why I'm here." Mary Rose got to her feet. "I'm just the aunt, so it doesn't matter what I think. Let's see if they'll talk to me."

She knocked on Trace's door first, though it was farther down the hall than his sister's. The bass vibrations rattling the door panel suggested that any sound short of a major explosion wouldn't get through to the boy inside. A twist of the knob demonstrated that he had, indeed, locked himself in. Mary Rose went back to Kelsey's door.

No loud music here, though the floorboards were shaking from Trace's stereo. "Kelsey, it's Mary Rose. Can I come in?"

She waited through a long silence.

"I'm not feeling good," Kelsey said finally. "Later, okay?"

"You think you'll be feeling better about this later?"

Another extended pause. "Aunt M, I don't want to talk about it."

"So we can talk about something else." Perhaps the

smell of whiskey on Kelsey during that hug at the soccer game Thursday.

She caught her breath. Only two days ago? Surely she'd been through at least a week's worth of upheaval already. First Pete Mitchell, and then the kids, and Pete Mitchell again...

After a minute, the lock clicked and the door swung back. Kelsey stood in the opening, blocking access to her blue-and-white bedroom. "Talk about what?" She looked altogether too tired and stressed for a fifteen-year-old.

Mary Rose winked at her. "Have you seen the new Brad Pitt movie? The man is totally awesome."

That got a small laugh. "Yeah, last weekend." The girl backed up and allowed Mary Rose into the room. "Matt Damon didn't exactly suck, either."

"And Damon's still single." Mary Rose sat on the end of the bed. "A definite advantage."

"Or how about Pete Mitchell?" Kelsey cocked her head and lifted a knowing eyebrow. "I thought he was extremely hot. For such an old guy."

Mary Rose felt a wave of heat wash over her, starting at the crown of her head and going all the way to the tips of her toes. "P-Pete Mitchell?"

"He said he was a friend of yours. I could stand to have such friends." She closed her eyes. "Those shoulders!"

"Um, yeah." Pete did have great shoulders. And the most intense silver eyes... "I knew him a long time ago. We, um, dated for a summer."

"And you let him go? Dumb, Aunt M. Really dumb."

At least Kelsey was talking to her, even if the subject was just about the most uncomfortable one imaginable. She managed a casual shrug. "Pete was too old for me back then—he graduated with Kate. You should stick to guys your own age."

Kelsey slumped onto the other end of the bed. "Like my social life isn't already a total disaster."

"Want to tell me what happened?"

"Ryan said he wanted to date other people, that he was bored." She glanced up, her brown eyes brimming with tears and anguish. "That I was boring. And the next week, he's going steady with Trisha Reynolds. A cheerleader."

Mary Rose let a moment pass. "I think this guy sounds like somebody you're well rid of."

"Oh, sure, if I enjoy Trisha rubbing my face in it every day during algebra. And if I enjoy going to parties by myself and not having a date for the prom."

"Being single isn't a bad thing, Kelsey. It's nice to run your own life without having to consult some man about what you're doing every minute."

Kelsey sat up against the pillows. "But you date, right? You've been dating the same guy for a long time."

"Well, yes." Mary Rose went to the window and stared down into the tops of the ligustrum bushes she hadn't finished trimming. "Martin Cooper. Most people call him Marty."

"Are you in love with him?"

How did this get to be such a difficult conversation? "I care about him, of course. He's a very nice, dependable guy."

"Has he asked you to marry him?"

"Um…yes."

"And are you?"

A reasonable question, one she should be able to answer. "I don't know."

"How could you not know? Either you want to or you don't."

"When you're older, it's not quite that simple. I've been on my own for quite a while. I'm used to living alone, and doing what I want when I want to. Being married means having to consider somebody else all the time." She laughed and turned back to the room. "Maybe I'm too selfish these days to get married."

"But I want to be your bridesmaid. You have to have a wedding so Kate and I can choose our dresses."

Mary Rose decided to steer the conversation into safer waters. "What color would you choose?"

Kelsey cuddled a pillow against her chest. "Anything but yellow. I look horrible in yellow. I think everybody does, don't you? *She* was wearing a yellow dress this morning, and she looked like a banana. Of course, that might have been because her stupid dress fit her like a banana peel."

For a second, Mary Rose was honestly puzzled. "She?" Then, just as Kelsey's face changed, comprehension struck. "Oh. Her."

Kelsey buried her head in the pillow. "The Bimbo." In a softer voice, she said, "The bitch."

Mary Rose put a hand on the girl's shoulder. "What did you fight with your dad about, Kelsey?"

"He had this dumb idea that we should all go to the beach together after school lets out. Have you ever heard anything so stupid? Like I want to be cooped up with *her* in the condo for a week."

"The condo?"

Kelsey peeked out of the pillow. "Sure. Good idea, huh?"

"Lousy idea. I'd have been furious, too. That's a family place. Your mother did all the painting and decorating."

"Exactly. So I told him what he could do with his beach trip and got the hell out of there. And I'll tell you something else." She sat up, her face red, her mouth firm, her chin in the air. "I am never going anywhere with him again. Whether she comes along or not. If he can't come live with us and make us a family like we're supposed to be, then I don't care if I never see him for the rest of my life."

At least she'd admitted how she felt. "He's made a lot of mistakes, Kelsey. But he's still your dad."

"Biologically. A real dad stays with his kids. That makes *him* a total loser. If he doesn't want me and Trace, we don't want him."

Downstairs, the doorbell rang. Looking out the window, Mary Rose saw an SUV parked at the curb. "Who drives a dark blue Yukon?"

Kelsey sat up straight. "That's Dad. I won't talk to him. I won't!"

"Shh. You don't have to. Your mother will take care of it."

"Oh, right. She couldn't keep him here, she can't get him back, and she can't get him to give her any money. What makes you think she can handle anything at all?" The contempt in the young voice bit deep. "Next thing I know, he'll be kicking my door down." Kelsey stared at the door with a mixture of fear and despair. And, Mary Rose felt sure, even a bit of hope.

"No, he won't kick your door down. I'll give your mom some backup. You stay put."

By the time she got to the top of the staircase, L.T.'s loud voice filled the house. "I'll see my kids any damn time I please. Like right now." He stomped out of the living room with Kate following, but stopped when he saw Mary Rose blocking his way up the stairs. He made a visible effort to recover his temper. "Hey, there, Mary Rose. I didn't know you were here. That your Porsche outside? Nice car."

A few times in the past, she'd thought he might be trying to flirt with her, but had refused to believe her sister's husband would be so dishonorable. Now she believed it. "Hello, L.T. Are you on your way out? Don't let me keep you."

L.T.'s hulking frame was as intimidating as his loud voice. At Mary Rose's words, his face, an older version of his son's, hardened. "I'm going to see Trace and Kelsey, first."

"Neither of them wants to talk to you, L.T. Why don't you let things cool off for a couple of days, then give them a call?"

He looked at Kate, then at Mary Rose again. "You can't keep me away from my kids. They're not even hers, for God's sake."

Kate gasped. Mary Rose tightened her hands into fists. "You've got one minute to get out of here, L.T. Then we're calling the police."

"This is my house. I make the payments. You can't kick me out."

"Watch me." Mary Rose turned and started back up the steps, to the phone in the upstairs hallway. L.T. stood his ground on the first floor as she picked up the phone and punched 911.

"I'd like to report an intruder," she said to the operator. "The address is—"

With a snarled curse, L.T. whipped around and headed toward the front door. He slammed it hard behind him;

the pictures on either side of the door frame jumped off their hooks and crashed to the floor.

On shaking knees, Mary Rose walked to the stairs and sat down on the top step. "Well, that was interesting." She took in a deep, shuddering breath. "What else could possibly go wrong today?"

THE PHONE RANG at eleven-fifteen that night. Mary Rose was sitting up with Kate, watching TV reruns and waiting for the kids to arrive home at eleven-thirty, as expected.

But as Kate listened to the voice on the phone, as her eyes widened and her face paled, Mary Rose knew that the quiet night was about to take a turn for the worse.

"What? What's wrong?" She got to her feet as Kate fumbled to replace the phone onto its cradle.

For an endless moment, Kate sat motionless, staring straight ahead without saying anything at all. Then she looked at Mary Rose, her eyes blank with shock.

"Kelsey and Trace are at the police station," she said finally. "They've been arrested."

CHAPTER FOUR

IN ALL HER LIFE, Mary Rose had never been inside the New Skye police station. The newness of the building surprised her, until Kate explained that this office had replaced the sixty-year-old municipal center only five years ago. Television dramas had conditioned her to expect small, dark—even dirty—rooms. But this large, open area was flooded with fluorescent light, painted a clean light gray, and could have been any ordinary business reception area.

Something else Mary Rose hadn't expected was the crowd of people occupying that bright space. Everywhere she looked, teenagers slumped on the chairs and against the walls. At least one adult flanked each child, and everyone seemed to be avoiding meeting everyone else's eyes. At a counter running the length of the room, police officers on the inside talked to parents on the outside, with a fairly high level of tension evident in all parties. No one was happy with this situation…whatever it was. Kelsey and Trace were nowhere in sight.

Kate gazed helplessly at the chaos, twisting her hands together. "What are we supposed to do?"

"What did the officer who called say?"

"To check in with the sergeant."

"Which one is that?"

"The one with the longest line," a short, tanned man standing near them volunteered. He had a firm grasp on the arm of a sleepy-looking girl about Kelsey's age. "Hey, Kate. I'm gonna give Les Hamilton hell when I get hold of him. What was he thinking, going off and leaving his kid at home to party? Did you know there wouldn't be any adults there tonight?"

Kate shook her head. Mary Rose thought back to the conversation as Kelsey and Trace left the house early that evening. Had Kate asked if there would be parents at home? Or had she just assumed? Surely she would be smarter than that…unless she didn't want to know, didn't want to face the conflict involved in dealing with all the facts.

She took hold of Kate's arm. "Let's go stand in the longest line."

After thirty minutes of watching parents argue with police and scold adolescents, their turn came to speak with the sergeant. Kate took a deep breath. "I—I'm looking for Kelsey and Trace LaRue."

The sergeant flipped through papers. "Right. Drunk driving—"

"Driving!"

"Vandalism, consuming alcohol while underage and possession of a counterfeit license." He glared at Kate. "You got a couple of real delinquents on your hands."

She gripped her hands together on top of the counter. "What kind of vandalism?"

"Mailboxes. Pulled over half a dozen boxes in the Burning Tree subdivision. Lucky one of the neighbors was awake and called the cops."

"What are you going to do to them?"

"That's up to the judge."

"They're going to have a trial?"

Glancing up from his papers, the sergeant must have seen how close to the breaking point the woman he was talking to had come. "A hearing," he said more gently. "In a day or two. All I need right now is for you to sign them out, take them home and keep them there. You are the legal guardian, right?"

"Yes, of course." She had adopted both Trace and Kelsey soon after her marriage to L.T. Kate put her wavering signature on the lines the sergeant indicated. "They won't get into any more trouble."

"Right." Skepticism weighted the one word. With a nod, he dismissed them, handing the papers off to another officer standing at his back.

In a few minutes the heavy door in the rear of the room swung open. Kelsey stumbled out, dazed and blinking. "Kate? Aunt M?"

Kate took hold of the girl's shoulders, gazing at her in the unforgiving fluorescent light. "Are you okay?"

Kelsey pushed her hair out of her eyes. "Uh…I guess so…"

"Come on, Kelsey." Mary Rose took the girl's limp hand. "We'll go get the car. You and Trace can meet us in front of the station," she told Kate, who looked nearly as dazed as her intoxicated daughter did.

Outside, the warm April night was scented with new grass and rain…and a hint of whiskey from Kelsey's direction. Mary Rose didn't pause to appreciate the atmosphere. Walking fast, she pulled the girl along behind her as she strode down the sidewalk. She didn't know about Kate, but *she* was mad enough to spit.

With the doors shut, she twisted around in the driver's seat of the Volvo to face her niece in the back. "What the hell are you trying to accomplish? Doesn't your family have its share of problems already?"

Kelsey drew up her knees and curled into a ball. "I'm gonna be sick."

"I hope so." Mary Rose turned to the steering wheel and started the engine. "I hope you're sick as a dog."

Trace and Kate walked out of the police station as Mary Rose pulled the Volvo to the curb. Mother and son got into the car without a word. The five-minute drive up The Hill and to the LaRue house passed in total silence.

Once inside, the kids started up the stairs to their rooms. Mary Rose opened her mouth to protest but, thankfully, Kate beat her to it.

"Not so fast. We are going to talk about this. Both of you come into the living room." Kate's voice was harder than Mary Rose had ever heard it.

And that steely tone achieved the desired effect. Trace and Kelsey retraced their steps down the stairs, then went to sit side by side on the love seat, facing their stepmother as she stood in front of the fireplace. Mary Rose retreated to the kitchen to start a pot of coffee. Against her inclinations, she closed the door to the dining room to give them privacy, so the voices—mostly Kate's, but sometimes the kids' as well—came to her as wordless mumbles.

More than half an hour passed before footsteps thumped on the staircase once again, announcing that the kids had gone upstairs. A moment later, Kate struggled past the heavy dining-room door and wilted into a chair at the kitchen table.

Mary Rose put a mug of sweet, milky coffee in front of her sister. "Was it very bad?"

"Very." Kate hid her face in her hands. "I ought to be stern and strong...but they're so terribly hurt already. How can I punish them when they're in such pain?"

That question didn't have an answer. "Did they have reasons? Excuses?"

Straightening her shoulders, Kate dropped her hands to curl her long, slender fingers around the mug. "Something to the effect that Trace's friends dared him to knock down the mailboxes and Kelsey didn't think she should let the boys take a car since none of them has a license."

"And she does?"

"Her learner's permit."

"What about the drinking?"

"Kelsey swears that she only had a couple of beers. She didn't realize how even that would affect her, because she'd never tried it before."

Damn. "Kate, that's not true."

"What do you mean?"

"When I saw her Thursday at the soccer game, Kelsey had been drinking."

"At school?" Her eyes widened in horror. "How do you know?"

"I could smell whiskey when she hugged me."

"Whiskey. And you didn't tell me?"

"I was hoping I was wrong."

"Oh, dear God." Kate put down her mug and stared into it blankly. "What am I going to do?"

Mary Rose put a hand on the soft, brown hair. "Katie, honey, I'm not sure. But we'll figure out something."

After a couple of minutes, Kate sighed and straightened up. "The reality is that they're begging for their father to notice what's going on. To come back home and take care of them. And all that will happen is that he'll yell at them—and at me—without changing the situation in the least."

"Would you take him back…if he asked?"

Kate squeezed her eyes shut. "I think I would have to." Tears crept out from underneath her lashes. "I don't know what to pray for anymore. Whether to pray that

L.T. comes home, for Trace's and Kelsey's sakes. Or...or to pray that he stays gone. For mine.''

Mary Rose leaned over to put her arms around her sister. And she wondered whether there was even one man on the entire planet worth the suffering he inevitably caused.

SUNDAY DINNER was a command performance for the Mitchell family. Pete and his brothers were expected to appear in time for the 11:00 a.m. service at Third Baptist Church and then to show up at the front door of the house they'd grown up in not more than thirty minutes after the closing hymn. Fortunately, their mother's way with oven-fried chicken and angel biscuits made the effort more than worthwhile.

''I took delivery on some engine parts this week shipped by your company.'' Pete handed the mashed potatoes to his older brother, a driver for one of the national courier services. ''The box was beat up all to pieces. What's with you guys these days? Playing dropkick with the merchandise in your free time?''

Rick plopped a mound of potatoes next to the chicken on his plate. ''What free time? I'm working overtime every night just to get the stuff out there. Talk to the guys at the airport. They're the ones who mangle the shipments. They put in their scheduled hours, watching the clock instead of their work, then head on home.''

''So few people understand the meaning of responsibility these days.'' Denise Mitchell got up to refill her sons' iced tea glasses. ''If the work can't be done in the time they're required to be at the job, they just don't finish. The younger teachers are especially guilty. That bell rings at three o'clock, they're walking out the door, without even taking papers home to grade.''

Still shaking her head, she went back to her seat at the head of the table. "And the way some parents send their children to school is shameful. I had a boy in just yesterday running a temperature of one hundred and two. He said he'd been sick all night but his mama made him come to school anyway."

Pete grinned. "Did you call her and give her a piece of your mind?"

"I did. But she couldn't leave her job, she *said.*" Denise sniffed in disbelief. "That poor little boy lay on a cot in my clinic until after two o'clock when she finally got there. I'm still thinking about calling Child Protective Services. We'll be lucky if a flu epidemic doesn't strike the whole school."

"She might be a single mom." Pete's oldest brother, Jerry, sat across the table. "Maybe she couldn't stay home because she'd lose her job and that's the only income the family has. Some women have tough choices like that to make."

Their mother sat up even straighter in her chair. "I had those choices to make, if you'll remember. After your dad died, I didn't have anybody helping me raise you three, with money or anything else. Yet I never sent you to school sick."

Jerry gave her an apologetic smile. "But not every woman is supermom. You've got special powers."

"Sometimes even two parents aren't enough to keep kids out of trouble," Rick said. "I heard at church this morning that the cops raided a big party last night, arrested the whole bunch."

Pete looked up from his plate. "Were they fighting? I swear, if any of the REWARDS kids were involved, I'm gonna take some skin off their hides."

"Nah, this was the right side of the tracks, up on The

Hill." As opposed to the "wrong side," Pete understood, where the kids in his rehabilitation program came from. "The beautiful people's kids were drinking, getting crazy. Some of them went out cruising, got picked up for driving drunk. There were some private mailboxes knocked down, cars vandalized. The cops found grass in the house. Er…marijuana," he corrected himself with a glance at their mom's frown.

Jerry shook his head. "Makes you question what the people with all that money have in their heads for brains, that they can't raise their kids right, keep 'em out of trouble."

Pete wondered if Kelsey and Trace had been at the party. He could imagine how upset Mary Rose would be if her niece and nephew were arrested. She'd been worried about them yesterday, obviously caring about the trouble they were having with their parents' divorce. Years ago, he'd been surprised at how *real* she was, how easy for a guy from the other side of town to tell his dreams to. To live his dreams with.

Not. Maybe if they'd been left alone, if the baby had lived, if they'd had a chance to work on building a marriage…

Regret stabbed him, stronger than anything he'd felt in a long time. Having Mary Rose in town was beginning to look like a recipe for the kind of remembering he really didn't like to do.

"Earth to Pete." A booted toe kicked his foot under the table. "Pass the gravy."

He looked blankly at Jerry. "What?"

"Gravy, man. You deaf?"

Pete reached for the gravy boat. "Nah."

Dumb, maybe. He thought about Mary Rose in her pink shirt and tight jeans, and sighed silently.

Really, really dumb.

STARING OUT her window on Sunday afternoon, Kelsey watched her father slam the door to his SUV and stride up the front walk. Seeing him two days in a row had to be a recent record.

She'd begged Kate not to call him, but that had been a waste of breath. At least he'd left the Bimbo at home. And that was the only good thing she could say about the afternoon ahead of them all.

The bell didn't ring, but she heard the front door slam shut. He must've walked in without even knocking.

His voice came up the stairs as loudly as if he stood just outside her bedroom. "Kelsey Ann LaRue, Trace Lawrence LaRue, y'all get yourselves down here right this minute." He waited five seconds. "Don't make me come up there. You're not too old for me to take my belt to you."

She remembered her last encounter with that belt all too clearly. Ignoring the pitch and twist of her stomach, Kelsey eased off the bed and walked slowly to open the door. Trace looked at her from down the hall, his face white with a combination of hangover and nerves. He hated it when their dad yelled.

"Come on." She tilted her head toward the stairs. "Let's get this over with."

Kate waited for them at the bottom of the steps, trying to smile but looking every bit as nervous as Kelsey felt. She'd never been arrested before, never done anything quite this bad. There was no telling what her dad would do about it.

He was staring out the French doors into the side yard, but as they stepped into the living room, he whipped around to face them. "Have you lost what brains you ever had? Bad enough you were drinking, but to get in a car and go knocking down mailboxes... In one of my neighborhoods, no less. What kind of stupid is that?''

Kelsey shrugged one shoulder. At the time, it had seemed immensely funny to knock over mailboxes that her dad's company had set up. Now she didn't have an answer.

"Don't give me that sullen face, young lady. You're gonna explain this until I'm satisfied with what I'm hearing."

Staring at his clenched fists, Kelsey got nervous. "I was drinking. Not thinking straight."

"No shit. And you dragged your brother along for the ride? I thought you might have more sense, boy."

Kelsey caught Trace's glance, knew he was wondering if she would give him away for having been the one to think up the stunt to begin with. "We didn't start out to—to cause trouble," she said, trying out her guiltiest look. "It just kinda happened."

"Yeah, right." He propped his hands on his hips and shook his head. "I'll just have to see what I can do to fix it, is all. I've got a call in to the D.A. If we're lucky, he'll be able to get this whole situation handled before the court system even sees the paperwork."

Kate stepped forward. "L.T., I really think Kelsey and Trace need to realize there are consequences to behavior like this."

He gave her a quick, contemptuous glance. "Oh, you can bet there are consequences." His gaze shifted to Kelsey. "You're not going anywhere but school for the next six months, you hear me? No ball games, no parties, nothing. You can sit here and twiddle your thumbs and think about how stupid you were last night. Same goes for you," he told Trace. "Forget the rest of soccer season. You're off the team."

"You can't do that!"

Kelsey watched her dad's face change and knew the protest was a mistake. Closing the distance between them, he took a handful of Trace's T-shirt and brought their faces together. "You want to watch me? I'm not having my boy raising hell in this town, ruining the reputation I've built these last ten years. You'll behave, or you won't leave the house."

Letting go with a shove that rocked Trace back on his heels, he whipped around to face Kate. "I don't know what you're thinking about, either, letting my kids go to a party like that. Anybody with common sense would know that a houseful of teenagers with no supervision means trouble." He sneered as he looked their stepmother up and down. "But you're not real strong in the common-sense department, now, are you? So let me make it plain. Keep those kids in the house, except when they go to school. Got it?"

Before she could say anything, he marched to the front door and slammed it one more time on the way out. In the silence, they heard the squeal of tires as he stopped at the corner, then roared away.

The three of them stood for a long minute without moving a muscle.

"I don't know what he'll be able to convince the district attorney to do," Kate said finally, and went to sit in a chair by the fireplace. "I wouldn't count on getting off without some sort of punishment from the court."

Aunt Mary Rose came in from the kitchen carrying a tray loaded with a plate of cookies, glasses and a pitcher of lemonade. "I gather the storm has passed. Y'all want something to drink?"

Kelsey looked at the tray, tried to imagine putting a cookie in her mouth or swallowing a sip of lemonade.

Tears burned her eyes and her stomach clenched. With a gasp, she turned and bolted up the stairs. She made it to the toilet in the hall bathroom just in time. Since she'd spent half the night throwing up and hadn't eaten breakfast or lunch, there wasn't much to lose.

Somebody started up the steps. "Kelsey?" Kate would want to make her feel better. Like that was even possible anymore.

Still retching, Kelsey managed to shut and lock the bathroom door. Then she curled up in a corner, buried her face in one of her stepmother's soft turquoise towels and cried.

WHEN HE CAME off duty on Monday afternoon, Pete got the message that the assistant chief of police wanted to see him as soon as possible. Without stopping to change his uniform, he signed out and then hopped in the Jeep for the drive across town to the police station. He had to wait about thirty minutes for another meeting to end, but finally got into the big man's office. "You wanted to see me, sir?"

"Yeah, Pete. Sit down." The assistant chief shuffled through some papers, tapped the stack on his desk and folded his hands on top. "I told you I'd get back to you as soon as our budget decisions were made."

"Yes, sir." This was not going to be good news.

"The city council handed down a fifteen-percent cut in next year's police department appropriation. We've frozen salary levels across the board, denied most new-equipment requisitions. But to meet the budget, we're gonna have to trim nonessential programs."

"Like mine." He'd talked himself hoarse over the years, arguing that taking care of the kids in the community was most definitely essential.

The man across the desk nodded. "I'm afraid so."

"You're closing us down?"

"No, no, son. It's not that bad. But we will be cutting back on your operating funds in the new fiscal year." He named a figure that slashed a third out of the money Pete used to run his REWARDS program.

Sitting forward in his chair, he tried to stay calm. "That's a problem, sir. The high school charges rent and custodial fees. I can't cover those expenses with the budget you've left me."

"You'll need to drum up some outside donations. The new budget starts in June, so you've got a couple of months." The assistant chief got to his feet, signaling an end to the interview. "You had the guts to get this program started, I have no doubt you'll figure out a way to supplement your funding." Wearing a politician's smile, he offered a handshake. "Good luck."

"Thank you, sir." Instead of punching him out, Pete shook the man's hand. He walked out of the police station with his jaw clenched, his fists at his sides to prevent himself from slamming them into walls, the way he wanted to.

Once in the Jeep, he took some of his rage out on the gearshift. After four years, he was beginning to see real progress resulting from his work with the REWARDS kids. A couple of his regulars had recently found steady jobs with the skills they'd learned. At least being at school on weeknights kept them from causing trouble somewhere else.

But without operating funds, he wouldn't be able to use the classrooms and the gym four nights a week. He'd have to cut back on the number of classes, on the nights they were offered. Turned loose, the kids would be liable to get into trouble. And his understanding had always been that he needed to produce measurable results—in other words, a low incidence of repeat offenders among the kids in his program—or REWARDS would be shut down.

Now he was damned if they hadn't gone and done it anyway.

And this was only Monday.

THE LARUE KIDS and their parents met with the juvenile-court counselor on Tuesday morning. Mary Rose waited outside the tiny office in a hallway filled with people, listening to the rise and fall of voices behind the counselor's door…the loudest being L.T.'s, of course. She wondered what had happened to the genial family man she'd thought her brother-in-law to be. L.T.'s temper had always been short, but she'd never known him to behave in such an abusive manner. Had Kate hidden this aspect of their lives all these years?

When the door opened, Kelsey and Trace emerged first, eyes downcast, shoulders slumped. L.T. practically seethed with temper.

Kate, however, looked relieved. ''There's a class tonight?'' She consulted a bright yellow paper in her hand, then looked over her shoulder at the woman behind her. ''They could start right away?''

''Definitely.'' The counselor nodded briskly as she took a file folder from a rack by the door. ''An instructor takes roll and turns in attendance records for each class, so the sooner you get started, the sooner the one hundred hours will be finished. I'll check on you every couple of weeks, see how it's going.'' She glanced at the file in her hand, then looked up and down the hall. ''Eric Hasty? And parents?''

The boy who responded traded shoulder punches with Trace as they passed each other.

"A friend of yours?" Mary Rose asked.

Hands stuck in the pockets of his baggy pants, Trace shrugged. "He's okay."

L.T. stopped in his tracks. "That the one who put you up to all this? I'll see he gets what's coming to him for dragging you into this foolishness." He turned on his heel, heading back toward the counselor's door.

"He's just a guy," Trace said desperately, trying to block his father's return to the office they'd just left. "Leave him alone, Dad."

"Please, let's just get out of here." Kate put an arm around Trace and moved him toward the elevator, where she held the door open until L.T. joined them. Without further incident, they made it to the street.

"My kids are forced to show up for some damn youth offender rehabilitation classes." L.T. shook his head in disgust as he put on his mirrored sunglasses. "I really thought the D.A. could do better for me than that."

Kate consulted the yellow paper again. "It will be all right. They offer some interesting options—auto-mechanics class, weight training, computer programming, martial arts—"

"Great. Just great. They'll learn how to be garage monkeys with a bunch of juvenile delinquents." Still muttering, he strode across the parking lot, slammed the door of his SUV and, as usual, gunned the engine before driving away.

MARY ROSE WENT WITH THEM that evening to New Skye High School, where the police-department–sponsored REWARDS program was housed. The object of the classes, so Kate said, was to engage teenagers in activities that kept them out of trouble with the law and introduced skills that directed them toward a self-sufficient future.

Several rows of the parking lot were filled. "This must be a popular program," Kate commented.

"Or else there are a lot of delinquents in town," Kelsey said. Then she sighed. "Including us."

Both kids lagged behind as Kate and Mary Rose walked to the open doors of the gym. Mary Rose glanced back. "You can't walk slow enough to get there after closing time, so you might as well come on." Trace rolled his eyes, but Mary Rose saw Kelsey's mouth twitch as if she wanted to smile.

Just inside the door, two female police officers in uniform sat at a check-in table. "Can we help you?"

"Trace and Kelsey LaRue," Kate said. "This is their first time."

The two women shuffled their papers. "I've got them," the younger one said. She scanned the report. "Right. One hundred hours in REWARDS Plus."

Kate, Trace and Kelsey all looked startled. Mary Rose said, "'Plus'?"

"Plus community service," the officer explained. "You're gonna be replacing all those mailboxes you wrecked. Meanwhile, here's the list of classes available." She handed Trace and Kelsey each the same bright yellow sheet of paper Kate had brought home from the counselor. "Every class is three hours twice a week. You can take two classes a week if the schedule fits. So, what looks good?"

The kids stared at the papers as if trying to read a foreign language. Mary Rose moved to read over Trace's shoulder. "Weight training is fun—you can do circuits that are as good as aerobics classes for getting your heart rate up." No response. "Word processing?"

Kelsey gave a snort. "Trace could probably teach the class. Do we have to do this? Can't we just pay a fine or something?"

"Yes, you do." Kate took the yellow sheet. "Money doesn't solve problems. Since you're so interested in driving, Kelsey, why don't you take the auto-mechanics class? Knowing how your car works and what to do when it doesn't is very smart."

The girl rolled her eyes. "I am not crawling underneath a car and getting all greasy."

"Trace?"

He shrugged a shoulder. "Whatever."

Kate turned back to the table. "We'll put Trace in the mechanics class. And Kelsey...in martial arts."

"What?" The girl stared at Kate with her jaw hanging loose.

"You can learn to defend yourself."

The younger policewoman nodded. "Okay. The auto shop is through those doors in the corner. The karate class starts in the gym in about fifteen minutes."

Kelsey and Trace still lagged behind as Kate and Mary Rose skirted the basketball court to get to the indicated doorway, so they switched places, putting the kids ahead to be herded, rather than dragged along. The hallway they entered was crowded and noisy. But the noise died down as the LaRue kids passed through, and groups of chatting teenagers stopped talking to stare. The conversations struck up again behind Mary Rose, low voiced but not inaudible.

"What they doing here? Slumming?" "Got busted at that party the other night. Guess the judge thought they needed to see how the rest of the world lives." "That bitch thinks she owns the planet. I like seeing her down here in the dirt with the rest of us."

Mary Rose started to turn back to deal with that comment, but Kate gripped her wrist and pulled her forward. "Here's the mechanics shop. Let's go inside."

Although she'd always been aware that the high school offered automotive-mechanics courses, Mary Rose had never visited the actual classroom. Like a car-repair shop, the space was divided into three bays, with overhead garage doors and the bewildering array of tools and equipment mechanics appeared to require to do their job. Tonight the doors were open to the cool spring breeze, though the smell of oil and gasoline and rubber remained strong. A car sat in each bay, hoods lifted in preparation for whatever arcane work needed to be done.

"This looks interesting," Kate said. Trace stared at the ceiling, his hands in his pockets, his shoulders hunched.

"*That* looks interesting," Kelsey murmured beside Mary Rose.

Following her niece's line of sight to the nearest car, Mary Rose smiled. Standing with his back to them was a well-built young man with glossy, black hair curling on his neck. Square shoulders and firm biceps showed under his white T-shirt, while faded jeans covered a great rear end, lean hips and long legs. "Oh, yes."

Another pair of legs in well-worn jeans extended from underneath the red-and-gold car. As Mary Rose watched, the strong thighs flexed to roll the dolly on which the man lay out into the open, revealing first a flat waist, a broad chest in a faded blue shirt, then powerful shoulders and arms. And, finally, a face.

Pete Mitchell sat up in one smooth movement, set his feet on either side of the dolly and stood up without a wobble. Only then did he glance in Mary Rose's direction.

His silver eyes narrowed for an instant, and his mouth

tightened. Just as quickly, though, his sexy grin reappeared.

"Well, well, well. Look who's here." He pulled a rag out of his back pocket and wiped his hands, then extended his right to Kate. "I haven't seen you in years, Kate. You still look wonderful." He shook Trace's hand, and Kelsey's. For Mary Rose, he had a nod. "The rest of your family and I had a chance to talk on Saturday." Leaning back against the door of the car, he crossed his arms over his chest. Mary Rose swallowed hard.

"What can we do for you tonight?" He looked from Kate to Trace to Kelsey. "Some kind of engine trouble you need to fix? Or…" His scan took in the folder of police department papers under Kate's arm. "Or have you got trouble of a different kind?"

CHAPTER FIVE

PETE KNEW EXACTLY why Trace and Kelsey LaRue had shown up at school tonight. He'd seen their names on the list of kids newly assigned to REWARDS. He hadn't expected them to sign up for *his* class, though. Neither of them seemed like the mechanical type.

And he sure as hell hadn't expected Mary Rose to come along with them.

While he was still dealing with the lack of breath seeing her had caused, he noticed Kate LaRue take a deep one of her own. "Trace and Kelsey have been in some trouble, and the judge assigned them to the REWARDS program. We...Trace thought learning about cars might be a good way to spend the time."

Trace pretty clearly thought nothing of the kind. He was looking around him with obvious contempt for the kids in the room and the enterprise itself.

Surprisingly, his sister had other ideas. "I think this class sounds like fun." Kelsey smiled at Pete, then doubled the wattage and aimed her beam at the boy standing to his left. "A lot more fun than karate."

Just what they all needed—adolescent hormones at work. Pete put out a hand and turned his assistant around. "Let me introduce you. Kelsey and Trace LaRue, this is Sal Torres."

The boys nodded at each other without enthusiasm.

Kelsey kept the smile going, but Sal only lifted an eyebrow and one corner of his mouth. "Hi."

That was all the encouragement Kelsey needed. "What are you working on?" She edged past Pete to stare under the hood of the Camaro. "Is it broken?"

Sal cast a dark glance at Pete and mumbled something in Mexican Spanish that was probably best left untranslated. "Nothing's broken. Pete races the car, and it needed tuning up."

"You race?" Mary Rose's blue eyes went round. "On a track?"

He felt his cheeks heat up with embarrassment. "Sure."

"Like NASCAR racing?" She actually sounded impressed.

"One of the NASCAR series, yeah."

"Do you win?"

"Sometimes."

Her gaze hadn't left his face. "I remember...you were always crazy about stock-car racing. You had a poster of...of—"

"Number 3. Dale Earnhardt. He'll always be the greatest." He became aware of Trace's puzzled stare. "I'm not on that level, and probably won't ever be. We have fun, though."

"How amazing." Mary Rose shook her head and, finally, shifted her intense consideration to the car. "Now that I look at it, I guess this isn't exactly the family sedan, is it? No passenger seat or back seat, and all those restraint belts." She glanced at Kelsey, who was trying to pump Sal for information. "Does he race, too?"

"Not yet. Sal's my pit crew."

"But you're training him."

Pete grinned. "Yeah. He's pretty good." Her grin in

return reminded him all too well of the wild, adventurous girl for whom he'd have given up racing and just about every other pleasure in life, that summer ten years ago.

"Hey, Mr. Pete, can you come over here?" The kids in the third bay waved. "We've got a question."

"Be right there." He turned to Kate. "That's the beginner car. Trace and Kelsey can start the class there. We'll be finished at about nine-thirty."

"Sounds good." She gave him a nod and a shaky smile. "I'll check in with the officers at the front desk to let them know Kelsey has changed classes."

Pete managed a quick glance at Mary Rose, but she was avoiding his eyes. He swallowed the disappointment. "Okay, then. Let's get going."

Kelsey looked at Sal, didn't get a response, and stuck out her bottom lip, but at least she followed. Trace stayed where he was.

Kate put a hand on his arm. "Go on, Trace. Mr. Pete is waiting for you."

"This is stupid." The words came out in a snarl.

"It's also the law," Pete told him. "Your options in this situation are pretty limited."

The boy stared at him for a second, then gave one of his careless shrugs and shuffled off in generally the right direction. Having scored the point, Pete didn't check again to make sure the kid joined the class. Chances were good that an escape attempt would occur sometime later in the evening. Until then, he'd give Trace the benefit of the doubt.

"Later in the evening" proved to be less than half an hour. Pete straightened up from an in-depth discussion of fuel injection systems and looked around to find Trace conspicuously missing from the faces around him. Bo

Scot and Eric Hasty, two other new additions to the program, had disappeared, as well.

"Okay, you guys spend a few minutes with the manuals," he told the rest of the group. "See if you can relate the schematics to what we've just been talking about. No," he told Kelsey as she started toward the Camaro… or more specifically, Sal. "You stay with this group. There will be a quiz when I get back."

Her blue eyes widened, but the rest of the kids made rude noises. "Yeah, right." "You always say that. When have we ever had a quiz?"

"There's always a first time." And tonight might just be the night, he decided as he headed for the open door of the bay. Not that failing a quiz would penalize these kids in any way—the REWARDS program didn't give grades. But a little shaking up never hurt anybody. And maybe he could come up with a reward for the ones who did well.

Stepping into the misty darkness outside the engine shop, he immediately caught the drift of cigarette smoke on the breeze. With silent footsteps, he followed the smell to the corner of the building and stopped there to listen to the conversation.

"Total waste of time," Bo said. "You need your car fixed, you take it to the mechanic. Who would buy a car without a warranty these days, anyway?" He peppered his comments with a foul word that had Pete itching to wash the kid's mouth out with soap.

"I can't believe I'm standing in there with all the low-lifes. You know, the ones who take remedial math and ESOL, and bring tacos for lunch." Trace took an audible drag on his cigarette. "Good ol' Mr. Pete should be doing his thing in Spic speak. They'd get more out of it."

Jaw clenched, Pete stepped around the corner, knocked

the cigarette from between Trace's fingers and ground it into the asphalt with the toe of his boot. "Those things'll kill you." Then he put a strong hand on Trace's shoulder and sent him back toward the light flooding out from the shop. "But you might not live long enough for the tobacco to get you if I hear you talk like that again." His glance at Bo and Eric had them dropping their smokes and following close behind.

Inside, Kelsey had gravitated to the Camaro again. Sal threw Pete a desperate glance as he approached.

"Come on, Kelsey. You're wasting your time." Pete nodded toward the first bay, where she should have stayed. "The only girls Sal pays attention to have four wheels and run on high octane."

Yet another pout distorted her lips. "Maybe he just hasn't seen the right model." She tossed her blond hair behind her shoulder and sashayed across the shop, with an exaggerated sway of her hips that evoked whistles and appreciative comments from all the guys…except Sal and Trace. Sal went back under the hood of the Camaro. Trace clenched his fists, ready to beat the rest of them to a pulp.

"Quiz time." Ignoring the groans his announcement inspired, Pete reached for his briefcase and took out a stack of diagrams he'd originally intended as a worksheet. "Grab a pencil and find a flat surface. It's time to show me what you've learned so far."

The quiz generated some peace and quiet and defused the violence potential. By the time even the most experienced kids had finished, nine-thirty had arrived and the class could be officially ended…a blessing and a curse, it turned out, since Mary Rose appeared in the doorway to collect Trace and Kelsey.

Pete didn't know how to avoid talking to her, so he

decided to get it over with as fast as possible. "Chauffeur duty?" he asked, leaning on the wall beside the door.

Mary Rose gave him that cool, infuriating smile. "Kate sat down for the first time today at about eight-thirty and fell asleep, so I came to get the kids."

Guilt punched him in the gut. "Sorry. I shouldn't be so sarcastic. I'm sure she's having a hard time and it's good she has you here to help out."

The infuriating smile softened to something more real. "Thanks. I hope so. Did things go okay tonight?"

Trace walked up just as she asked the question, and Pete could sense the boy's tension over just what he would reveal.

Pete shrugged. "Sure. The first night's always rocky, but I think Trace and Kelsey will settle in fine. I'll look for them on Thursday, right?"

"If we can peel Kelsey away tonight, first." Mary Rose's gaze went beyond him to where Kelsey stood by Sal at the Camaro. *Again.* "Kelsey!" Even raised in a shout, her voice retained the husky softness that had always made Pete think of velvet and old lace. "It's time to go."

Heels clicking on the concrete floor, Kelsey crossed to the doorway. "What's the rush? I was saying goodbye."

Mary Rose ushered her charges out the door. "The counselor gave you a curfew, remember? And we're almost past it." She glanced back at Pete, hesitated, then smiled again. "You must be good with the kids. They really seem to like you."

The compliment left him speechless, his jaw hanging loose as he watched her walk away from him down the hall. Tonight she wore a white sweater that just grazed the waist of her snug black pants. When she reached out to hold the door, he thought he got a glimpse of smooth, tan skin where shirt and slacks didn't quite meet. The very idea set his pulse to pounding.

He turned back into the auto shop. "Something heavy," he muttered, heading toward the Camaro. "Give me something really heavy to carry around for an hour or two."

Still leaning under the hood, Sal turned to give him a grin. "Girls are hell, aren't they?"

Pete groaned and scrubbed his face with his hands. "Man, you don't know the half of it."

AT SCHOOL ON WEDNESDAY, Kelsey used her network of informants to gather as much information as possible about Sal Torres. He was now going through the eleventh grade for the second time, she learned, because he hadn't passed his math or English courses last year. He'd been kicked off the varsity soccer team for the same reason, despite being a star player. The oldest of seven kids in his family, he drove a beat-up Taurus with a crucifix hanging from the rearview mirror.

Lisa got her the real news. "He's a member of Los Lobos. That's the gang all the Mexican kids want to join."

"Los Lobos? The Wolves?" A shiver of fear traced its fingers over Kelsey's spine. "Sounds kind of dangerous."

"Anna Maria wouldn't say much. She's going with Paco Hernandez, another Lobo, and she said they get in trouble if they tell anything that goes on with the gang."

"If Sal's in the REWARDS program, he must have done something to get in trouble with the police. Something to do with the gang, you think?" She knew what Kate would say if she wanted to go out with a gang member. As for her dad… The thought made her smile. "Where do you suppose Los Lobos hang out for lunch?"

On the basis of a little deductive reasoning, they found Sal and his gang behind the auto shop. Fortified with Jack Black and ginger ale, Kelsey had no problem approaching her quarry, even when he frowned and turned a shoulder in her direction.

"That's not a very nice way to say hello." She moved around to face him, close enough that she could smell his cologne. Musky, spicy. Very nice. The bright sunlight turned his skin to a deep brown, picked up gold highlights in hair she would have sworn was solid black.

He rolled his eyes. "I don't want to say hello."

"Why not?"

"Because you're trouble. I don't need no more trouble."

"How do you know?" She took a step closer and smiled when he backed up.

"White girls are always trouble. You got a dad who thinks he runs this town. That makes it worse."

So he'd found out about her, too. "My dad doesn't give a shit what I do."

Sal laughed. "That's what you think. Until he finds out you're chasing some wetback. Or would he use Spic?"

"He won't know one way or the other." Reaching out, she ran a finger along his smooth, tanned wrist. "Even if he did, it might be worth it."

"You smell like whiskey." He took the soda can from her fingers and sniffed it. "Drinking in school? You're not just trouble—you're dumb trouble. Stay away from me, girl. I don't need somebody like you in my life." Pivoting on his heel, he walked away, dumping her drink into the trash can he walked by.

Lisa came closer. "That, uh, didn't go well, did it?"

Kelsey blinked away tears. "He's going to be sorry."

"What are you going to do?"

"I don't know yet. But I swear...Sal Torres is going to regret turning me down."

SAL WATCHED Kelsey LaRue stomp into the school building. Then he leaned back on the warm brick of the wall behind him, closed his eyes against the sunshine and blew out a long breath.

Quite a package she was, from the gold curls and big brown eyes to the sexy curves and the great legs. Full of fire, too. A man couldn't ask for more passion in a woman. Or more trouble.

He'd told her the truth. The last thing he needed in his life was an Anglo girlfriend. Her dad would freak. *His* dad would freak...and Mano Torres got ugly when he got mad.

"She's something." Joey Feliz joined him at the wall. "And she wants you."

"Nobody gets everything they want."

"You made her mad. She'll cause trouble."

Sal thought about his restless sleep last night, the way Kelsey LaRue's pout tempted him to smile, the way her walk tempted him in other ways.

"She's already caused enough trouble," he told Joey. "I'm not giving that girl a minute more of my time."

His friend's disbelieving laugh echoed Sal's own doubts.

ALREADY RUNNING LATE on Wednesday night, Pete stopped at home to feed Miss Dixie and let her out, then decided to grab his own supper at the diner before his REWARDS class started for the night. When he pulled into the parking lot, he saw Abby Brannon around the corner of the building, scrubbing at the brick wall near the back door.

"Hey," he called as he got close. "Shouldn't you be inside serving up somebody's dinner?" Then he got a look at the wall, and swore. "When did this happen?"

Orange, black, white and blue graffiti had been spray painted across the blank red wall. In addition to a few obscenities and a clever comment or two, the wall was covered with the signs of some of the local gangs, each one scrawled over another. The only sign that hadn't been obliterated in some way was a double *L*, marking the diner as Los Lobos territory. Clearly, this was a turf war in progress.

Abby shook her head. "Last night sometime. The dinner rush is slow tonight—who would want to come into a place marked up like this, anyway?—and Dad can handle it. This is the first real break I've had to get out here today. Stupid punks." She swiped the back of her wrist over her eyes and went back to scrubbing.

Pete reached for the brush. "Let me do that for you."

"No." She warded him off with both hands raised. "I need to do this, or I'm gonna start breaking glasses. You go order something to eat. I'll get it done."

Given that the paint wasn't coming off very well, Pete didn't think so. But he understood the need to feel as if she was doing something. He put a hand on her shoulder and gave her a squeeze. "Have at it. But I'll be back on Saturday to help."

Forehead creased, Abby nodded, still focusing on the wall. Inside the diner, Pete got an earful from Charlie about outlaw kids and the responsibility of the police to protect private property. His country-fried steak dinner didn't go down very well.

"You got some of these idiots in those classes you teach over there at the high school," Charlie pointed out. "Doesn't look like they're learning much."

Pete couldn't argue with the facts. "No, it doesn't. But I have to keep trying, Charlie. Things won't get better if somebody doesn't try."

"Whole bunch of 'em should be locked up, if you ask me. If they was in jail where they belonged, my wall wouldn't be messed up."

No, but the kids would be. Pete kept the comment to himself. "I'll see what I can find out, maybe track some of them down and get them over here to help clean up."

"Yeah, sure." Charlie gave a dismissive wave and limped back to the kitchen. Pete finished his coffee with a distinct lack of enthusiasm for the classes ahead of him. Some of those gang members no doubt were in the REWARDS program. He knew of one for sure, the last kid he wanted to suspect of this kind of crime. And the first one he had to consider.

Because Sal Torres was the leader of Los Lobos.

MARY ROSE DIDN'T WANT to admit that she looked forward to taking Kelsey and Trace to their REWARDS class on Thursday night. There could be only one reason to anticipate driving two sulky kids to a program assigned as punishment for their bad behavior.

She really hated to think that she simply wanted to see Pete Mitchell again. That she was wearing a cropped top and jeans because she knew how sexy the outfit looked on her, that she'd dabbed on Chanel's Coco scent because it was the perfume that made her feel...young.

These were the mistakes she'd already made once in her life—that summer with Pete, when she'd dressed for him, dreamed about him, lived for their time together.

The end result of all her effort was heartbreak. So why would she choose to repeat the experience?

What she chose was to avoid the question altogether. *Just helping Kate out,* she told herself. *That's all I'm doing.* Ignoring the butterflies in her stomach, she walked behind Trace and Kelsey as they dragged their feet across the gym floor and down the hallway to the mechanics shop.

As an excuse for lingering, she made sure both kids got inside the door and across to the bay Pete had taken them to the first night. She noticed that Kelsey tilted her chin and turned her head the other way as she passed Sal at the Camaro; she also noticed the way Sal's gaze followed Kelsey to the other side of the shop, his expression a combination of hunger and regret that she found worrisome. He was, no doubt, a nice enough boy, but Kelsey didn't need man trouble in her life. Her father supplied more than enough for all of them.

"A little young, don't you think?"

Mary Rose jumped and looked up to find Pete leaning on the doorjamb right next to her. "What?"

He nodded in Sal's direction. "He's only seventeen. Just barely legal."

Heat flared in her face. "I don't know what you're talking about."

Pete flinched, then offered an apologetic grin. "I know. You were staring at him, and I made a tasteless joke. Sorry."

"I think he likes Kelsey." She felt compelled to make him understand. "The last complication we need."

"I think it's the other way around. She wouldn't leave him alone Tuesday night." He studied the room for a second. "But she's ignoring him now. That's interesting."

"No, that's strategy." When he looked at her again, Mary Rose nodded. "Playing hard to get, you know? Guys always want what they think they can't have."

"Oh, yeah?" He raised his eyebrows. "Giving her lessons, are you?"

"Of course not. Why would you think—" She caught the twinkle in his eye. "Oh. Another joke."

"The best defense is a good offense."

"Now you've completely lost me."

His gaze veered away from hers. "Good." Then he straightened up away from the wall and looked at her again. "So what do you do, down there in Charleston? Besides getting a great tan."

Mary Rose fought down the pleasure of knowing he'd noticed. "Investment banking."

"No kidding? High finance and all that?" He whistled long and low. "Pretty impressive."

She could feel herself blushing again. "It's not Wall Street. I help the bank's clients invest their savings wisely."

"Little old ladies and their money?"

"A few old men, and some not-so-old ones, too. It's always a good idea to plan for the future."

"No doubt about that." But his agreement was a little absentminded, and he appeared to be thinking about something else entirely.

So much for the cropped top and tight jeans. She couldn't even hold his attention through a short conversation. Stepping backward, she gave him a wave. "I—I'll see you later. When I come back to get Trace and Kelsey."

"Sure." Pete lifted a hand in farewell, but he was still a million miles away.

Mary Rose stalked out to the Volvo, intending on

heading straight back to Kate's house to gorge herself on whatever concentrated form of sugar and fat came to hand first. But as she started the engine, the lights of Charlie's Carolina Diner across the street caught her eye. She found herself remembering how a Super Dooper Triple Scooper Banana Split—SDTS, for short—had always made even the worst test grade seem less of a tragedy. Tonight's fiasco with Pete seemed to call for just such drastic measures.

The bell jangled as the diner door closed behind her. This late, only three people remained in the dining room—a dark-haired man with his back to her in a booth near the door and a woman and young girl at one end of the counter. Mary Rose took a seat at the opposite end of the long stretch of green Formica. By the time she'd settled her purse, Abby Brannon stood in front of her, hands on her hips, a mock frown on her sweet face.

"Mary Rose Bowdrey, it's about time you got around to coming by. I know your sister's a great cook, but she deserves a day off now and then."

"Tell Kate that, why don't you? She won't let me take her out to eat." Heedless of napkin holders and salt and pepper shakers, they managed a hug across the counter. "But nobody makes a banana split like Charlie. Can I get an SDTS?"

"Charlie's already gone home. Will you settle for my handiwork?"

"As if you didn't make them most of the time, anyway. Of course." She sat down on the round stool to watch as Abby efficiently assembled an extravagant creation of fruit, ice cream, toppings, whipped cream, nuts and maraschino cherries. When the heavily laden glass boat came to rest in front of her, Mary Rose could only sigh. "I hate to spoil it by taking a bite."

Abby snorted. "Well, then, we will have a mess."

"You're right. Artistic scruples be damned." She spooned up the first luscious helping of fudge sauce, strawberry preserves, chocolate ice cream and banana. "Mmm. Perfect."

"Hey, Mom, don't we need one of those?" The girl at the other end of the counter was eyeing Mary Rose's dessert with envy. "I could study better with a little banana split under my belt."

"Or you could be bouncing off the ceiling with a major sugar high," her mother said severely. Then she grinned. "Got the muscles to make another one, Abby?"

"I lift weights every morning, just to be ready. Hey, Mary Rose, you remember Jacquie Archer? She graduated with Kate and me. Jacquie, Mary Rose is Kate Bowdrey's sister."

Jacquie nodded in Mary Rose's direction. "It's good to see you again. This is my daughter, Erin."

"Hi, Erin." She looked to be about Trace's age, but without the veneer of sophistication Kate's children wore these days like a suit of armor. "Jacquie, you were the equestrienne, right? Bound for the Olympics? Are you still riding?"

"Only for fun—Erin's the one with the serious ambitions these days. I'm a farrier."

"A farrier...you mean, you shoe the horses?"

"That's right."

Abby put an SDTS in front of the Archers. "There you go. Enjoy."

"All right!" Erin dug in with enthusiasm.

Mary Rose returned to her own dessert. "I didn't know women did that kind of work. You must be in really great shape."

Jacquie held up a finger, asking for a moment's pause

while she savored a spoonful of ice cream. "There's a lot to be said for just knowing the right way to swing a hammer."

Footsteps approached from behind them, then the man alone in the booth put his check and some bills on the counter near the register. "And a l-l-lot to be said for a woman w-willing to swing a—a hammer at all. If you ever get t-t-tired of horses, Jacquie, I can always use a g-good c-carpenter."

Jacquie laughed. "I never get tired of horses. But I'll keep the offer in mind."

"You d-do that. 'Night, Abby."

"'Night, Adam." She put his money in the cash drawer. "See you tomorrow... He eats here every evening," she told Mary Rose, after the door had closed again. "I never saw a man with less domestic interest. Even Pete Mitchell eats at home occasionally."

Mary Rose kept her eyes on the banana split, but her curiosity couldn't be contained. "You don't think Pete does much around the house?"

"I can't see that he'd have the time, given his job and the hours he puts in with REWARDS. Between heading up the program and teaching classes most nights, he can't be home much."

Now she did look up. "Pete heads the REWARDS program?"

Wiping down an already spotless counter, Abby nodded. "Came up with the idea, broached it to the police department and the city council, drummed up the community support to get the program started, and runs it pretty much by himself."

How much more impressive could the man get? "Does the program achieve its goals? Do the kids he works with turn their lives around?'' This time she wasn't just giving in to curiosity.

"I know for a fact that many of them have," Abby said. "I think some kids get their act together while they're under Pete's influence, but when they go back to the old neighborhood, they fall back into old habits. He hasn't figured out the answer to that part of the equation, and I know it frustrates him a lot. And now the city council has seen to it that he might not get the chance at all."

"What do you mean?"

"The city's in a major budget crisis. They're cutting school funds for next year, city employee salaries, and even the police department budget. What do you think will go first—operating expenses for law enforcement, or a rehabilitation program for problem teenagers?''

"I can tell you that." Jacquie slid off her stool and came to the register, leaving Erin to finish up the banana split. "The good old boys in the political system aren't going to sacrifice law and order for a bunch of 'delinquents.' Pete's funding is going to be cut, and I hope he's looking for other sources. Otherwise..." Shaking her head, she took her change back from Abby. "Otherwise, REWARDS will be history. Along with a lot of the kids Pete could have rescued." She put a hand on Mary Rose's shoulder. "Good to see you. Give Kate my best."

"I will." Mary Rose spooned up the last swirls of fudge and ice cream and thought over what she'd just learned. Over the years since their aborted marriage, she'd managed to barricade her mind against Pete Mitchell, to stop herself from wondering where he was or what he had done with his life. She couldn't have gotten on with her own, otherwise.

And now she discovered that while she was pursuing

her narrow goals—earning an MBA, finding a good-paying job, funding an elegant Charleston condo on the harbor and a flashy car—Pete had been doing really heroic things for his community.

Not a comparison to be proud of.

Back at the school at nine-thirty, she was still feeling ashamed. She intended to collect Trace and Kelsey and sneak out without speaking to Pete. Really, what did she have to say to him that mattered?

But he was waiting at the door, his face lit up with excitement. "Mary Rose, I want to talk to you." His big, calloused hand closed around her wrist, pulled her into the shop. He didn't let go right away, and the warmth of his fingers against her skin drove her heart rate into triple digits.

She tried to focus. "Is something wrong? Did Trace give you trouble tonight? Where's Kelsey?"

Pete shrugged. "Trace is acting like a jackass, but that'll get better. Kelsey's finishing up an assignment in the back room." He turned to face her, and his gray gaze practically burned her with its intensity. "Listen, I have a great idea. You work at a bank, right?"

"Right." If he didn't let go of her soon, she wouldn't be able to think at all.

"So you're really good at checkbooks and bank statements, credit cards and all that stuff."

"I can balance my checkbook, yes. Can't you?"

"Sometimes. But that's what I'm saying. You've got great skills that everybody needs to function as an adult. Skills these kids could use in order to be successful in their lives."

As if he'd just realized he was still holding her wrist, he let go and stepped back, putting his hands in his pockets.

"So what do you say, Ms. Mary Rose Bowdrey? Can I convince you to help me set these kids on the right track? Will you join the REWARDS teaching staff while you're in town?"

CHAPTER SIX

ONCE THE IDEA of getting Mary Rose to offer a financial-skills course occurred to him, Pete struggled to stay focused on the night's lessons. It was such a brilliant idea, he couldn't believe he'd never thought about adding that kind of class to the program. Most of the kids in REWARDS came from families that lived from paycheck to paycheck, at best. They had no concept of financial planning, saving money, or investing.

But Mary Rose could teach them.

She was staring at him as if he'd suggested she dance naked on the hood of the Camaro. "You want me to teach?" Her voice squeaked on the last word.

"I think you could do some of these kids a world of good, showing them how to manage their money. It's one thing to give them the skills to go out and get a decent-paying job. But if they blow it all on credit card debt, what good have we done? You could talk about savings accounts and investments and retirement plans, pensions—"

"You mean all the subjects I spent six years in college learning about?"

He shrugged. "Not in as much depth, of course. Hell, if you just taught them about checking and savings accounts, that's more than they'd probably learn from anybody or anywhere else."

"Pete…" She looked beyond him, watching the kids

bent over engines or, like Trace and Bo and Eric, standing in a corner wasting time. "Do you really think they'd be interested?"

"Probably not." Her gaze flew back to his, her eyes wide. Pete opened his hands to signal surrender. "It's math, Mary Rose. It's schoolwork. That's not where these kids put their time, given a choice. But *you* could make it interesting. You could show them why they need to know this stuff."

"How?"

"I'm not sure yet. We can talk about it. All I need from you is an agreement to offer the class. We'll start with just one night a week, see if we can get some interest drummed up."

But Mary Rose was still frowning. "I won't be here too long, you know. Just until Kate's life settles down. I need to go back to my own job. My own life."

The timing was perfect—after the impending budget cut, he probably wouldn't be able to afford even the rooms he used now and definitely wouldn't have space for a new class. But in the meantime, Pete knew Mary Rose could give the kids something to think about. "So you'll help me plan a curriculum, and then we'll get somebody local to step in and teach when you leave." Something about those last words didn't feel right, but he ignored the warning. He tried out a grin. "Come on. You can't trim bushes all the time."

"No, I can't." She took a deep breath. "Okay. I guess I can at least help you set up the class, maybe get it started. I do think it's a good idea. I didn't have a clue about how checking accounts worked until I went to college."

"That's fantastic." Pete resisted the urge to give her a hug. He didn't want to scare her away. "I really appreciate your help and the kids will, too. When can we get together to talk about the details?"

In her hesitation, he saw his own concerns. Spending one-on-one time with Mary Rose Bowdrey could be asking for trouble. She'd already stirred up too many memories, too many feelings he thought he'd buried a long time ago. Seeing more of her might make resisting those feelings a losing battle.

Nah. They'd been kids that summer. Being an adult meant using logic, meant controlling impulses. He was an adult. He could do this.

"Um...why don't you call me," she said finally. "I need to get Trace and Kelsey home to finish their schoolwork."

"Sure. I'll give you a call tomorrow sometime. Have a good evening. And thanks again. This'll be great." He turned away, made himself walk across the garage, made himself ignore the urge to whistle in satisfaction. This was for the kids, after all.

Nothing personal about it.

SAL KEPT AN EYE on Pete as he talked with Kelsey LaRue's aunt. There was something fairly intense going on there, for sure. As long as Sal had known him, Pete had kept a low profile where women were concerned. He didn't talk about them much and he spent most of his time on the car or with the REWARDS program.

Something about this particular woman, though, had Pete looking as if he'd just won the Daytona 500.

Shaking his head, Sal glanced in the opposite direction, where Kelsey was doing her best to make him sorry he'd turned her down. Tight, low-riding jeans and a T-shirt that showed off her belly button pretty much did the trick. His palms tingled every time he got a glimpse of the smooth, pale skin at her waist. Her blond hair gleamed under the lights of the garage. She'd passed close enough as she walked by before class to give him a whiff of her perfume…and it wasn't an innocent scent. It wasn't cheap, either, or too much. Just tempting as sin.

He turned back to the Camaro, trying to concentrate on the timing adjustments he wanted to make. But Kelsey wouldn't leave him alone, even after she left the building. One glance from those deep brown eyes was enough to rev up his personal engine.

After turning off the lights in the other bays, Pete walked over. "So, are we going to be ready to race next weekend?"

Sal straightened up, grateful to be called away from his thoughts. "Think so. Just needs the final tune-up."

"Good. I'll send in the registration." He lowered the hood as Sal turned to put his tools in the chest. "I, uh, heard there's been some trouble in the neighborhood."

One of the things Sal liked most about Pete was that he didn't try to use slang that didn't belong to him, didn't use "'hood" as if he were part of the culture.

But that courtesy didn't entitle the highway patrolman to privileged information. "Nothing new," he said with a shrug.

"That's not what I hear. I hear the Los Lobos sign has shown up in some new places."

"Nowhere it doesn't belong."

Pete shifted his balance. "If you get picked up by the police, even just for questioning, our deal's off. No more racing. No more work here in the shop. Remember?"

"I remember." And he was grateful for the opportunity. That didn't mean he could discard his honor.

"I'm having a hard time seeing how you can stay on as the head of a gang bent on trouble and not get pulled in yourself. Want to explain how you're gonna manage that balancing act?''

''No.'' Sal wouldn't say more. And he couldn't abandon his brothers in the gang. But there were layers of members between him and what was actually going on with Los Lobos these days. Pete didn't need to know the details.

''Great.'' The other man took a few angry strides away, then turned and came back to where Sal had stopped to shrug into his shirt. ''You've got the brains and the ambition to be more than just another punk, Sal. If you don't get away from the gang, though, you might as well forget about any real success. I'd be sorry to see things turn out that way.''

Sal closed the doors to the bays without saying anything in response. His face still flushed with anger, Pete locked up, and they went down the empty hallway to the gym.

The school custodian was pushing his wide broom across the floor. ''Everybody out, Pete?''

''That's everybody, Mr. Davis. We'll let you lock up.''

The custodian nodded. ''See you Monday.''

''Sure thing.'' Pete pushed open the door and Sal stepped after him into the night air. Across the street, Charlie's Carolina Diner stood dark and quiet. But Sal glimpsed a shadow slipping along the wall. Los Lobos? Or a member of their current rival, Los Presidentes? He was too far away to tell.

They walked to their separate cars, parked a couple of spaces apart. Pete unlocked his Jeep, then turned to look at Sal again. ''I can't do this for you,'' he said. ''You're the one who chooses.'' With that parting shot, the trooper got into the Jeep and drove off.

Once Pete was gone, Sal sprinted across the street into

the darkness under the diner's tattered awnings. While he didn't intend to cause trouble, he did want to know exactly what was going on.

Easing silently to the corner, he peeked around the edge. At the far end of the wall, a short, chubby dude he didn't recognize was spraying the bricks with paint. Whoever he was, he wasn't Lobos. And he wouldn't be allowed to spoil Los Lobos work.

Sal hit the guy at full speed; they went down together with a grunt and the clatter of the paint can. A couple of punches to the face and throat left the fat guy begging for mercy. Sitting back on his heels, Sal allowed the wimp to get free and stumble away. As he flexed his shoulders, clenched and unclenched his fists, he knew he'd have his own set of bruises tomorrow.

But when he took up the can of silver paint the Presidente had dropped, when he crossed out the eagle the other gang used as a mark and found a nice, big, blank space for the Lobos double *L,* Sal tried to believe a few bruises were a small price to pay.

SINCE MARY ROSE had been taking them to and from just about everywhere all week long, Kelsey knew something was up when Kate drove them home from school Friday afternoon. As soon as they got into the house, her stepmother wanted to talk "for a minute." Trace made a fast escape upstairs, and Aunt M was nowhere to be seen.

Stalling for time, Kelsey unloaded her backpack to the floor with a sigh of relief. "What do we have to talk about? What's there to eat?"

Kate sat down at the kitchen table and motioned her to do the same. "You told me that last Saturday night was the first time you had tried alcoholic drinks."

Uh-oh. She sank into the chair. "And?"

"That's not true, is it?"

"I told you I hadn't ever had beer before. That was true."

"But you were drinking whiskey at the soccer game last week."

Damn you, Aunt M. "A little."

"How often do you drink?"

"Just every once in a while, Kate." She called up her wide-eyed, innocent stare. "Really. When somebody else is, maybe."

Her stepmother gazed at her for a long time. "I don't know if I can believe what you say. It seems there have been so many lies recently. How do I know I can trust you?"

Kelsey reached out a hand, which Kate took in both of hers. "I swear, I don't drink that much. You know there's no liquor here, and where else would I get it? Just sometimes at parties the kids have drinks, you know? But I can't go to parties anymore. So I can't even drink on the weekends." Thank God for Lisa and the flask of Jack Daniel's she kept in her locker at school.

Kate pressed a kiss to Kelsey's fingers. "I know this has been a terrible few months, Kelsey. I can only imagine how you're suffering. But we're going to get through this dark time, I promise. Just…leave the alcohol alone, sweetheart. It'll destroy you. And you're too young to ruin your life."

"I know." And she did. It was just that school was so unbearable, with everybody looking at her, talking about her dad and his mistress, and seeing Trisha and Ryan together all the time… And then there was Sal, who wouldn't give her the time of day. "I'll do better, I promise."

For a little while, she even meant it.

DURING A LONG MINUTE after she stepped into the diner on Friday night, Mary Rose thought Pete had stood her up. He wasn't anywhere to be seen in the crowd. Considering all the second thoughts she'd endured in the last twenty-four hours, she didn't know whether to be glad or sorry.

Abby Brannon brought a tray of plates to a booth near the door, made sure everybody had what they wanted, then came over to Mary Rose. "He's outside," she said with a smile. "We're having some trouble with graffiti, and he's looking at the mess they've made of our wall. But he reserved a booth and asked me to get you settled until he came in."

Nerves jumping, Mary Rose managed a smile of her own. "That sounds good. But I'm sorry you're getting vandalized. Is this the first time?"

Abby led her to a booth toward the back. A spray of live azalea blossoms graced the vase on the table, replacing the diner's usual silk carnations. "Over the years, kids have expressed themselves on our walls occasionally. But this time we're dealing with gangs trying to claim turf. Not nearly so forgettable as 'Go, Chieftains.'" She sighed and shook her head. "Can I get you something to drink?"

Mary Rose had taken only a couple of sips of excellent iced tea when Pete came through the front door. Her heart actually did a somersault at the sight of him. He wore khaki slacks and a blue buttoned-down shirt with the sleeves rolled back—nothing special or fancy, but the fact that he'd gotten dressed for this "meeting," that he had worn something besides his uniform or the T-shirt and jeans she'd seen him in this week, gave a new meaning to the whole evening. Her own struggle to choose clothes—a long green linen skirt and camp shirt in sunny yellow—seemed worth the effort, somehow. They both cared about the impression they made.

She didn't have time to heed the warning bells going off in her brain. Pete had reached the table.

"Hey." He slid into the seat across from her, flashing a grin that could melt chocolate. "Sorry to keep you waiting. I guess Abby explained what's going on."

She nodded. "It's hard to imagine gangs operating in New Skye. It's such a little place. Los Angeles, New York, Chicago, sure. But *here?*"

"Gangs are everywhere. Thanks, Abby." That grin showed itself again as Abby set down another glass of tea. "All it takes is kids who feel like outsiders, who don't have a strong family, who need to belong. Most towns have kids like that these days."

Mary Rose's laugh was a combination of worry and bitterness. "Sounds like Trace and Kelsey."

"There are white gangs, though that's not the typical picture. But Trace and Kelsey don't have to turn to crime for cash, and they're probably not prone to violence. Those are the real problems."

"I hope you're right." She stirred her tea with her straw. "The fact that they were arrested last weekend isn't very reassuring."

Pete reached over and stroked the back of her hand with his fingertips. "You're here and you're doing everything you can to get them straightened out. That's really important. Most of the REWARDS kids don't have anybody who cares so much."

Now her heart had started pounding and she couldn't breathe. But she wasn't eighteen and they were here on business, something she needed to keep firmly in mind.

"So…" She sat back, managing to slip her hand away from his touch. "Tell me what exactly I'm supposed to do with this financial-skills course."

Pete's mouth straightened into a thin line. He picked up the menu and opened it up between them like a wall. "Let's order up some food first, okay? I'm starving."

Despite the tension between them, by the time Abby arrived at the table with two platters bearing the specialty of the house—cheeseburgers and fries—Mary Rose had taken several pages of notes. She still had reservations, but she couldn't help getting excited about the possibilities of the class.

"We could spend a couple of sessions on interest—compare a savings account earning interest and a credit card charging interest. That's a pretty dramatic contrast, don't you think?"

Pete dunked a fry in ketchup. "Definitely."

"Do you think these kids are likely to need to know about stocks and bonds? The market is fairly complicated, and I'm not sure I'd do much more than confuse them if I tried to cover even the basics."

"Why don't you leave that until after the important stuff? Then, if you have time and they're interested, go for it. By the way, are you planning to eat any of your dinner?"

She looked up from her notes to find him grinning at her. "You haven't taken a single bite," he said with a nod at her plate. "I'm beginning to understand how you've stayed so slender all these years. You just don't eat."

"I eat," she said defensively, and finished off a French fry to prove it. He thought she was *slender*. So much nicer than *thin* or *skinny*. A romantic word, *slender*. A caring word.

As if what he thought mattered. After cutting her burger in half, she bit off a healthy chunk. "See?"

"That's better." He picked up his own sandwich and they ate in silence for a few minutes. Abby stopped by to refill their glasses, but hurried away with just a smile and a quick "Everything okay?" which left them on their own again. If they weren't going to talk about the class, what should she say?

Finally, she gave in to her curiosity as a way to fill the conversational gap. "Have you lived in New Skye ever since…" The divorce? "Ever since you got out of the law enforcement academy?"

"I have, in fact." He pushed his empty plate away. "Miss Dixie and I have a house over in Drummond Hills. Not too big, but it's enough for us."

A chill washed through her that had nothing to do with the ceiling fan circling lazily above their table. She hadn't given a thought to the possibility that there was a woman in his life, hadn't even considered asking. He didn't wear a ring, but she'd known other completely faithful men who avoided jewelry. L. T. LaRue had worn a thick, diamond-studded wedding band. And look where Kate had ended up.

"That's…nice." She avoided Pete's face, trying to recover her balance, trying to forget some of the wee-hours fantasies she'd indulged herself in recently. "Dixie's a sweet name. Is she from New Skye, too?"

"Nope, she came from a farm out of town. Her mother's a champion breeder. I was lucky to get one of the pups."

"Pups?" Staring at the man across the table, she realized she'd been completely and unrepentantly duped. "Miss Dixie is a dog?"

"Best little beagle you could ask for." He gave her

that grin, the one which turned her insides to jelly. "Why, what did you think I meant?"

She threw her napkin at him. "You know I thought you were talking about a woman, you jerk. I don't remember you having such a—a sick sense of humor when we...before you...back then."

Pleased with the results of his joke, Pete smoothed her napkin and tucked it under the edge of her plate. "Kids at that age take themselves too seriously to have a real sense of humor. I've learned to lighten up."

"I don't know that it's an improvement." The red in Mary Rose's cheeks, the way she avoided looking at him, spoke of an embarrassment out of proportion to the situation. She took an audible breath. "So are you married? I mean, again?"

True confessions. "I was. I've been divorced about three years now. How about you?"

"N-no."

"You don't sound so sure." As a result, his gut had tightened up like a drum.

She took a deep breath. "I...I've been seeing someone pretty steadily for a couple of years. But there's no date. No ring." She smiled and fluttered those elegant fingers at him.

"I noticed," Pete said, and watched her eyes widen until he thought he could get lost in the deep, deep blue. So now they had it out on the table—neither of them attached. And both of them, he thought it fair to say, attracted. Again.

But surely he'd learned his lesson in the relationship department, enough so that he wouldn't make the same mistakes nowadays that he'd made in the past. Even though Mary Rose tempted him powerfully to forget everything he knew about himself. And her.

He broke contact with that sea-blue stare and, thankfully, saw Abby heading their way. Picking up a menu, he put them back on level ground. "What do you want for dessert?"

Mary Rose took a few seconds to answer. "Oh... nothing, thanks. Just some coffee."

"Are you sure? Abby's pies are not something you want to dismiss lightly."

"I remember." He glanced up and saw that her smile had taken on a brittle look.

"So what's next?" Abby flipped the page on her order pad. "Lemon meringue? Apple? Strawberry? Carrot cake?"

"Just two coffees." Pete shrugged at Abby's amazed stare. "We're satisfied with the wonders of your cheeseburgers. Some acts are too hard to follow, you know?"

Like the woman across the table.

Since the dinner crowd had departed, they finished their coffee and their plans for the class in the quiet of the almost-empty diner. Mary Rose didn't give him a hassle about paying for their meals, a respite for which Pete was intensely grateful. Even as infrequently as he dated, he'd gotten tired of haggling with women over who paid for what. She let him open the door for her, another courtesy he appreciated. Outside, the springtime darkness stroked gently across his face. A deep breath brought the scent of new leaves, green shoots, damp earth.

"Nothing like a Southern night," he commented as he walked Mary Rose across the deserted parking lot to her Porsche. "Or a great car. Too bad you don't get to exercise its full potential."

She glanced up at him out of the sides of her eyes as she unlocked the door. "Who says?"

That smile of hers always got to him. Arms crossed, he leaned against the Porsche's bumper. ''As a state trooper, ma'am, it's my duty to warn you that there's nowhere in this part of the country outside a racetrack you could drive this vehicle up to its maximum speed.''

''I'll keep that in mind.'' Mary Rose put an elbow on the car's roof and faced him. Once again, she was close enough to touch. ''Thanks for dinner.''

''You're more than welcome.'' Moonlight played in her hair, shadowed her eyes, defined her cheekbones and shoulders and the curves of her breasts. He was all too aware of the long, elegant legs under her skirt, the glimpse of bare skin at the throat of her shirt. Keeping his hands off her was taking all the willpower he had.

And it wasn't enough. Tested beyond the limits of his strength, Pete lifted his hand to the soft fall of gold-and-silver hair, let his fingers curve around the nape of her neck to draw her close, even as he bent his head to bring their mouths together.

He tasted coffee laced with cream and sugar. But under that, an essence he'd never forgotten, a sweetness that drove him instantly from wanting to craving. With a sigh, he folded his arms around Mary Rose Bowdrey and surprised them both with the passion that shook him.

She'd forgotten how big he was, Mary Rose realized. He surrounded her like the night, filled her with the same sense of infinity. His lips moved over hers, demanding… then gentle, playful…and then intense, until she couldn't follow the mood anymore, until she could only let her head fall back against his arm while Pete Mitchell took whatever pleased him. She had no doubt that, in the process, he would please her, too.

At the sound of shattering glass, Pete jerked his head

up. The rest of his body was like a rock above her. They stood that way for seconds, until the sound came again.

"What is it?" Mary Rose whispered, barely able to breathe. "Where is it?"

"At the school." He levered himself away from her, took hold of her shoulders and pushed her down into the seat of the Porsche. "Lock your doors, then call 911. Then go home. In that order. Got it?"

She nodded, but he was already running away from her, toward the school. Alone.

After she called the police, she sat with the doors locked for a few seconds, trying to recover her emotional balance. Finally, remembering the gang signs painted on the wall of the diner, Mary Rose edged the Porsche into the black shadows looming over the rear parking lot of New Skye High.

AS HE ROUNDED the corner into the darkness behind the New Skye gym, Pete heard gasping breaths of laughter and several pairs of footsteps running away from him. Without a weapon, without backup, there wasn't much he could do to stop them. He stood with his hands on his hips, getting his breath back and swearing at the stupidity of teenagers. Or was it gangs?

With a sudden roar, the powerful Porsche engine came up behind him, its headlights showing him the departing shadows of three teenage boys, now a long way beyond his reach. In front of him on the asphalt, shards of glass from the high windows in the gym lay scattered like diamonds in a coalfield. Most of the debris would have fallen inside. He winced, thinking of Mr. Davis's dismay at the damage to the highly polished floor.

Then he saw the writing on the wall. Spray painted vulgarities, crude, suggestive pictures…and gang marks.

Something about those bothered him, but he didn't have time to figure out what, as two patrol cars pulled up behind Mary Rose's Porsche. First, he would make a report, then give a certain stubborn woman a piece of his mind. And then figure out what it was about the gang signs that struck him as wrong.

The two police officers weren't the brightest crayons in the box, so it took him a while to get to the second part of his agenda. The Porsche was blocked in, though, so Mary Rose couldn't leave until he'd said his piece.

Which he did, leaning over the door as she looked up at him from the driver's seat. "What the hell did you think you were doing coming over here? I told you to go home. You can't follow a simple direction?"

She blinked up at him. "I didn't think you should be back here in the dark all by yourself."

He blew out a frustrated breath. "I go into situations like this, on my own, all the time. That's what I get paid for. You, on the other hand, do not."

Now she rolled her eyes. "Don't give me the macho protective-male act, Pete. I thought you needed some light and maybe somebody around in case you got hurt."

"But not *you*." A little blunter than he'd intended, but what would he have done if she'd been hurt? Or even threatened with hurt?

She stared up at him for a minute, her eyes narrowed, her face still. "Fine. Tell those two…gentlemen…in back of me to get out of my way and I'll get out of yours." When he didn't move, she glanced up. "That means you have to let go of my car. Now."

He stepped back; Mary Rose slammed the door almost before he got his hand out of the way. Without waiting for the patrol cars to move, she turned the Porsche on a dime, edged between one of the cruisers and the chain-link fence surrounding the school property, then gunned the engine and sped off into the night.

Pete hung around with the police while they investigated the scene. He talked to Principal Floyd when he arrived, and stared at the two gang marks for Los Lobos on the back wall of the gym, trying to figure out why they disturbed him.

Finally, he went home to Miss Dixie. But instead of concentrating on the basketball playoff he'd wanted to see, he found himself thinking back over the last run-in with Mary Rose. What had he done wrong? He'd made her mad again, but why? All he'd wanted to do was keep her safe.

"Goes to show," he told the beagle as she lay beside him on the couch while he rubbed her stomach, "that I don't have a clue. Whatever I do backfires. 'Cept with you, Miss Dixie." He pulled her up on his chest to rub her ears. With a sigh, she collapsed bonelessly on top of him. "You're the only female I was ever good enough for, the only one I could ever make happy. And it's you I'm sticking with!"

PETE WAS ALREADY at work on the Camaro when Sal arrived on Saturday morning. He didn't look up as the boy got out of his car, but he was aware that Sal walked back toward the gym…to stare at last night's handiwork, no doubt.

"Nice, huh?" he asked as Sal came to stand beside the Camaro.

"For a fake."

Pete straightened up from underneath the hood. "What do you mean?"

Sal shrugged. "The technique is wrong. Somebody tried to make it look like Los Lobos did the job, but they missed some of the details. Close, but no cigar, as they say.''

"Another gang?"

"Nah. They'd put up their own sign. I'd say some white boys looking to make trouble. But that's just a guess." He leaned a hand on the fender and looked down into the engine. "So we got a week until race day. What else can we do to tune this baby up?"

Soon enough they were deep into the fine points of the engine. But Pete had to wonder if Sal was telling the truth as he saw it...or pulling a fast one on somebody he saw as just another representative of the law.

In other words, the enemy.

CHAPTER SEVEN

PETE FOUND Mr. Floyd waiting for him when he got to the gym Monday night. "I need to talk to you for a minute."

"Yes, sir." He dropped his gym bag on the floor and set the crate in which he kept files and paperwork for the REWARDS program on the check-in table. "Everything okay? No more vandalism?"

"Not last night, at least." Mr. Floyd was about the same height as Pete's six-two, but he carried an extra forty or fifty pounds. He always seemed to be overheated, and his collar always looked too tight. "No, this is about the rental fees for the gymnasium and classrooms."

Pete shut his eyes for a second. "Yes, sir?"

"Well, you know they've cut the school budget for next year, and we'll be making do with ten percent less funding than in the past. So, in order to make ends meet, we're going to need to raise our fees for the use of the building, effective immediately. And for custodial services, of course."

"Mr. Floyd, you must have heard that the police budget got cut even more than the school budget did. Which means my funding through the department got slashed. I don't have the money to pay higher fees. If you give me a couple of months, I'll find some sponsors to help with expenses. But right now, I just don't have any extra money. I was hoping our rental fees could stand as they were." *As the contract states,* he wanted to say, but didn't. If the principal chose, he could end the contract right here and now. And then where would REWARDS be?

Mr. Floyd nodded. "I understand your problem, and I applaud the good work you're doing with these kids. But I'm responsible for the welfare of this school, and I'd be remiss in my duty if I didn't make sure that our financial needs came first. I'll send you a revised schedule of fees, and we can discuss what changes need to be made in order to keep your program running." He gave Pete a clap on the shoulder and stepped outside. "Have a good evening."

"Yeah, right," Pete muttered. "Kind of like telling the victim of the guillotine to sleep tight."

He was still frowning when Mary Rose came through the door, followed by Trace and Kelsey. Although her chin was up in the air, as if she wanted to convey that she was still mad, he saw her face change, saw concern take over. She shifted her briefcase to her left hand and put her right hand on his arm. "What's wrong?"

"Financial stress. Nothing for you to worry about." He had a feeling he should worry about how much he enjoyed having her hand on his bare skin. Those kisses in the parking lot of the diner had been on his mind all weekend.

But right now Mary Rose was all business. "Tell me what's wrong. Are you losing funding for the program?"

"Not completely. But I'm getting squeezed from both ends—fewer resources, higher fees." And he'd just expanded the program to include her class. *Great thinking, Mitchell.*

"You need outside sources of money."

"Tell me something I don't know. But the folks with

money to give away aren't usually interested in spending it on 'delinquents.' They'd rather support the art museum or the historical society. Makes fund-raising a real challenge.''

''Kate must know some people who would help. I'll talk to her as soon as I get a chance.''

''That'd be great. I appreciate it.'' She gave him a smile and headed across the gym toward the door to the classrooms. It was a long walk and gave him plenty of time to appreciate the rear view of Mary Rose Bowdrey wearing a short, slim, blue dress and high heels—her bare arms, her slender legs, the bounce of her hair and the sway of her hips.

Too bad he didn't have time for a cold shower before his class started.

SAL SHOWED UP for the Making Money Work class on Monday night because Pete asked him to, as a favor, so there would be somebody in the room besides the LaRue kids. Good call on the trooper's part, because when seven-thirty arrived there was only the three of them in the room with Ms. Bowdrey.

To give her credit, she took the lack of attendance with just a blink. ''I'm glad to see you,'' she told them, just as though there was a kid sitting in every desk. ''But I wonder why the three of you have to occupy the three farthest points in the room. Could you move up to the front? That will make it easier for us to talk.''

From the side, Sal could see Kelsey's pout, but she got up and went to a desk in the front row. Trace slouched into a seat one row back. Sal moved up to the first row, but left an empty desk between himself and Kelsey. The blonde's cute lower lip stuck out even farther. She was looking extremely hot tonight in a tight, crinkly shirt and jeans. But Sal was trying not to notice.

"Much better." Ms. Bowdrey smiled and came around to sit on the front of the desk. She wore a nice dress that skimmed her curves and ended just above her knees. Pete would be impressed when he saw her. "Now, the first thing we want to do when talking about money is establish some goals. Trace, what do you see yourself doing in five years?"

The kid shrugged one shoulder. "Don't have a clue."

"Are you going to college? Will you be in a job? Living on your own, at home?" Trace turned his head away without answering.

His aunt took his attitude in stride. "Well, think about it for a minute. Kelsey, how about you?"

"I guess I'll be in college." She cast a sidelong glance at Sal, which he did his best to ignore.

"How are you planning to pay for that?"

"My parents, of course."

"Okay. What about spending money?"

"I guess I'll get an allowance, just like now."

"And does your allowance last until the next installment?"

"Of course not. They only give me thirty dollars a month. How am I supposed to survive on thirty dollars?"

Sal choked. Kelsey rounded on him. "What are you laughing at?"

He shook his head. "Some families don't get thirty dollars a month to *live* on."

"Are you implying I'm spoiled?"

"You said it, I didn't."

As Kelsey's hands curled into fists, Ms. Bowdrey broke in. "Sal, where do you see yourself in five years?"

His turn under the microscope. He sat back in the chair. "I guess I'll be working on cars somewhere."

"Your goal is to work in the auto-repair business?"

"I guess so."

"Do you plan to work for someone else, drawing a salary? Or would you be interested in owning a shop? Being the boss?"

That wasn't something he let himself think about too much. "Owning your own place takes a lot of cash."

"True. Would you be interested in knowing how to get enough cash to run your own business?"

"Maybe." As if he could ever reach that high.

"So let's see what we can do about that."

To his surprise, the next hour turned out to be fun. Pete's lady seemed to know her stuff, and the worksheets she handed out talked about crazy characters and funny situations that made him and Kelsey smile, even if Trace's sour attitude didn't change much.

Sal was also surprised at how easily he understood the problems. Math had never been his subject but then again, what had? He got the idea of interest right away, though, and reconciling checking-account statements made complete sense.

Ms. Bowdrey gave them a break about halfway through the class. Trace took off fast; Sal got out of his desk and went to stare out the window into the darkness. Los Lobos would be on the move about now.

Behind him, Kelsey gave a groan. "I can't do it. I get a different number every time. This is impossible." She flipped her pencil across the room.

He turned to face her. "It's just math. Nothing to get upset about."

"You can say that because you understand. I hate being stupid."

"You aren't stupid, Kelsey." He walked back to her desk. "You're just not looking at the problems from the right direction." He braced his left arm on the desk and bent over her, close enough that her hair brushed his ear and her perfume washed over him. The smooth skin of her cheek caught his eye, and he struggled to control his reactions. "Think about it like this…"

Mary Rose came back into the room after getting a sip of water to find Sal instructing Kelsey on reconciling account statements. She wondered if he needed to be quite so close, but whatever he was saying appeared to be completely in line with the subject, and they were so deeply focused she hesitated to interrupt. How much trouble could there be in working on checking accounts?

Much more problematic was that Trace didn't come back to class after the break. They started without him, and since he hadn't contributed while present, the class lacked nothing when he wasn't there. But Mary Rose worried, nonetheless.

About nine-fifteen, she left Sal and Kelsey in the classroom with compound-interest problems and roamed the hallways, looking for Trace. The auto-mechanics shop was closed and she didn't find him in any of the rooms she peeked into. Finally, she went to the gym, hoping he'd dropped her class in favor of a basketball game or… or something.

There was no basketball game going on in the gym. Out in the center of the court on a blanket of blue mats, a bunch of barefoot kids in white robes and pants were going through the motions of a martial arts discipline, with Pete moving among them, correcting, explaining, complimenting. He wore the same dress as the students, with a brown belt instead of white. Mary Rose knew nothing about martial arts except that a brown belt signified a high degree of proficiency. Leave it to Pete to be good at this, too.

He saw her as she hesitated in the doorway. With a word to the students, he came across the floor. "Something wrong?"

"I can't find Trace. He didn't come back after the break."

Pete shook his head. "That kid is cruising for trouble. Let me get my class finished and we'll hunt him down." He put a hand on her shoulder and squeezed. The gesture really did make her feel better. Not to mention breathless.

When he came back, he'd slipped on a pair of sandals. "I'm betting he's out back, smoking with his buddies. Let's try there first."

"Smoking?" She hurried to keep up with him. "Trace smokes?"

"I caught him out here last week." He pushed open the back door, where cigarette smoke tainted the air. "Yeah, it's a hard habit to break. LaRue, you're an idiot."

Seconds later, three boys shuffled into the hallway ahead of Pete. "Bo, Eric, you're not even supposed to be here tonight. You didn't sign in. That'll get reported to your juvenile services counselor, probably add a few hours to your time. Same goes for you, LaRue. I warned you last time. I imagine your parents will have something to say about the smoking. I see cold turkey in your immediate future."

Pete escorted the other two boys to the gym to wait for their parents. Mary Rose walked with a silent Trace back to the classroom. Just outside the door, she put a hand on his arm and stopped him. "I don't understand. Why are you trying so hard to get into trouble?"

Hands in his pockets, he stared at his shoes.

"Trace, I expect an answer."

"I don't have anything to say."

"We used to be friends. You used to talk to me."

"Well, things change, right?"

"I don't want to make the situation worse for your mother, but I'm going to have to tell her you've been smoking."

"So tell her. Tell the old man while you're at it. We haven't had any fireworks for several days now. I'm sure he misses acting out his parental role." He turned his back and walked down the hall. "I'll be in the gym."

Mary Rose was beginning to understand exactly why Kate was so tired. She turned into the classroom, just wanting to gather up her papers and get home...to find Sal and Kelsey wrapped around each other, engaged in what looked to be an intense and dedicated kiss.

KELSEY WASN'T SURE exactly how it had happened. She really was trying to follow Sal's explanations about compound interest, but she couldn't concentrate on numbers when he leaned so close, when he smelled like some exotic spice, when his brown skin was so smooth and touchable. Without really thinking about it, she'd reached out to stroke her fingertips over his wrist, the back of his hand. She heard his breath catch, felt him go still. And then he was down on his knees beside her, his hands framing her face, bringing their mouths together.

Never had she been kissed like this. She recognized experience, and gentleness. He knew what he wanted, but he didn't take more than she could offer. The problem was, the more he asked for, the more she *needed* to give.

When he lifted his head, she didn't understand at first. He was breathing fast, his eyes black as he stared at her. His hands were gentle on her shoulders for another second.

"Kelsey?"

And then he was standing several feet away. Kelsey pushed her hair back and looked to the doorway where Aunt Mary Rose stood staring at her.

"Kelsey, what…?" She pressed her hand to her throat. "Sal, it's time for you to go home."

"Sure. G'night." Without looking at either of them, he left the room.

Kelsey was still having trouble breathing. Not to mention thinking, beyond remembering how wonderful Sal's lips felt. She jumped when Mary Rose sat in the desk next to hers—she'd forgotten her aunt was still here.

"Are you okay?" Mary Rose's soft hand covered hers. "Did he hurt you?"

"Oh, no." How could anything so amazing hurt? "No…he just kissed me."

"That's good. But is it a good idea?"

"Is what a good idea?" She wasn't following the conversation too well.

"Getting involved with Sal. He's older than you, Kelsey."

"So?"

"And more experienced."

Definitely. "What difference does that make?"

"He might expect more than you're prepared to give." More than everything? "You're just upset because his skin is darker than mine. You don't want me involved with a Mexican."

"His nationality has nothing to do with it. His culture is different, though. And he's been in trouble with the law, more than once. This doesn't sound like the kind of guy you need to be with. Too many conflicts."

"Good grief, it was only a kiss." And this postmortem

was spoiling everything. Kelsey got to her feet and went to the door. "He didn't ask me to marry him or anything. Relax, Aunt M. My virtue is still intact."

Though, she would admit that Sal might just be persuasive enough to make a girl reconsider her intention to stay a virgin until marriage. He possessed a masculine power she'd never encountered in another boy.

And, already, she craved another taste.

KATE WAS WAITING for them in the living room when they got home. "You're home early. How'd the class go?"

While Mary Rose was framing an answer, Kelsey slipped behind her and ran up the stairs. Trace clumped after his sister, and their doors slammed simultaneously.

"Mary Rose?"

She faced her sister. "There were three kids in the class tonight—Trace and Kelsey and that boy who works on Pete's race car, Sal Torres. Things went okay for the first half, but when we took a break, Trace didn't come back." She explained what he was doing when they found him.

"Smoking!"

Might as well get everything out in the open. "And when I got back to class, I found Sal and Kelsey... kissing."

"In the classroom?"

"Um, yes."

Kate stood up, then sat down again. "This just gets worse and worse. Trace is smoking, Kelsey's drinking and...and making out with boys she barely knows. She's only fifteen. He's only thirteen. What in the world is going on?"

Mary Rose sat in a nearby chair and reached out to hold Kate's hands in her own. "You've said already... it's all about L.T. His leaving has completely disrupted their world. I don't know that you're going to be able to solve these problems by yourself, because you're not the real source. Have you thought about taking them to a counselor? Maybe all of you need some outside help."

"I suggested that to L.T. when he first left. He wasn't interested."

"So you and the kids can go without him."

"Perhaps." She leaned back in the chair and closed her eyes. "But I have to talk to them first."

"Not necessarily." Mary Rose met her sister's questioning stare with a shrug. "I talked with Kelsey a little about why Sal might not be a good choice for a boyfriend. And I'm pretty sure Trace knows why smoking is a bad idea. They might appreciate not being called on the carpet for a change."

Kate closed her eyes again. "Not forcing another confrontation? That seems so easy, it can't be a good idea." When the phone rang, she winced. "Who would that be so late?"

"I'll answer." Mary Rose went into the kitchen and picked up the extension there. "Hello?"

"Mary Rose, it's Pete. I thought I'd check up on you and on Trace. Y'all got home okay?"

The warmth of his voice weakened her knees. She felt for a chair at the table, eased into it. "We did, thanks. The atmosphere is a little strained, but we're home."

"I talked with Sal and he said he enjoyed your class. I imagine he'll get a few of his friends to show up for the Wednesday session. Those desks will be filled in no time."

Did he also tell you I caught him kissing Kelsey? Somehow, it seemed like a betrayal to share that incident. "He's a very bright boy. I imagine he could go as far as he wanted to."

Pete sighed. "Yeah, but he isn't used to looking at wide horizons, so I'm not sure where he'll actually end up. And he does have a record with the juvenile court."

She stopped breathing. "For what?"

"In the past, he's been involved with Los Lobos, a Hispanic gang with a reputation for violence, some drug involvement, vandalism. I don't know if he's still involved—I can't get him to talk about it anymore. But his last arrest had to do with a gang fight."

That put the situation in a different light altogether. "He's interested in Kelsey, Pete. We can't let her get involved with somebody like that."

"Listen, I don't want you to get the wrong picture about Sal. That arrest was a couple of years ago. He works with me in the REWARDS program now because he wants to, not because he's assigned there. He's no bigger risk to society at this point than Trace is. Or Kelsey, for that matter. She's the one who was driving drunk, without a license."

"But she's younger than Sal, a lot more innocent. He's a real threat to her safety. And her future."

There was a long pause. "I'm getting echoes from the past here. Seems to me your parents said pretty much the same thing, ten years ago."

Another silence passed while Mary Rose struggled with the need to defend herself. "That's not the issue. Kelsey is at an incredibly vulnerable point in her life. A relationship with Sal will just make everything worse."

"And what do you want me to do?"

"I think you could talk to him, explain that with the

upheaval in her family, Kelsey really doesn't need a boyfriend.''

"Sometimes a boyfriend can be a real help."

"Not when you're this young." How much less would she have suffered if she'd never gotten involved with Pete Mitchell?

"I guess you have the experience to back up that opinion," he said, as if he'd heard her thoughts. "I'll talk to Sal, remind him that he doesn't need the hassle of dealing with a princess and her family. See you Wednesday."

Pete hung up the phone without giving the woman on the other end a chance to object. He hadn't been this mad in years. Mad enough to spend an hour getting the kitchen perfectly clean, then attack the bathroom, do the laundry, which had been piling up for a couple of weeks…okay, maybe a month…and bundle up the accumulated newspapers for recycling. Miss Dixie sat on the couch and stared at him as if he was crazy.

About midnight, he finally calmed down and sat down. "'Somebody like that'" he mimicked as Miss Dixie pricked her ears. "Sal's just a regular kid. Pretty much the same as I was at that age. Okay, I wasn't in a gang. But as far as her parents were concerned, I might as well have been. And I didn't mean any harm to Mary Rose. I would have taken care of her, given her everything I could, kept her safe. I'm betting Sal would do the same."

Nevertheless, he decided to talk to Sal on Tuesday night. Watching the boy with Kelsey in class, he could tell that something had changed. There was still plenty of tension between them, but not the antagonistic kind. He began to understand why Mary Rose was worried.

He didn't know whether to be glad or sorry that Kate picked up the LaRue kids that night. The prospect of seeing Mary Rose in the evening added a certain brightness to his day. Even when she made him mad, she got his blood flowing with a rush he hadn't known in quite a while. But hadn't he already decided that was a rush he could live without?

Once the classroom had cleared out, he walked over to the Camaro, where Sal was still tinkering. "Got it set?"

"Think so." Sal straightened up. "We'll find out Saturday."

"Yeah." Pete jammed his hands into his pockets. "Listen, I need to check with you on something."

The boy carefully laid a wrench in the tool chest. "What?"

"It's about Kelsey LaRue."

Sal's face hardened. "I got nothing to say."

"Her aunt says you and she are...involved."

"Her aunt is wrong."

"You're not interested?"

He got a one-shouldered shrug in reply. When he crossed his arms, expecting a better answer, Sal rolled his eyes. "Hey, she's a real hottie. Who wouldn't be interested?"

The disrespectful attitude was reassuring...but unacceptable. "You shouldn't talk about a girl like that, Sal. Whether you're interested or not."

"Quit hassling me, okay? I'm just trying to tell you there's nothing here to talk about."

"I'm glad to hear it. 'Cause I can tell you from experience that getting involved with the pampered-princess type is a recipe for disaster, unless you come from the same side of town."

Sal's glance was too perceptive. "You and the aunt had some good times, huh?"

Pete felt his face heat up. "I've made a few mistakes

over the years, and one of them was believing I could make that kind of relationship work. It's a waste of time.''

"I believe you, man." Sal pulled his shirt on. "Don't worry about me. I'm more interested in what's happening on Saturday than anything else. You ready to roll?''

"One hundred percent." Relieved to have the conversation done with, Pete closed up the shop and said goodnight to Sal.

But he wondered, as he drove home to Miss Dixie, if he'd just been made the victim of a major snow job. If Sal had lied to him, then Mary Rose was right and there was more to the situation with Kelsey than the boy wanted to admit.

"Another replay of *Romeo and Juliet*," Pete said with a groan. "Only this time, I get to be the hard-hearted, can't-see-the-truth-until-it's-too-late adult."

He shook his head, anticipating all the complications in the near future. "Thanks, Mary Rose. Thanks a lot."

KELSEY KNEW the moment Sal came into the classroom Wednesday night. The air prickled against her skin, seemed to crackle around her, even though she stopped herself from turning to look at him. She heard the whisper of his jeans as he slid into the desk a row back and several seats over. He wasn't coming too close. But he was there, and she knew he was thinking about her, too.

Four other kids showed up that night. Ricky, Joey, Benita and Ava were part of Los Lobos, she knew from what Lisa had found out about the gang, and were probably there because Sal had told them to come. But that was okay—Mary Rose obviously liked having the extra kids in class.

Even better, they distracted her at break time. Sal left

the room right away, but Kelsey pretended to work on some problems for a few minutes, to make it look as if she didn't care one way or the other. With only about five minutes left, she put down her pencil, picked up her purse and headed for the door.

"Kelsey? Where are you going?"

She turned her most innocent look to the front of the room. "Just the bathroom, Aunt M. I'll be back in five. Promise." Outside the door, she headed in exactly the opposite direction.

How she knew he would be there, Kelsey wasn't sure. But when she pushed open the door into the pitch-black garage, there were lights on in the office in the back corner. As she came close, she saw Sal leaning back against the desk, hands in the pockets of his jeans, staring at the floor as if he was waiting for something. Someone. Her.

He looked up as she came to the door. "Hey."

She moved into the office. "Hi."

"Not a good idea, you following me like this."

"Who says? More important, who cares?"

"Your parents will. Your aunt." But he reached out, closed his fingers around her wrist, pulled her close.

Kelsey stepped between his feet, set her hands on his shoulders. "I'm the one who matters. And this is what I want." She put her palm against his cheek, and he leaned into her touch with a sweetness that stole her breath. "How about you?"

Sal closed his arms around her waist, tight. "Let me show you what I want."

"HOW'D IT GO TONIGHT?"

Mary Rose looked up to see Pete in the doorway. She was feeling good enough about the evening to give him a wide smile. "Very well. Sal brought some of his friends, and they really livened up the class. Even Trace participated a couple of times. I think we all had fun."

"I'm glad to hear it. I figured if Sal was interested, he'd bring along more kids." He came across the room and propped one hip on the corner of the desk. "I...uh...talked to him by the way. He says there's nothing going on between him and Kelsey."

She kept her eyes down as she closed the latches on her briefcase. "They both left the room tonight at the break, but came back separately just as I started class again. I don't know if they were together or not." Then she looked up at Pete. "But I know there's something in the air when they're in the same room. A...a kind of electricity. It's impossible to miss."

As Pete held her gaze, she knew he understood what she meant, because it was happening at that moment, between the two of them. She was completely aware of him—the strength in his shoulders and arms under the white robe, the pulse beating in the hollow of his throat, the shape and texture of his mouth. His very stillness told her he was thinking...feeling...much the same thing.

"Aunt M? You ready to go?"

Kelsey's voice broke the moment. Mary Rose dragged in a deep breath and picked up her briefcase. "I'm coming, honey. Right this instant." She felt Pete's eyes on her as she went to the door. Turning to face him required another deep breath. "I—I guess I'll see you next Monday night. Have a good weekend."

He stood and came toward her, flipping the light switch as he passed. "I expect it'll be a great weekend. I'm racing on Saturday."

"Well, then, have fun. And drive safely."

"I'll do my best."

For a few seconds they stood together on the border between the lighted hallway and the dark classroom. Mary Rose stared up into Pete's shadowed face, saw him debate what he was about to say. She heard him swallow hard in anticipation.

"You wouldn't...I guess...be interested in coming out to watch me drive Saturday. Would you?"

Oh, my stars. The strength of her longing to do just that shocked her. For a minute she couldn't think of anything but how much she wanted to say yes.

"That's okay, don't worry about it." Pete dismissed the invitation with a wave of his hand. "I know it's not your kind of entertainment. I wasn't thinking."

"No, no, that's not it at all." She put a hand on his arm. "I think watching you race sounds like a lot of fun."

"You do?" His silver gaze was worried, vulnerable. Underneath her hand, his skin was warm, a little rough with hair. She fought the urge to stroke him, to explore further.

"Yes, I do." Mary Rose hesitated another moment, then gave herself up for lost. She sent Pete a flirtatious glance. "You know how much I like speed. What time should I be ready?"

CHAPTER EIGHT

"LaRue party? Let me show you to your table."

This old-fashioned steak house wasn't Kelsey's favorite restaurant, but after two weeks of restriction, she wouldn't argue with the chance to get out of the house on a Friday night. Even Trace brightened up a little bit at the thought of spending a couple of hours somewhere besides his bedroom.

Kate and Aunt M settled across from each other at the square table, and Kelsey sat opposite Trace. The four of them wolfed down cheese spread and crackers while the adults talked about REWARDS—something to do with needing more money to keep the program running, and Kelsey had to bite her tongue so she wouldn't make a comment about what she thought they could do with the whole idea. They had just started on their salads when the hostess showed a couple to the table in the corner, directly in Kelsey's line of sight.

It was her dad and the Bimbo.

Thanks to a planter, Mary Rose couldn't see that corner of the restaurant, and Trace and Kate were facing the opposite direction. That left Kelsey as the only witness. She pretended to eat, all the while watching the cozy couple hold hands, clink glasses, whisper to each other, as if they'd read the manual on being romantic and were following every rule.

They looked so happy. Her dad seemed relaxed, as he

hadn't been at home for a long, long time. He only had eyes for his date, didn't seem to notice anybody else in the room.

Kelsey blinked back tears and looked down at her steak. She couldn't possibly eat a huge hunk of meat, not with her stomach twisting and turning inside her. Even without forcing another bite into her mouth, she thought she might be sick.

Kate put a hand over hers. "Are you okay? You're not eating."

For once, telling the truth wasn't hard. "I feel sick."

Immediately, Kate's cool hand came to her forehead. "Do you have a fever? Sore throat?"

Kelsey could only shake her head. If she tried to talk, she really would throw up.

"Let's take the food home and eat there." Mary Rose signaled the waitress and the next few minutes got busy with paying the check and transferring all their meals into take-out boxes. Meanwhile, the couple in the corner billed and cooed like the lovebirds they were.

Fortunately, her dad and the Bimbo went to the salad bar just a minute before Kate and Mary Rose would have seen them when they stood up to leave. Somehow, they all managed to get out of the restaurant with only Kelsey the wiser. Even Trace didn't realize how close they'd been to a real disaster. The thought of Kate coming face-to-face with the Bimbo gave Kelsey the shivers.

She trembled all the way home. Aunt M walked her upstairs and tucked her into bed while Kate made hot tea with lemon and honey. Then they both sat in her room, talking about nothing important, kind of waiting for her to feel better, she supposed.

Finally, though, they left her alone. With the door shut,

she was free to give in to the tears that had been waiting since tonight's first glimpse of the man she still wanted to call Daddy.

AFTER COMMITTING herself to spending the evening at the racetrack with Pete, Mary Rose hoped for harsh winds and drenching rain. Even in the sunny South, April weather could be unpredictable, right?

But Saturday dawned as a perfect spring day, with soft air and clear skies. She had no excuse for backing out on this date, unless she confessed to a bad case of nerves. And she didn't want to admit that weakness, even to herself.

So she dressed in jeans and sneakers, put her hair in a ponytail in readiness for the sports cap Pete had said was a requirement for racing spectators, and went downstairs to drown the butterflies in her stomach with iced tea and a couple of Kate's chocolate chip cookies.

Her sister was sitting at the kitchen table with papers spread everywhere. "I'll move some of these," she said as Mary Rose poured herself a glass of tea and refilled Kate's. "You're all set for the racetrack?"

She couldn't confess the way her heart pounded at the prospect of seeing Pete again. "Should be interesting. I hope I don't come back deaf. What are you working on?"

"The plans for the Azalea Festival Street Fair. There's a committee meeting here tonight. I can't believe we've got just four weeks to bring it all together." Kate rubbed her eyes with her fingertips. "Why do I volunteer for so much?"

"Because you're good at it, because you care about making your community a better place?"

"Or because I was trying to escape what was going

on at home. Staying too busy to notice that L.T. was...
straying...and how unhappy Trace and Kelsey were."

Mary Rose sat down at the space Kate had cleared.
"You're being too hard on yourself. You're close to the
kids, you know how they're feeling. As for L.T., well,
he was pretty careful to hide what was going on, wasn't
he?"

"All I can say is that I didn't know until he told me.
But I should have questioned the late nights at work, the
weekend 'meetings.' I was just so grateful he wasn't here,
raising a fuss..." Kate shook her head. "That's a terrible
thing to say, being glad your husband isn't at home. But
he's always so hard on Trace and Kelsey. Never gentle,
rarely supportive. We were all so tense when he was
around, afraid to put a foot wrong."

"I think it sounds like a good thing he's gone."

"That's a mean thing to say." From behind them, Kelsey's voice trembled with hurt and anger.

Mary Rose hadn't heard the girl's footsteps. She turned
to face her niece's outraged face. "I'm sorry, honey. But
your dad doesn't seem to have been an easy person to
live with."

"Maybe *we* were the problem, did you ever think
about that?"

Kate started out of her chair. "Kelsey—"

"Maybe he felt like all we wanted was more money.
Which meant he had to work harder, and he was tired
when he got home, but then he was supposed to do stuff,
take us places, go to Kate's stupid charity parties and all.
Maybe he got involved with the Bimbo because she
didn't make him run around town, because she let him
just—just rest. Maybe it was all our fault, and you're
sitting here talking about him like he's some kind of
monster!" With a sob, Kelsey spun around and ran

through the dining room. This time, they heard her feet pounding on the stairs and the slam of her bedroom door.

Picking up her glass with two shaking hands, Mary Rose took a sip of tea. "How can she be so confused? He got involved with another woman—a twenty-year-old, no less—for rest and relaxation?" She shook her head, tempted to laugh…except for the tears in her eyes. "Poor Kelsey."

Then she realized that Kate had broken down, crying relentlessly with her head buried in her arms on top of the paper-strewn table. "Oh, Katie. I'm so sorry. This is such hell for you." Arms around her sister, she held on through the sobs and went to the bathroom for tissues when the sobs reduced to sniffles.

"I'm the one who's sorry." Kate sat up, finally, still blotting her eyes. "I shouldn't have let myself go like that. It doesn't help."

"I'm not sure. If you need to cry, that might be the best thing to do." She'd cried gallons during her first semester at college, so much that her roommate had gotten fed up and moved in with someone else. Being alone had suited Mary Rose just fine, allowing her to endure her agony without a witness.

Gathering up the mountain of used tissues, Kate dumped them into the garbage compactor. "I suppose I really need to go up and talk to Kelsey. Again. What time are you leaving?"

"Pete said he'd be here at four."

"It's ten of, right now." Turning, her sister gazed at her with concern in her red-rimmed eyes. "Are you sure this is a good idea? I mean, spending time with Pete Mitchell…do you think it's safe?"

Mary Rose carried her glass to the sink. "Truthfully, I don't know."

"I thought you and Marty Cooper were getting pretty serious."

"We've been going out for quite a long time. He's mentioned marriage. But—" She took a deep breath. "I can't say I'm convinced. It's all very civilized and organized. Just not...persuasive."

"Are you using Pete as a test?"

"I—" Mary Rose closed her eyes, appalled at the thought. But, really, had she thought about Marty at all since Pete stopped her on the interstate? Didn't that pretty much sum up her feelings? "Out of sight, out of mind" was not a good omen for a marriage.

On the other hand, she had never, ever managed to forget Pete Mitchell.

The doorbell rang, and she looked at Kate. "Saved by the bell. I'll be back pretty late, so don't wait up." She kissed her sister on the cheek, grabbed her purse and went to the front door.

Pete stood on the front porch—big, dynamic, sexy as sin in his tight T-shirt and jeans, and obviously as wound up as a ten-year-old boy with a new bike. "You look great. Ready to see some major racing action?"

Mary Rose couldn't help grinning in response. "I wouldn't miss it for the world."

WHEN KELSEY OPENED her bedroom door, she thought her stepmother's face looked as bad as her own, red-eyed and splotchy. But that didn't call up much sympathy. "What do you want?"

"World peace?" It was a reference to a line from one of their favorite movies. Once upon a time, Kelsey would have smiled.

Today there didn't seem to be much to smile about. "Not likely. So if that's all..."

Kate put her hand on the door as it started to close. "Kelsey, you know that's not all."

She suddenly lost the energy to keep fighting. "Fine. Come in. Say whatever it is you think you need to say."

"I'm not sure I'm the one who needs to talk. I'd rather listen."

"This is going to be a very quiet conversation. I don't have anything to say."

"Are you feeling better? After last night?"

"Oh, sure." Once she'd thrown up the cheese and crackers and salad and honey tea, her stomach had settled down.

"Seeing your dad in the restaurant upset you, didn't it?"

Kelsey let her jaw drop. "You knew he—they—were there?"

Her stepmother nodded. "The people I could see were whispering, nudging each other, even pointing. I took a quick peek over my shoulder to see what was going on."

"You didn't say anything."

"What was there to say? If we'd stormed out in a huff, everybody would have been talking about it today." She gave a sad smile. "I was really grateful you weren't feeling good, though. You looked so sick, it gave us a great excuse to leave."

"But when we got home…"

"You were in no mood or condition to talk about it. And I'm pretty sure Trace didn't see anything, so there wasn't any point in getting him upset, too."

"No. Trace doesn't notice much these days." She knelt on the window seat and put her elbows on the sill, catching the cool breeze as it came through the screen. "He looked…happy." In a whisper, she added, "Without us."

"I can't explain that," Kate said. "Except that perhaps he's enjoying a kind of freedom from responsibility. Like going to a resort for your vacation, where you don't have to think about housework or meals because someone is doing it all for you. Your dad might enjoy feeling like he's on vacation from all his family obligations."

"I don't like being an obligation."

"Nobody does."

"Why doesn't he miss us?"

"He will, eventually."

"And he'll come back?" Kate didn't say anything. Finally, Kelsey looked back at her stepmother. "Well?"

"I can't promise that. I don't know what he'll do."

"But you would let him come back, right? So we could be a family again?"

Kate pushed her hair away from her face. "I can't commit to that right now, Kelsey. It would depend on a lot of things."

"Like what?"

"What your dad had to say, what he would commit to…it's very complicated."

"Why would it be complicated? If he wants to come home, that's all that counts."

"I have to be able to trust him, honey. To know that this kind of situation won't happen again."

"You're going to make rules, aren't you? Make him promise all sorts of things." Kelsey pounded her fist against the seat cushion. "You're going to punish him for leaving."

In her lap, Kate's hands had clenched into white-knuckled balls. "I don't want to punish him. But I deserve respect, as a person and as a wife. If he can't respect me, how can I live with him?"

There should have been an answer to that question, a

way to persuade her stepmother that taking her dad back was the right thing for all of them.

But Kelsey couldn't find that right answer, couldn't see through the complications to any kind of solution. With a sigh, she put her head on her arms and let the breeze blow through her hair.

"I understand you're interested in a boy you met at the REWARDS program," Kate said after a while. "He works in the auto shop with Mr. Pete?"

Fear and anger exploded in Kelsey's chest. She sat up straight. "I don't know who you're talking about."

"The boy Mr. Pete introduced us to the first night of REWARDS. Sal...Sal Torres."

"And what else did Mary Rose say?"

"You don't need to be sarcastic, Kelsey. She's worried about you."

"Well, she shouldn't be. Sal's just a boy at school." If they knew any different, they'd probably chain her to the bedpost and never let her out of her room again.

"Mary Rose said you were kissing him in the classroom Monday night."

"Shit!" She jerked to her feet. "Can't I have any privacy? Does my whole life have to be up for inspection? So I kissed him. Big deal, okay? I've kissed lots of guys and I'll kiss lots more. Leave it alone. Leave me alone."

"I'll say this, and then I will leave you alone." Kate went to stand in the doorway. "Sal has been involved with a gang. He has a police record. We—"

Kelsey laughed. "So do I."

Her stepmother took a deep breath. "We don't know his family, his background, anything at all about who he is. I knew a great deal about your dad before I married him...and look how things have turned out. You want to be very sure you can trust the person you care for. We don't want to see you hurt, Kelsey. It's our responsibility and our joy to take care of you. Please, please consider carefully before you get involved with someone like Sal. You could make a mistake that affects the rest of your life.''

Without waiting for a response, Kate stepped into the hallway and closed the door. Kelsey threw herself on the bed, her face buried in the pillows.

She wanted a drink. But her weekends were dry these days because Kate didn't keep liquor in the house except for special occasions.

Even more than a drink, she wanted Sal. Wanted his arms around her, wanted his mouth moving over hers. He gave her a high without a hangover. Kelsey giggled at the thought.

Then she rolled across the bed to the phone. Lisa answered on the first ring. ''What's up?''

''Can you get a car tonight?''

''Maybe. Can you get out of the house?''

''Late. Say eleven-thirty. Meet me at the corner.''

''I'll be there.''

''See ya.''

Lying on her back, Kelsey stared up at the fluffy white clouds painted on her blue ceiling. Tonight she would get a drink and some time with Sal. He wouldn't be easy to find, but she knew where to start searching.

On the south side of Boundary Street.

PETE SENT SAL ahead to the track with the trailer while he picked Mary Rose up in his Jeep, which, though not very elegant, was a lot cleaner than the truck.

''Here's your official number eighty-nine Pete Mitchell cap.'' He dropped the gold hat with red lettering on her lap as she buckled her seat belt.

"You're number eighty-nine? Let me think…the year you graduated?"

"You got it."

She set the hat on her head, pulled her blond ponytail through the back and turned for his approval. "Does it look okay?"

"Fantastic." Just like everything she wore. Or, he was sure, when she wore nothing at all. Pete cleared his throat. "So, have you ever been to a car race?"

"This is my first."

He'd been her first in other ways, too. *Down, boy.* "This is Street Stock racing—the cars are basically your ordinary Detroit product with the engines modified for more power and the exteriors painted for racing."

"Yours is the Camaro, right?"

"An '86. Very cool to look at. Crazy to drive."

"So is this like a NASCAR race? A huge track, deafening noise, cars hitting walls—that sort of thing?"

Pete grinned. "Hopefully not hitting walls. The track is only half a mile, and we do forty laps. It's pretty loud, though. I brought you some ear protection."

"To wear over the hat? What a fashion statement."

"You'll look great, regardless."

Mary Rose seemed to hold her breath for a second. "So…what happens when we get there?"

On the forty-minute drive to the speedway, he explained the way a race worked—practice sessions, the qualifying heats and the race itself. Mary Rose asked intelligent questions about the engine and the tires, about the driving skills needed to compete.

"You sure you haven't watched a few races? Or driven them?" He chuckled. "Come to think of it, the speed you were making coming into town that day, you probably do know a good bit about what it takes to keep a car under control.''

''I read a lot of car magazines before I decided to buy the Porsche. I guess I picked up on some of the racing details.''

He was worried that she would be disappointed by the speedway itself. After all, it was just a small, privately owned asphalt track with aluminum bleachers and a single concession stand, not a big, impressive stadium like Daytona or Charlotte.

But Mary Rose took everything in stride. She stood by while Pete and Sal unloaded the Camaro, fetched drinks and sandwiches from the cooler as they worked, held his helmet as he donned his racing suit and boots. During the prerace inspections and the practice runs, she watched and listened, but never got in the way.

For a princess, the lady demanded precious little attention.

Then it was time for the qualifying run. Pete took hold of his helmet, but before he could put it on, Mary Rose put a hand on his arm.

''A kiss for good luck,'' she said and, leaning close, pressed her lips to his.

His pulse, already skipping, went into high gear. ''That's sure to get me the pole position.'' He looked at Sal, gave him their usual prerace nod. ''Let's do it.''

Mary Rose watched as Pete climbed feetfirst through the window of the Camaro, buckled the five safety belts and settled himself in the seat. With the flick of a switch, the engine rumbled and snarled its way to life. Then Sal came to stand beside her and together they watched the gold-and-red race car ease out onto the track.

Sal touched her arm with his fingertips. ''Pete wanted

me to help you find a good seat.'' He nodded toward the stands. ''This way.''

He led her to a spot high in the bleachers. ''You'll see most of the race from here. I need to stay in the pit, in case something goes wrong, but I'll come get you when the race is done.'' Before she could even say thank you, he'd turned away and jogged down the steps, disappearing into the crowd.

It occurred to her that she should say something to him about Kelsey. But that might ruin the night for all of them. Maybe after the race, she could corner Sal for a few minutes, suggest that he choose someone else to help him improve his kissing techniques.

Having resolved that issue, she sat with her elbows on her knees and watched as the pack of cars swept around to the far side of the track, then raced back toward the bleachers with a collective roar that shook her all the way to her spine. Pete's car was in the center, seemingly blocked on four sides by other racers. But on the next curve, the clump of cars broke apart, with a couple sliding up the bank toward the wall, some falling away slightly, while others held their course. As they rumbled into the back straightaway, Mary Rose saw the gold-and-red Camaro swerve to the inside and then slip through a small space between two other cars. All at once, Pete was out in front. He kept his lead as the throng of cars took the last turn and he crossed the finish line first, with the nearest car almost a full length behind him.

But, he'd told her, this was just the first qualifying heat. Another group of cars would run the same two laps, and the top racers from that group would join the fastest from Pete's heat in the final race. She watched the second round with less interest, wishing she could be down in the pit with Pete, even if that meant merely watching while he and Sal performed the arcane adjustments that would make the Camaro run its best.

She was behaving like a teenager, she realized, willing just to watch and be ignored. What had happened to the mature, independent woman she had worked so hard to become?

The second heat finished up, and the final set of cars moved out onto the track for the race. The red-and-gold Camaro was at the head of the group, on the inside of the curve. Pete had gotten the advantage he wanted, she saw with a smile. Maybe her kiss really had been good luck. That was all it meant, of course.

With the wave of a green flag, the pack of cars leaped forward. The noise level rocketed to unbearable. Mary Rose put on the ear guards Pete had given her and sighed with relief. Watching the race was exciting enough. She didn't have to hear it, too.

Each lap of the track passed in mere seconds. Following the gold-and-red Camaro on its repeated revolutions made her dizzy, especially on the turns, but she couldn't look away, couldn't resist the fascination of following the driver she knew to be Pete as he blazed around the racetrack. He held his position in first place through ten laps, even with a black-and-green car constantly menacing his rear bumper. Whenever that second car made a move, a shift to the right, to the left, Pete blocked it. His focus would have to be phenomenal, to drive at such high speeds and yet be aware of the competitor in his rearview mirror.

At the beginning of lap twelve, Pete was still in the lead, with the black-and-green car riding just to his rear on the right side. The two vehicles swept out of the front stretch and into the curve, the second-place car inching forward.

For no reason that Mary Rose could see, Pete's Camaro suddenly grazed the inside wall, scraping along the concrete block with a shower of sparks. The black-and-green car moved to pass just as the Camaro jettisoned off the barrier; the two racers collided, sliding up the bank of the curve toward the outside. While the rest of the pack drove furiously onward, the Camaro and its nemesis slammed into the outside wall, spun around and around and then slammed again before slowly sliding to a stop.

Paralyzed, Mary Rose watched the crash, saw men running toward the two cars, saw the ambulance lights approach. In seconds, the emergency vehicles blocked her view of the mangled cars, so she couldn't see whether the drivers got out, couldn't tell whether Pete was okay or...

She gripped her hands tight together, held her feet and legs exactly parallel, took evenly spaced, controlled breaths. She couldn't allow herself to think, or even move, because if she opened her mind at all, the impossible, the unbearable would make itself known.

And so she sat in a vacuum of thought and sound, watching the other cars drive at a slow pace around and around the oval while the disaster was dealt with. The ambulance lights clicked off, the vehicles drove away, and she didn't consider what that might mean. Wreckers came onto the track and towed the Camaro and the black-and-green car away. Though she looked for Pete and Sal among the men working, the crash site was too far away, her mind too numb to take in details. She didn't try to assess what kind of damage had been done. She simply sat with her hands gripped together, waiting for the world to somehow fall back into proper orbit again.

With the track clear, the race resumed. Mary Rose

stared at the cars going round and round. She noted the checkered flag as it flashed down. Somebody had won.

Just at that moment, a pair of hands jolted her back to reality by taking the ear guards off her head. Sound rushed painfully into her world. Wincing, Mary Rose looked up and found Pete sitting on the bench beside her, his face black and sweat-streaked, his grin as wide and wicked as always. A quick glance showed her the remarkable absence of broken bones or even bruises. Without another thought, she surged toward him, closed her arms hard around his neck, buried her face under his chin.

"Thank God you're all right." She was crying and didn't care. "I thought you must be dead."

Chuckling, Pete pulled her closer still, rubbed his cheek against the silky blond ponytail. "There were a couple of seconds there when I thought so, too." He stroked her back, feeling the sweet curve of her spine through the T-shirt. "But they don't make us put all that safety gear into the car for nothing. Roll bars, head protectors, belts...they serve their purpose now and then." She felt so good, tight against him like this. Even though his body was starting to ache like a sore tooth, he could have sat there on that hard bleacher all night long, holding Mary Rose in his arms.

After a few minutes, she loosened her grip a little. "What about the other guy? Is he okay?"

"The jerk has a broken ankle. It's the least he deserves, trying to pull a stunt like that on a little track like this."

"What did he do?" To his delight, instead of pulling away with the question, she nestled into his chest again.

"Tried to bump me out. A really bad idea all around, on a small track like this. He's lucky he didn't kill us both."

Now she did sit up, and he reluctantly let her go. "What about your car? Is the Camaro fixable?"

With a sigh, then a groan, Pete got to his feet. He held Mary Rose's hand as they made their way down the steps to the ground. "The body is pretty much a wreck. I don't know about the engine. We'll just take her home and see what we can salvage. Nothing else to be done."

At the bottom of the bleachers, she put a hand on his chest. "Oh, Pete, I'm so sorry."

"Me, too." He shrugged, wincing at the pull of muscles in his back. "But those are the breaks. Nobody gets out of this sport without the occasional crash. The cars can be fixed, or replaced. We're lucky that we're walking away relatively whole." Then he shook his head. "I did want to win tonight, though. I wanted to give you that checkered flag."

"I would have treasured the flag." Mary Rose smiled at him, and her eyes shone bright blue in the stadium lights. "But I'm happy just knowing you're safe and sound." Her arms came around his neck again and she stood on tiptoe, close against him. "Nothing matters as much as having you right here, right now."

Then her mouth claimed his, and the night exploded with a fireworks display like nothing he'd ever known.

CHAPTER NINE

THE CATCALLS and whistles from the folks on the bleachers finally broke them apart. Pete stepped back, let his hands come to rest on Mary Rose's shoulders. "I...uh...think this isn't the kind of action the crowd came to watch."

Her cheeks flamed. "I guess not. Is there somewhere I can hide?"

He turned her toward the exit and kept one arm around her as they walked. "How about just going on home? Sal's already headed out with the truck."

"Sounds good." When he opened the door to the passenger side of the Jeep for her, she paused. "Do you feel like driving? I can take the wheel if you want." Eyes laughing, she marked a cross over her heart with one finger. "And I promise to stick to the speed limit."

A stiff neck and back warred with his upbringing as a gentleman. Or his macho instincts, depending on the interpretation. Upbringing won. "Nah, I'm okay. It's a short drive."

Mary Rose sighed and shook her head, but hopped into the passenger seat. "If you say so."

Country music from the radio filled the silence as he aimed the Jeep for New Skye. Since it was Saturday night, all the songs seemed to be about partying, getting drunk, and partying some more. Not exactly romantic.

Pete finally put in a Tim McGraw tape he knew would be mostly mellow. At least they could talk over the lyrics.

His passenger turned sideways in her seat. "Do you always listen to country music?"

"Most of the time. Do you hate it? We can find something else."

"No, no, it's okay. I don't listen to any kind of music, really. If my radio's on, it's usually tuned to the daily financial report."

"I'm still trying to picture you as an investment wizard. I would never have imagined it that summer." He glanced over, saw her frowning. "Sorry. I guess that's the wrong thing to say."

"No, don't apologize. I was pretty much an airhead in high school. I got accepted into the university, but I didn't have a clue about what I would do when I got there. Not until…" She cleared her throat. "Well, I guess my priorities were rearranged."

"How was that?" He gave in to his curiosity and asked, though he wasn't sure she would answer.

A long minute passed. "Guys, dating, the whole social scene just didn't mean much," she said finally. "I didn't seem to have anything in common with the students who lived for the weekend and the parties. Even after I…felt better…there was just too big a gap between my… experience and theirs. So I concentrated on my courses, found out I really liked math and accounting and economics. Pretty weird, but that's the way it turned out."

"So have you worked in Charleston since you left school?"

"I started out in a bank in Chapel Hill, where I went to school, then moved to a branch in Charlotte. I got a better offer from a different corporation and they sent me to Charleston. I've been there for four years now. I'm wondering if it's about time to move again.''

''Why not just settle permanently?''

''In business, you don't generally advance in the job if you stay in one place. Most executives move around a good bit.''

''And you want to advance?''

''I—I suppose so. What else would I do?''

''Get married, have a family?'' Really tricky ground, here. But he wanted…needed…to know. ''You said there was a guy you'd been dating.''

''Yes.'' Needing as much space as she could get, Mary Rose turned to face the windshield, put her feet squarely on the floorboard. ''I don't plan to have a—a family. Whether Marty and I get married or not.'' Surely he would take the hint and change the subject.

Instead of letting it go, he pressed harder. ''Because of your career?''

''Why else?'' This was not a subject she wanted to think about, or talk about with anyone, especially Pete Mitchell. Gripping her hands together, she looked out the window, saw only her reflection against the darkness and, behind her, Pete's shadowy profile in the dashboard lights. He seemed to be waiting for even more explanation. ''I've seen how hard Kate works to take care of Kelsey and Trace. I couldn't possibly manage my career and…and children.''

Couldn't possibly bear trying to have another child. But she had never said that to a living soul. Including herself.

''Do you sleep with him?''

She bit back a gasp, whipped her head around to stare at the man across the car. ''What business is that of yours?''

"After that kiss at the speedway, I'm thinking it's very much my business."

"Oh." That hadn't been her intent. She'd been so relieved to have him safe, so thankful, she'd just followed her impulse to let him know. How could she make Pete understand that he'd misinterpreted the gesture?

How could she be sure he had?

"Well?" He was going to push her for an answer to his question.

The quickest way to end this conversation was to give him his answer. "N-no. We aren't…intimate."

"Ah." Hearing the satisfaction in his tone, she wanted to slap him. She certainly didn't want to talk to him anymore.

Which turned out to be just as well, because they'd already reached the outskirts of New Skye. Kate's house was only a few minutes away; he would take her there and the night would be over. And that would be best for both of them. Pete was tired, sore. He was reading things into the relationship that shouldn't be there. Tempting her to do the same.

"You haven't had much to eat," she found herself saying. "Are you hungry? Would you like to stop somewhere?"

"I'm starving, as a matter-of-fact. But I'm not exactly cleaned up. You wouldn't want to be seen with such a derelict."

"You're not a derelict. I'd invite you to Kate's house and make us something, but she's having a meeting tonight. I expect you would probably feel better with a shower, anyway."

"No problem. You want to come to my place? I've got spaghetti and frozen garlic bread. Maybe even some lettuce for a salad. And you can meet Miss Dixie."

Warning signals blared in her head, but his smile urged her to ignore them. "I think that sounds like a lot of fun."

He stopped the Jeep in the driveway of a neat brick bungalow with blooming azaleas along the walls and a tall magnolia standing sentinel by the street. Mary Rose caught a glimpse of bright eyes and perked ears in the picture window before the curtain twitched down. With the Jeep doors open, she heard a series of frantic yips and barks coming from inside the house.

Pete wore the grin of a proud father. "That's Miss Dixie. She's usually pretty happy to see me get home." As soon as he opened the front door, a bundle of fur bounded into his arms. "Yes, sweetheart, I know it's been hours." The dog licked his face as he crooned to her. "Oh, yeah, baby. I love you, too."

Mary Rose couldn't help smiling at the nonsense. Finally, Pete turned the beagle to face her. "Mary Rose Bowdrey, meet my roommate, Miss Dixie. Dixie, darlin', this is Mary Rose. You be a good girl, okay?"

The dog went still in his arms, only her nose twitching as she surveyed the other woman. Mary Rose put a hand out to be sniffed. "Hey, Miss Dixie. I'm glad to meet you." Carefully, she stroked two fingers over the silky head. "You're a pretty girl, aren't you? A little jealous, too?" Dixie suffered the attention for a few seconds, then pointedly turned back to Pete.

Pete stared at the dog, his eyebrows drawn together in a frown. "I've never known her to be so unfriendly. Usually she's all over anybody I bring home."

"Maybe she doesn't like my perfume."

"That'd be bad taste on her part." He turned and walked toward the back of the house. "I'll put her outside. Make yourself at home while I grab a quick shower.''

A vision of Pete naked, with warm water glazing his skin, flashed into her mind. Mary Rose shook her head hard and sat down on the sofa, sifting through the magazines on Pete's coffee table, mostly law enforcement publications and racing rags. The summer they were together, she recalled, he'd read all the golf journals...and the racing rags. Some things never changed.

But some things did. Ten years ago—July 7, to be exact—she'd married Pete Mitchell. They'd lived together for a little over a month in the one-room apartment he had rented, sharing the cheap furniture that came with the place, subsistence groceries, and the red Mustang her parents had given her as a graduation present. Not to mention fantastic sex.

These days, she could afford a luxury condo in Charleston, a Porsche and the finest restaurants in the country. Pete was doing pretty well for himself, she thought—this house wasn't large but had been recently renovated with new windows, new paint and refinished hardwood floors. The sofa and armchairs were leather, the TV and sound system big and state-of-the-art. And then there was the race car. Chances were good that such powerful engines carried a hefty price tag.

After ten years, they were obviously different people, at different points in their lives, than the kids they were long ago. Mary Rose didn't act on impulse anymore. She considered options, made plans, evaluated results. Yet after ten years, here she was again...in Pete Mitchell's place.

Somewhere in the back of the house a faucet screeched, and the sound of water stopped. She imagined him standing in the tendrils of steam, running a towel over his shoulders, his chest and belly, his thighs. At twenty-one he'd still been a little rawboned, a bit lanky. Now he was all solid muscle, finely shaped.

And her palms were damp, her breathing shallow at the thought. An ache was growing deep inside her, an ache she recognized from long ago but had ruthlessly suppressed since.

Mary Rose jerked to her feet, turned toward the front door. She ought to leave. Right away.

"That's a definite improvement." Pete came into the room on bare feet, smelling of soap and hot water, wearing jeans and a chambray work shirt with the tail out. Grinning, he put a hand under her chin and lifted her face for a quick kiss. "Great ideas you have. Now let's see about some food."

And just like that, she lost the chance—and the will—to escape.

TRACE KNOCKED on her door just as Kelsey was opening the window to make her getaway. She thought about pretending she was already asleep. But if he found out differently, he'd be really pissed, maybe enough to tell Kate what she'd done.

So she let him in. "What do you want?"

He glanced around and immediately saw the loosened screen. "You're going out? Where?"

Kelsey tried out a nonchalant shrug. "Lisa's picking me up. We're gonna cruise around."

"More likely, you're going looking for that Spic."

"Don't call him that." She pushed her brother in the chest with both hands. "Don't use that word."

"Why not? That's what he is. You're all worked up over some stupid wetback."

"He was born here. He's as American as you are."

"Which is why he hangs out in a gang called Los Lobos, right? Sounds real American to me."

"What is your problem? So his parents came from Mexico. Nobody's a native American—all our families came from somewhere else."

"But most of us try to blend in, you know? We're not celebrating some other culture, and at the same time taking advantage of what America can offer."

"You sound like Dad."

"Yeah, and you can bet he's gonna be extremely pissed when he finds out you're hot for somebody like Torres."

"He won't find out if you don't tell him."

"You think Kate won't say anything?"

"She doesn't like it when he yells."

Trace sat down on her bed and propped his elbows on his knees. "Kate's a wimp, that's for sure. Maybe if she'd stood up to the old man occasionally, he wouldn't have gotten bored and gone looking for somebody else."

The clock on the bedside table read 11:20 p.m. Lisa wouldn't wait more than five minutes. "I've gotta go, Trace."

He rolled his eyes. "God save me from lust-crazed females." At the door to the hallway, he turned back. "You're asking for disaster, messing with Sal Torres. He's got a tough reputation, with girls and anybody who crosses him. I don't think you know what you're getting into."

"You and everybody else," Kelsey muttered as he shut the door behind him. Dismissing the train of thought, she slung her purse over her shoulder, pushed open the screen and swung her leg over the windowsill. In another minute she was shimmying down the main trunk of the old oak tree, then running along the sidewalk, praying

Lisa had waited. Only when she caught the silver gleam of Lisa's mom's Jaguar did she slow down a little.

"Hey, girlfriend," Lisa said as Kelsey bounced into the seat. "Where we headed?"

"The wrong part of town." Kelsey grinned. "The south side of Boundary Street."

PETE WAS an exuberant cook, splashing water and oil and sauce over the counter, scattering lettuce as he made a salad. Mary Rose cleaned up behind him, marveling at his unconcern. "It's quicker to clear as you go."

"But not as much fun," he insisted, dumping the spaghetti into a colander in the sink. "I don't have any wine around, but I do have cold beer. Want one?"

She couldn't remember the last time she'd actually had a beer. "Why not?" As she set the bottles down on the table, there was a scratching sound at the back door.

"That's Miss Dixie. Would you let her in?"

Mary Rose pushed open the screen door. Miss Dixie hesitated, as if she wasn't sure she had come to the right place. "It's okay, Dixie. Come inside."

Pete glanced over from the salad. "Come on, sweetheart. Got some spaghetti for you."

Ignoring Mary Rose completely, the dog trotted into the house and went to sit by Pete's feet. He picked up a clump of pasta he'd set on the counter to cool and dropped it in front of Dixie on the floor. Two seconds, and the whole lump had vanished. "She really likes spaghetti," he explained with a grin.

"Obviously."

During dinner, Mary Rose rediscovered the sharp pleasure of drinking cold beer and the even more intense excitement of Pete's undivided attention. He coaxed her to talk about the vacations she'd taken to the Caribbean,

Europe and California, and about her little old lady clients. In return, he told stories about the little old ladies he'd stopped for speeding, and how some of them cussed him out when he gave them a ticket.

"Always in a perfect Southern accent, of course."

She laughed until the tears poured down her cheeks. "Oh, I know…they can be so feisty. If they think you've made a mistake with their money, they'll raise holy hell until you either fix it or prove you're right."

Pete gathered up their dinner plates and took them to the sink. "And give you their life story while they're at it."

Mary Rose followed him with the serving dishes. "Oh, yes. All the children, and the grandchildren and what each of them is doing now…"

"And what they would think if they knew you were mistreating their sweet granny like this." He shook his head as he rinsed off the silverware. "Pretty amazing, to think of having that much family. Kids and grandkids."

She didn't know what to say. "Are your brothers married?"

"Not yet. Jerry's been with his girlfriend for a couple of years. But no wedding plans. Really frustrates my mom. She, of course, wants grandbabies."

"I know. My parents thought Kate would have her own children, but I guess that won't happen now."

"We're all such a disappointment to our folks."

"You could still have a family, for heaven's sake. You're only thirty-one."

"Nope. I gave it a shot with Sherrill, but things didn't work out."

"Sherrill." His second ex-wife? Other ex-wife? "What happened?"

"She didn't like being a trooper's wife. Worried all

the time that I'd get hurt or killed, until the worry killed the marriage.''

''I'm sorry.''

''Me, too. I would have enjoyed coaching Little League. But, hey, I've got the kids in the REWARDS program and Miss Dixie. I'm doing okay.''

''I'm glad.''

He turned off the overhead light, so only the lamps from the living room lit the kitchen. Then he put his hands on her upper arms. ''And you're okay, too. Right?''

She took a deep breath. ''I am.''

''I think it's great that we got a chance to see each other again, to find out that we've moved on with our lives. We're not stuck back in that summer, sad and bitter.''

''No.''

''So now the question is…what happens next?''

''Next?''

His palms moved over her skin, pushing up the sleeves of her T-shirt, then smoothing down to her elbows and back again. Mary Rose shivered under the caress.

''I keep thinking about you, plotting and planning how to see you again,'' he said in a low voice. ''And God knows you're the most desirable woman I've ever known. I'm wondering if we could make more of this than just a trip down memory lane.''

''I don't know, Pete. I'm only here for a little while.''

Somehow, without her noticing, he'd backed her up against the counter. ''I understand. All the better, maybe. We go in with our eyes open, no teenage hormones to contend with.'' Bending his head, he set his mouth against her throat. ''Only adult desires to worry about. I want you, Mary Rose.''

Her knees buckled as his lips moved over her skin. She caught at his shoulders and his arms came around her waist, holding her against him. And then he brought their mouths together, a desperate meld of lips and teeth and tongues as they struggled to get close, then closer still. Running her hands under Pete's shirt, Mary Rose encountered smooth, hot skin, felt the rumble of his groan in her own aching breasts.

He lifted his head, stared down at her with that incendiary gray gaze. "Stay tonight. Please."

Every nerve in her body screamed yes. But the slight space between them allowed her brain to regain some measure of control. She shook her head. "Not tonight, Pete. I have to think about this. I don't mean to tease you, but...I have to think."

His arms dropped and he stepped to the side to lean on the counter, hanging his head between his shoulders. After a minute, he blew out a sharp breath. "Sure. I understand." Another few seconds, and he straightened up, gave her a brief grin. "I'll get my car keys and take you home."

In his bedroom, Pete reached for his other jeans, lying across the foot of the bed, then dropped to sit there, elbows on his knees and head in his hands.

Man, he'd been carried away. Another few minutes with Mary Rose's soft hands on his skin, he wasn't sure he could have stopped.

And that was a dangerous state of affairs. Losing control was for kids. He didn't play the relationship game for keeps anymore, because he sucked at it. And Mary Rose had made it clear that she wasn't staying around. This was strictly a temporary connection, at best. If he couldn't keep his perspective, he'd be better off never getting involved at all.

When his heartbeat had gotten close to normal again and his body was more or less relaxed, he slipped into some loafers, fished out his keys and went back to the living room. Mary Rose sat in one of the armchairs, gazing across at Miss Dixie, planted squarely in the center of the sofa. "She didn't want to share."

Even female dogs were confusing him tonight. "I don't know what's with her. We'll have a talk when I get back. Are you ready?"

"Sure." As she got to her feet, she wobbled a little, and he put a hand out to steady her. Mary Rose flinched.

"Whoa." He put both hands up in a gesture of surrender. "You don't have to be scared of me. If you don't want this to go one step further, just say so. I'll never touch you again."

She sighed and shook her head. "It's not you I distrust, Pete. It's myself."

And with that flattering confession, she walked out the front door.

CROSSING BOUNDARY STREET was like driving onto a different planet. The houses were small, run-down. Instead of coffee shops and interior designers' showrooms, there were bars and pawnshops and convenience stores with signs in Spanish. Men and boys congregated on corners and leaned against the walls of buildings, most with bag-covered bottles in one hand and cigarettes in the other. Sometimes they yelled out as the Jag went by, but Kelsey didn't understand what they said, which was probably just as well.

Lisa drove as slowly as she dared, and Kelsey scanned the parking lots, but Sal wasn't so easily found. They circled around by the school and the diner, both of which were deserted. At the stoplight, Lisa leaned her head back against the seat. "Any other ideas? If not, I'm getting sleepy. Maybe it's time to go home."

"No, I know we can find him. It's not that big a town." The only alternative she could think of was his home, though she couldn't imagine anybody who wasn't grounded actually being in their own house on a Saturday night. Still, she'd looked up his address in the school directory, just in case.

They had to consult the map in the glove compartment to find the street Sal lived on. When they came to the corner, instead of turning, Lisa stopped the car. "It's a dead-end road. I don't like that very much."

"What could happen?" Kelsey didn't like it, either. But they'd come too far to back out now. "He won't be there, anyway. So we'll just look and go home. Okay?"

"I dunno." Despite her doubts, Lisa nosed the Jag onto Sal's street. This was the most disreputable place they'd seen yet. Beat-up cars lined both curbs, leaving only the middle of the road for driving. Lisa sat up straighter, clenched her hands around the steering wheel. "This is looking really, really bad. I think we should leave."

"Let's just see his house. Please? It's 344."

Her friend glanced to the house beside them. "This is 304. His house is at the other end of the street, Kelsey, and I'm gonna have to back out. I can't take this car home with any dents. I'm getting out of here."

"Fine." In the seconds it took Lisa to shift into reverse, Kelsey jumped out of the car. "You go. I'll get Sal to bring me home."

Lisa yelled out the window as Kelsey headed farther down the road. "Dammit, you don't even know he's there!"

Kelsey didn't stop. She heard the Jag's engine roar,

and figured Lisa had backed out and gone home. Walking with her head high, she held to her course down the broken, bottle-cluttered sidewalk. Sal would be home. He would be glad to see her.

Now there were footsteps thudding behind her—somebody running, closing the distance between them. Her heart jumped into her throat; she wasn't sure whether to run, or to turn and face the person behind.

A hand clutched at her shirt. She shrieked and spun around to see Lisa standing there, panting. "What are you doing?"

"I couldn't let you go down there by yourself, you idiot. I parked the car around the corner. If it gets stripped, we're in seriously deep shit."

Kelsey decided not to worry about it. "You're the best, Lisa. Let's go."

They walked the rest of the way down the dark street, past couples necking on front porches, past men with bottles of liquor in their hands who stared blindly into the night. As they approached the last house, it became obvious that a party was in full swing. Salsa music blared out of the open windows. Inside, the lights were dim but they could see bodies writhing and wriggling to the beat. The crowd overflowed to the porch and the small front yard, drinking, dancing, singing.

"Maybe he is home." Kelsey smiled. "Let's go in."

She recognized a few faces as she and Lisa struggled through the crowd in front of the house, but most were strange to her, and considerably older. Many of the dancers stopped and stared as she passed, then turned to each other and began talking in excited Spanish. Kelsey swallowed hard and kept going. When she found Sal, everything would be okay.

They finally got to the front door, where a tall, thin

guy with a mustache stood leaning against the screen with his arms crossed over his chest.

"Excuse me," Kelsey said. "Can we get by?"

"You got an invitation?"

"Do I need one?"

His smile was a sneer. "Anglos always need an invitation."

She flipped her hair behind her shoulders. "Is Sal inside?"

"Who's asking?"

"Maybe somebody could tell him Kelsey is here. I think he'd want to know."

Mr. Mustache turned and spoke to someone beyond the door. Then he looked at Kelsey again. "We'll see if he's home."

Lisa tugged on her sleeve. "Let's split, Kelsey. This is looking really, really bad."

There seemed to be just guys around them on the porch now, most of them wearing expressions that reminded Kelsey of sharks circling an injured seal. She wasn't sure she and Lisa would be allowed to leave if they wanted to.

Forever passed while she waited. Trying to stare down the hot eyes running over her, Kelsey was afraid if something didn't change in another minute, she would start to cry.

Behind her, Mr. Mustache shifted quickly and the screen door opened. Somebody grabbed her shoulder and jerked her around. She found herself staring up into Sal's furious face.

"Don't you have any brains at all?" he demanded. "What the freakin' hell are you doing here?"

CHAPTER TEN

"I WANTED TO SEE YOU," Kelsey tried to explain.

But Sal wasn't listening. As he glared at the guys gathered around them on the porch, the circle widened, broke, disintegrated. Even Mr. Mustache disappeared, until it was just Lisa and Sal with her by the front door.

He glanced at Lisa, then looked at Kelsey again. "At least you brought somebody with you. And I assume you drove. Where are you parked?"

"Around the corner," Lisa said.

"You walked down the street." It wasn't a question. He said something under his breath in Spanish. "Great. Let's go." Not gently, he pushed Kelsey toward the steps.

She caught the porch-rail post and turned to protest. "Can't we stay at the party? Looks like fun." Smiling, she put a hand on his chest. "I'd like to dance. With you."

"Not a chance." His fingers closed around her arm and he pulled her down the steps. "This is no place for you."

"It's where you live."

"Exactly." Laughter followed them as he dragged her across the yard and then up the street, with Lisa close behind.

"What's wrong?"

He stopped and turned to face her. "Those people aren't members of the country club. They are not people you should know."

"Because they belong to Los Lobos? Like you?"

"They're different than you. They don't trust you. And so you can't trust them."

"I trust you."

"Bad idea." He started up the street again, but his hold on her arm was gentler than before.

"You wouldn't let them hurt me."

"I might not be able to stop it."

"Of course you could. You're the leader, right?"

They reached the corner. Sal looked around and saw the Jaguar. "You left a Jag parked in this neighborhood? You're lucky there's anything left to drive." He waited while Lisa unlocked the doors and got behind the wheel. Then he took Kelsey to the passenger side. "Get out of here. Don't ever come back."

In the light from the streetlamp, his face was cold, hard as stone. She reached up to touch his cheek. "I want to know you. I want to be part of your life."

"You don't know anything about my life."

"So show me. Tell me."

"Kelsey…" He shook his head. "You don't have a clue about what you're asking."

"I'm asking to be with you. That's all."

For a long time he stared back the way they had come. Then he looked down at her again. "You tempt me beyond hope, little girl. Come on then. See how the rest of the world lives."

Just like that, with an arm around her shoulders and a wave to Lisa, Sal took her once more down that dark, fearsome street.

KATE STARTED COOKING early on Sunday morning because their parents were coming for dinner after church.

Even though she'd arrived home after midnight and then spent several restless hours thinking about Pete, Mary Rose joined her, hoping to ease the overall stress of the situation. Getting the kids up in time for the eleven o'clock service was a major undertaking; Kelsey literally had to be pulled from her bed. She was barely coherent even when showered and dressed, and still bleary-eyed when they got back home from church.

Of course, their mother remarked on it. "You're looking rather…tousled," she told Kelsey, stroking a hand over the girl's hair. "Not at all your usual well-groomed self."

"Sorry," Kelsey mumbled. She did look exceptionally tired and pale.

Mary Rose put a hand on her forehead. "Are you feeling okay?"

"I'm fine." Placing extra emphasis on the last word, she pulled away and went to sit in the corner of the living room farthest from everyone else.

Her grandmother clicked her tongue. "Such manners." Then she subjected Mary Rose to the same scrutiny. "Your eyes are red today, too. Were you out late last night?"

Having done what she could to improve the problem, Mary Rose wasn't happy to have it pointed out. "A bit later than usual," she admitted, only belatedly realizing her mistake.

Frances Bowdrey's eyes took on a sparkle of avid interest. "Really? Did you have a date? Someone I know?"

She'd never been a good liar and had learned long ago not to bother trying. "Um, yes. Pete Mitchell."

Her mother stared for a moment, her lips parted slightly. It was her father who said, "Pete Mitchell? The golf caddie?"

Mary Rose couldn't help laughing. "That was ten years ago. He's a state trooper now, Dad."

"What's he doing here?"

"He lives here, always has. Remember, he graduated in Kate's class." Time to end the conversation before things got more complicated. "I think I'll see if there's anything I can do to help Kate with lunch."

But her mother followed Mary Rose into the kitchen. "Why in the world would you go out with Pete Mitchell? Hasn't he done enough damage in your life?"

Kate looked up from the mashed potatoes, her eyes wide and concerned. With her back to her mother, Mary Rose made a face. "Can I help you?"

"Um…set out the glasses and pour the tea?"

"Sure." She walked in and out of the kitchen three times with her mother right behind her.

"Mary Rose, I expect an answer to that question."

Her dad came in and stood behind his chair at the head of the table. "I'd be interested in the answer, as well."

When she got the last glass poured, she turned. "It's not all that complicated, or all that important. He's the organizer of the rehab program Trace and Kelsey are in. He asked me to teach a class, and then he asked if I wanted to see him drive a race car. That sounded like fun, so I said yes."

"Race cars?" Frances put a hand to her throat.

"You mean NASCAR?" her father asked.

"Street Stock cars," Mary Rose explained. "Some drivers do go on to the NASCAR circuit from there."

"My heavens." Her mother pulled out her chair and sat down. "Why would you ever be interested in something so…so loud? And dirty, and grotesque?"

"Hardly grotesque, Mother."

"Common, then."

"I think it's cool." Kelsey looked more alive than she had all day. "That Camaro is awesome."

"Not so awesome today. Pete crashed last night and there was some serious damage to the car."

"Dangerous, as well." Frances set her silverware a little straighter on either side of the plate. "Really, Mary Rose. I thought you had better taste. In men and in entertainment."

"Men don't come much better than Pete, Mother. He's honorable, dedicated and responsible. I don't know if I'll ever go to another race. But I enjoyed the one I did attend." Biting her lip against further recriminations, she went to the kitchen to help Kate bring out the food.

In the midst of getting everybody served, Kelsey piped up again. "So did you date Mr. Pete in high school, Aunt M? Is that how everybody knows him?"

A day for truth. "We went out together after I graduated. He was working at a golf course on Hilton Head. A couple of friends and I spent the summer down there."

"Was he gorgeous back then? I mean, he's kinda old now. But I bet he was hot when he was my age."

Mary Rose smiled, remembering just how hot Pete had been. "Definitely."

"Why'd you break up?"

She hesitated a second too long. "It was obvious," her father said, "that Mary Rose and Pete Mitchell were not the same kind of people and didn't belong together. She went on to college and an enviable, successful career. While we certainly need law enforcement officers and it's admirable that Pete Mitchell does his job so well, the two of them were clearly not compatible. Fortunately, Mary Rose realized that fact and we were able to extricate her from a serious mistake."

Finding her hands clenched in her lap, Mary Rose relaxed her fingers and smoothed her napkin. "You put things so well, Dad. So...clinically."

Kelsey studied her plate for a while, then looked up. "What does 'a serious mistake' mean? Were you engaged?"

Mary Rose suddenly got tired of the game. "Let's lay the facts out for everybody. Pete and I were involved that summer, and I became pregnant. So we got married, but I lost the baby. And since there really wasn't a reason to be married anymore, we divorced. I went on to school, he attended the law enforcement academy, and we hadn't seen each other until I came to town a couple of weeks ago."

"And now you're dating again?" Kelsey's eyes went soft. "Wow. That's so romantic."

"No, it's incredibly foolish." Frances's voice was its most acerbic. "I'm sure Mary Rose realizes that nothing has changed. Relationships are most successful when we choose people who are similar to us in background, education and interests. Like Martin Cooper. Have you heard from him since you've been here, Mary Rose?"

She realized she could barely remember what Marty looked like. Light blond hair, horn-rimmed glasses, blue eyes? Or were they green? "He was going out of the country on business for several weeks."

Kelsey set her glass down with a thunk. "I don't see why you have to choose somebody who's just like you. Isn't it more interesting to have differences to talk about and explore?"

"That's a possibility," Kate said. "But—"

"But it's more likely that the differences will provoke disagreement." Frances nodded decisively, as if she would get the final word. "You'll understand as you get older, dear, that it's best to mix with your own kind of people."

"Even if they're boring?"

Mary Rose and Kate laughed, and even Trace snickered.

Frances cleared her throat. "If you think someone is boring, you are probably not trying hard enough to know them."

"I've known most of the guys in my class since kindergarten, and they're all the same. All boring."

"You're fifteen. In a few years, everything will be different."

Mary Rose wanted to ask how everything would be different in a few years for Kelsey, when nothing had changed in the ten years since the summer she spent with Pete. But they'd skirted enough controversy for one Sunday dinner. Time to change the subject.

"So, Dad, how's your golf game?"

It did occur to her, later in the afternoon after the dishes were put away and her parents had gone home, that Kelsey had an ulterior motive for debating the caste system as it existed in New Skye. She tracked down her niece to the hammock strung between two maples in the back of the yard.

"Mind if I join you?"

Kelsey opened one eye, obviously debating an honest answer. "Not at all," she lied.

Mary Rose pulled a lawn chair over and sat down. "It's a great afternoon for a nap. Not too hot, not at all chilly."

"Mmm."

"I won't keep you awake long, Kelsey. But I wanted to finish up the discussion at lunch."

"'Bout what?"

"The real problem in dating somebody who's very different from you is that the differences themselves can be the reason for the attraction. You don't see the person themselves, just the—the exotic aspects that are exciting simply because they're unfamiliar."

She didn't open her eyes. "Is that what happened with you and Mr. Pete?"

"N-no. Despite what your grandmother says, we weren't so different. She just doesn't want to admit that she's a snob."

Kelsey laughed. It was a nice sound, one they hadn't heard much lately.

"But somebody like Sal is very different, because of his culture. He may be a wonderful guy," she said, holding up a hand as Kelsey started to protest, "but you can't be sure it's not the difference you're attracted to. And differences aren't much of a foundation for a real relationship."

With an abruptness that set the hammock into a wild swing, Kelsey turned on her side, setting her back toward her aunt.

Mary Rose wearily pushed herself to her feet. "I get the message, honey. I hope you do, too."

SAL WOKE UP, rolled over to look at the clock and groaned: 3:00 p.m. As if he didn't have enough to answer for, he'd slept through Mass. All of them. Maybe Mama wouldn't yell if he promised to go to Vespers.

He pulled on clothes that he could wear to church and stumbled out into the deserted front room. Given how many people had been here last night, the place didn't look too bad. He'd picked up all the bottles and cans before he went to bed, of course. Mama and the kids must've cleared away the food mess. Hard to tell there'd been a party at all, except for the aroma of beer hanging in the air. By the time the old man got home, he'd be so drunk he probably wouldn't notice.

But right now the house felt empty. "Where is everybody?" He was surprised to realize that raising his voice didn't hurt. For once, on a Sunday, his head wasn't killing him. Having Kelsey here meant he'd had to stay fairly sober. Most weekends, he drank until he passed out. Like father, like son.

And he couldn't remember the last time he'd partied just to have fun. Usually, there was business involved—deals to make, plans to draw up. But last night had been about her. About them. About dancing, talking, eating. It had been a long time since life had been so simple.

"Sal!" Eight-year-old Tina ran in through the front door and grabbed his knees, followed by the rest of the little ones. "We went for ice cream. I got a red one." "Mine was blue." "I got yellow." Maria, the youngest at four, dropped the last of her green treat on the floor and started to cry.

"Oh, Maria." Sal crooned to her as he took the towel his little brother brought him and mopped up the floor. "So sad. But there will be more next week. I promise."

"So you finally got yourself out of bed." His mother came through the door. "And what about church? What about your soul?"

"I can go to Vespers, Mama. My soul will be okay." He got up to give her a kiss. "But you should have waked me up. I would have taken the children for their treat."

"I needed a walk." She sat down heavily on the sofa. "Exercise is good for you, they say."

"Cleaning houses all week isn't exercise?"

She shook her head. "Not the same. And it's such a beautiful day. You should all be outside playing," she told the children. "Go, enjoy the weather. You'll be inside all week at school." When the room had emptied, she looked at Sal again. "So, you had an Anglo girl here last night? As your date?"

Sal went to the window to watch as a game of hide-and-seek got organized. "I know her from school. That's all." He wished that could be all. But every time they were together, Kelsey seemed to get a tighter grip on him.

His mother shook her head. "I keep telling you—stay away from the gang, stay away from Anglo girls. And do you listen?"

"No." He went to sit beside her and kissed her cheek. "But I love you."

She patted his shoulder. "You talk too smooth. Go to Vespers. And bring home pizza for dinner. I promised your brothers and sisters."

"Will do." He left her to her Sunday-afternoon nap and went out to his car. On the way up the street, he saw his father walking home from whatever bar he'd spent the day in. Mano Torres stepped down off the sidewalk, requiring Sal to stop and roll down the window. "Hey, Papa."

"Where are you going?"

"Vespers."

Mano nodded. "Slept through Mass again." He grinned. "Smart boy." His mood was mellow this afternoon. Maybe they could get through the weekend without a fight.

Without warning, Mano's beefy fist shot through the open window, grabbed the collar of Sal's shirt. "Well, listen to this, smart boy. You bring a white girl into my house again, I'll beat you 'til there's nothing left of that pretty face any sane woman would want. Got it?"

Sal jerked free, but didn't answer.

Mano pounded his fist on the roof of the Taurus. "You hear me, boy?"

"I hear you," Sal said wearily, as he put the car in gear and drove away. "I hear you."

LISA TRACKED Kelsey down at break time Monday morning. "Well? What did you do? What happened?"

She was still feeling wrung out from getting home at dawn Sunday morning. "Danced. Talked. Drank beer until I thought I would explode."

"Did you get any time alone with him?"

Kelsey shook her head. "We stayed at the party the whole night." Even though she'd hinted several times—maybe more than several, since there were some blank spots in her memory—about getting somewhere "quieter."

"So you didn't see his room?"

"No."

"Were his parents there?"

She shrugged. "I didn't meet them."

Lisa leaned back against her locker door. "Man. Doesn't sound like it was worth staying for, if you ask me."

"You'd be wrong. I had a great time."

"Why?"

"It's hard to explain. But once they figured out that I was with Sal, there was this attitude…like suddenly I was more important. I mean, all the guys were incredibly macho, and they treated the girls like dirt. Not me, though.

Because of Sal, they were polite. Got me drinks, food, whatever I wanted. I know it was just that they were trying to make points with him. I really liked it, though. Then Sal drove me home and we sat in his car for a while and just talked as the sun came up. It was cool.''

''You're too much.''

''I know.'' Kelsey grinned just as the bell rang. ''And today he told me to meet him for lunch out behind the gym. How cool is that?''

''Wow....''

MONDAY NIGHT saw even more students in Mary Rose's class, which would have gratified her except that the discussions tended to get out of hand, with the kids more interested in making jokes than in learning the material. At break time, they all stayed in the classroom. Kelsey stood in a group with Sal and his friends, whom she seemed to know pretty well. Trace still sat at the back of the class, but tonight his friends Bo and Eric came in to talk to him. In effect, the population was divided into two groups—the Hispanics plus Kelsey on one side, and the rich white boys on the other. Mary Rose found the division quite disturbing.

She waited until Pete finished with his judo class to talk with him about it. He listened, but then shrugged. ''That's the way the whole school fragments. Hard as we try, these kids resist mixing.''

''But Kelsey appears to have bridged the gap.''

''Because she's interested in Sal. When the relationship cools, she'll be back on the other side.''

''You think it will cool?''

''Don't most of them at that age? Teenagers don't stick with one partner for very long.''

''I guess you're right.'' She sighed and looked toward

the door where Trace and Kelsey waited. "I hope you are, anyway. Good night."

"Mary Rose." He held her back with a hand on her wrist. "I know you said you had to think about…things. And I don't want to pressure you. But I was wondering if you'd like to have dinner with me on Friday night."

She hadn't thought about much besides Pete since Saturday night. "Why?"

He blinked in surprise. "Why?" At last he released her wrist. "Well, because I like talking to you. Being with you. All the usual reasons."

"But—"

"But?"

"We aren't going anywhere. We can't."

Pete's face hardened. "Because of that other guy? Have you decided he's the one you want?"

"No. This has nothing to do with him." Poor Marty. He would be hurt. Though not, Mary Rose was sure, devastated. Neither of them cared enough for that. "But my life is in Charleston and yours is here. There's no common ground."

"I think you're wrong about that." Without moving a muscle, the man beside her somehow became more focused, more intense. "I think the way we feel about each other is common ground. I'm not ready to throw out the possibilities between us for a little detail like lifestyle. Give this a chance, Mary Rose. Who knows what we could find?"

I know, she thought. *Heartbreak.* But she also knew he was wearing down her defenses. Not that those defenses had been very strong to begin with.

She groped for sanity one last time. "We gave it a chance before, Pete. Look what happened."

"We're older. Smarter. We can handle it."

He was so certain, so confident. Mary Rose shook her head, but smiled at the same time. "I guess dinner would be harmless enough fun. Where are we going? What should I wear?"

His sexy grin rewarded her courage. "Do you still like picnics?"

FRIDAY WAS A DAY of sunshine and showers. Mary Rose watched the weather anxiously and was relieved, around midafternoon, when the clouds seemed to be breaking up.

"The grass will be wet," she commented to Kate as they planted impatiens in the front flowerbeds. "I don't remember—do the botanical gardens have picnic tables?"

"And shelters, so you can be dry if it starts to rain again." Kate sat back on her heels. "I don't think I've ever seen you quite this anxious about a date."

Mary Rose paid careful attention to taking a seedling out of its plastic sleeve and placing it in the hole she'd dug. "I'm not anxious. I just want things to go well."

"My guess would be that Pete will enjoy your company whatever the weather. If you can say the same about him, then you're all set."

"Pete's always good to be with." She tamped the dirt firmly around the little plant with her fingertips. "I just wish…" Kate didn't push, and after a minute or so she went on. "I just wish I knew whether letting this…this situation continue was a good idea."

"Situation?"

"He…I…we…"

"Are physically attracted to each other?"

Mary Rose nodded, feeling her cheeks flush.

"Not surprising, considering how things worked out the first time around." Her sister gently set a plant in place. "I can't remember what it felt like to be that crazy for somebody. Maybe I never have been."

"L.T.?"

Staring sightlessly at the wall of the house, Kate shook her head. "I was flattered that he paid attention to me because he was so much older. After we got married, I thought he was a good lover—he had to be, since he'd been married before. But I never craved being with him." With a shrug, she went back to work. "Maybe I'm not cut out for that kind of passion. Anyway, you and Pete are hot for each other. So—"

"What an elegant way to put it."

"I have teenagers. So what's the problem?"

"I don't sleep around."

"I didn't suggest that you do. You're not sleeping with anyone else right now, are you?"

"N-no."

"Have you and Marty…"

Mary Rose shook her head. "He doesn't press very hard when I say no."

Kate laughed. "And somehow I'm pretty sure the same cannot be said of Trooper Pete Mitchell."

"Um, no."

"So you're free to let the situation, as you call it, develop any way it wants. Why don't you just relax? See where things lead?"

"I don't like to relax. I like to plan and predict."

"Mmm, hmm. Great qualities in an investment adviser. Totally useless when it comes to love."

"Not love." The idea panicked her. "We tried love and it didn't work. This is just…just…"

"Okay, lust. That can't be planned, either." Kate got to her feet. "Speaking as somebody who blew her first chance and might never get another, I say go for it."

"Why do you think you won't get another chance? What's to stop you from getting involved again?"

"There aren't that many candidates in a town this small. And Trace and Kelsey are being hurt enough. I think they would resent any new relationship I tried to develop."

"They'll be out of the house in a few years. You need your own life."

Kate smiled. "I'll live vicariously through yours. Go get dressed. I want to see you in that outfit we bought."

AT SIX O'CLOCK, Mary Rose opened the front door wearing the sky-blue pants and square-necked shirt printed with dragonflies that she and Kate had gone crazy over that morning.

Pete grinned as he looked her up and down. "I won't lose you in the dark. You look great, as usual."

"So do you." The evening was warm enough that he'd worn shorts, showing off the strength and shape of his legs. "We'll be the best-looking pair at the park."

His hand floated lightly at the small of her back as they went down the walk toward his car. "We could be the *only* pair in the park. Those clouds are piling up again in the west. Everybody else might just decide to stay home."

"It's not going to rain again. I won't allow it."

Pete opened the passenger door to the Jeep. "Well, then, we're covered. Let's have a picnic."

The gardens were gorgeous. White and pink dogwood trees bloomed lavishly at each turn of the path, with late tulips and early irises nodding at their feet. Pansies had been tucked into every conceivable nook; some of the camellias were still putting out freshly ruffled flowers. Carrying a sturdy picnic hamper in one hand and a cooler in the other, Pete led the way to a table on the edge of the natural area, where the panoramic view took Mary Rose's breath away.

"Now I remember why I love the South." She drew a deep breath, inhaled the green fragrance of grass and a mixture of sweet floral scents. "Spring is something we enjoy outside because it's warm and sunny. Not like up North, where it can be cold even with the flowers blooming."

"I definitely agree, though I imagine lots of northerners wouldn't. Help me spread this cloth." He'd brought a blue-checked cloth, even matched it with blue paper plates.

"Color coordination?" Mary Rose winked at him. "I'm impressed."

"Don't be. I borrowed my mom's stuff."

"You should have taken the credit. I would never have known."

He snapped his fingers. "I always forget that part."

The menu was straight out of Southern mythology—fried chicken, potato salad, iced tea and pound cake. "Let's practice that taking-the-credit trick again," Mary Rose suggested, using her fingers to eat the chicken like a good Southerner should. "Did you make all this food?"

Pete closed his eyes, pretending to concentrate. Then, shaking his head, he shrugged. "Can't do it. Some incurable truth gene, I guess. There's a great shop in town that fries chicken like Mama used to before we all discovered the evils of saturated fats. I just asked them to put together something we would enjoy."

"They succeeded beyond all expectation." Mary Rose polished off her chicken leg and reached for a third. "I haven't enjoyed food so much in years."

And he hadn't enjoyed being with a woman so much

in...well, at least a decade. Not to mention that she could get him hot just by licking her fingers...like right now. He stirred on the bench, looked out over the garden. "Uh-oh."

As they'd concentrated on the food, clouds had crept over the sky. Now the straight lines of a rain shower could be seen in the distance. Heading their way.

Mary Rose followed his line of sight. "Oh, no. Maybe it'll pass by? Or come and go really fast?"

"We can find out."

That first shower did sneak by with not much more than a mist blown under their shelter. Following behind it, though, came a heavier, longer rain. The sky lowered, settled in.

"This is looking like an all-nighter." Trying to hide his disappointment, Pete finished packing up the hamper. Big boys weren't supposed to throw temper tantrums. But, damn, he'd wanted more time with her tonight. "And a premature end to the evening."

"What time do the gardens close?"

"When it gets dark—maybe an hour or so from now."

Mary Rose got to her feet and stuck her hand out from underneath the shelter, catching the rain in her palm. "It's really warm. And there's no breeze. Want to go for a walk?"

He winced. "I hate to admit it, but I didn't bring an umbrella. So much for 'Be Prepared.'"

"Were you a Boy Scout?" When he nodded, she shook her head. "I didn't know that. Though I probably should have guessed. Anyway, we'll get wet whatever we do, right? I mean, we'll be drenched walking to the car."

"True."

She gave an elegant shrug, then held out her hand to him. "So why don't we enjoy the rain first?"

Grinning, he took hold of that hand and pulled her out into the open. "Good question, Ms. Mary Rose Bowdrey. Why don't we do just that?"

CHAPTER ELEVEN

THEY PLAYED like children, chasing each other across the grass, hiding behind trees, competing to see who could go highest on the swings. And the rain continued to fall...warm, gentle but steady, refreshing the gardens as well as Pete and Mary Rose.

While they were still on the swing set, the sun finally set behind the clouds. A figure approached out of the deepening twilight, an older man in a raincoat and hat bearing a Parks Department insignia. He didn't look particularly happy. "Hey, you two. Time to go home. It's getting dark. And I'm ready for my dinner."

"Yes, sir. We're on our way." Pete held out his arms as Mary Rose reached the top of her arc; she stretched out her arms and jumped from the swing, landing against his chest. He was warm under the wet shirt and shorts. When his arms closed around her, she warmed up, too. Quickly.

That heat didn't fade on the walk to the car, because Pete held her hand the whole way, toting the empty hamper and cooler with the other arm. They didn't say much on the short ride to his house, but the air quivered with what they didn't put into words.

He turned to her once he'd stopped the Jeep in the driveway. "I just assumed...would you like to come in and dry your clothes before you go home? Or I can take you home wet, if you want."

Mary Rose knew what she wanted. Did she dare take it? How would she survive leaving Pete Mitchell a second time? Was the pleasure worth the eventual cost?

She stopped thinking. "I'd like to get dry."

He grinned, and her stomach jumped in anticipation. "Come on in."

Miss Dixie met them at the door and scrambled into Pete's embrace. Tonight, he didn't respond with quite the same enthusiasm. "Yeah, baby, I love you, too. Let's put you outside. I'll give you some dinner in a minute."

He sent the dog out the back door, then looked at Mary Rose as she stood dripping on his kitchen floor. "Um...I guess you need something to wear while your stuff is in the dryer. Hold on." In a few seconds he came back with a T-shirt and gym shorts. "Not exactly elegant, but I won't tell anybody."

"Thanks." Mary Rose scooted into the bathroom, trying to cope with the idea of wearing Pete's clothes. *Wearing Pete's clothes without underwear,* she thought, with her whole face heating up as she pulled on the shorts and dragged the shirt down over her bare breasts. *Oh, my stars.*

Then she glanced at the mirror and let out a horrified shriek.

"What's wrong?" Pete's voice came through the closed door. "Are you all right?"

"Y-yes. I just didn't realize how awful I looked. The rain...my makeup...and the hair." Mary Rose moaned. "You could have told me."

"Can I come in?"

"No." She sighed. "Yes. You've already seen the worst."

He opened the door. "I don't see anything wrong."

"You've lost your eyesight." But she hadn't, and seeing him in the same clothes she was wearing—dark green shorts that revealed most of his tanned thighs, a tight gray T-shirt designed to show off his muscles rather than hide them—made her feel self-conscious in a very provocative way.

"Well, okay, the mascara is a little smudged." Taking a washcloth off the towel rack, he came close and tilted her chin up with his knuckle, then dabbed at her eyes.

"And my hair looks like straw—straight and sticky. I never leave the house without a session with the curling iron. This is why."

"It just needs to be combed." Pete turned her away from him, then began to stroke a comb through her hair, pulling gently away from her face, up off her neck. "Sorry to say, I don't have a hair dryer."

"I don't suppose you need one, with yours so short." She closed her eyes, soothed like a purring cat by the motion of his hands. "This is wonderful."

He took the one step that brought their bodies together. "I can make it even better." The comb vanished; his hands capped her shoulders and his breath blew over her ear. "Stay with me tonight, Mary Rose."

She took a deep breath and leaned back against him. "I can't stay the whole night. Kelsey and Trace…I don't think it would be good for them to see me come in the morning after. You know?"

His sigh was outside of her, yet somehow inside, as well. "Yeah, I know." He turned her to face him and his palms came up to cup her face. "We'll just have to do our best with the time we have."

They made slow progress toward the bedroom…taking steps between kisses, halting all too often to rediscover the curves and angles and planes first learned years ago. Pete tugged the T-shirt over Mary Rose's head, discarded his own, then pulled her tight against him. They met flesh to flesh with a gasp, a groan.

"You're gorgeous," he murmured, skimming his lips along her collarbone. He slipped his hands up over her ribs, weighted his palms with her firm, small breasts. "Amazing."

"Pete." She arched up as his mouth claimed her sensitive skin, suckling her gently. "Oh, please…"

"What can I do for you, sweetheart?" Her hands clenched on his shoulders as he moved his attention to her other breast.

"I…need…" She ran her knee along the outside of his thigh, pressed intimately against him.

"Oh, yeah." Pressing her back into the wall, he lifted her off the floor, wrapped her legs around his hips. "Better?"

"Mmm." She moved with him in a sensual, mind-blowing dance. "I want you inside me. Now."

The invitation nearly ripped the lid off his control. But he had enough brains left to remember the basics. "Hold on, honey. You're goin' for a ride."

With his hands braced under her sweet, round rear end, he carried her to the bedroom, then set a knee on the bed and slowly laid her down. The sight of her, pale and smooth on his dark blue bedspread, took his breath away. "Incredible." He bent to kiss her swollen mouth, got lost all over again in the glories of her body. Soon they were both naked, wrapped up tight in each other, on the very edge of Paradise.

One more time, he drew back. With protection in place, he returned to Mary Rose's open arms. "Okay, babe. Let's fly."

SHE DRIFTED out of a deep, satisfied sleep to the accompaniment of Pete's snores.

As full consciousness returned, though, Mary Rose realized the chest under her cheek rose and fell peacefully, easily, in a different rhythm from the snoring sounds. She stirred a little more, lifted her head.

Pete's arm tightened around her shoulders. "Where're you going?"

"Just wondering what that noise is."

"Noise?" He listened for a few seconds. "Miss Dixie. Must be playing with a toy."

"Oh." She collapsed thankfully on her resting place again, maybe even went back to sleep, because the small bounce on the bed barely registered.

But the cold, wet nose pressed into the small of her back certainly did. "Ow!" She jerked upright and turned wildly, looking for the source of her torture. "That's...that's mine!"

Miss Dixie had joined them on the bed and was now in the process of curling herself into a nest just under Pete's arm, where Mary Rose had been lying. Around her neck were the shreds of what had been a very expensive bra.

Pete opened his eyes. "Oh, damn." Then he started chuckling. "Miss Dixie, I don't think ice blue is your color." Untwining the scraps of silk and lace from the dog's head, he didn't quite manage to keep a straight face. "But I bet it was pretty on you," he told Mary Rose. "I'll buy you another one."

She gingerly took the cloth out of his hand. "Do you suppose she ripped up the rest of my clothes? I guess we left them lying on the bathroom floor."

His eyes widened. "I'll check." He came back looking relieved. "Everything else is okay, and I put them all in the dryer. You," he told the dog, lifting her off the bed, "have been a bad girl. Go sleep on the couch. Tonight is not your night for snoozing in my bed." There was a whimper on the other side of the shut door, then a disgusted snort and the receding click of toenails on the wooden floor.

Pete surveyed Mary Rose from across the room. "You, on the other hand, are right where you belong." He climbed back into bed and pulled her into his arms. "Unless you want to go out in the living room and watch TV with Miss Dixie?"

"Not a chance." She relaxed against him, ran her hands along his back, over his tight butt, down his thighs. "I'm staying right where I'm at."

PETE ESCORTED HER up the front walk of Kate's house at about 1:00 a.m. "Thank you." He rubbed his lips over hers, a light caress that quickly turned into a deep and ardent involvement. With a groan, he finally pulled away. "I don't want to let you go. But I will." He put his hands up in surrender and stepped back. "As long you say I can see you again this weekend."

Mary Rose was still regaining her breath. "Sunday, for lunch? Kate usually does a really nice dinner after church."

"Uh…sure. Sounds great. What time should I show up?"

With the details settled and one last kiss, he left her in the open doorway and went back to the Jeep. The engine sounded like thunder in the quiet, damp night, fading away to nothing as he turned the corner. Mary Rose stayed outside a minute, listening to the crickets, enjoying the smell of spring rain, and then finally, with a sigh, turned into the house and shut the door behind her.

When she looked up, she met Trace's suspicious gaze.

She jumped and gave a silly squeak. "You scared me. I didn't know you were there."

"I figured that out." He looked her up and down. "You look like you've been in a boat wreck."

Her outfit had not dried wrinkle free. "We, um, played around in the rain some and got wet." That sounded innocent enough, and had the virtue of being the truth.

But Trace wasn't satisfied. "It stopped raining hours ago."

"Well, we went to Pete's house to dry my clothes."

"Blowing on them through a straw, or what?"

"Trace, what is the matter with you?"

He gave a disgusted shrug. "Nothing. Forget it."

Mary Rose held him by the arm when he would have gone up the stairs. "No, I won't forget it. You're upset with me and I want to know why."

"I just didn't…" He ran a hand over his hair. "Hell. I just didn't think you did things like that."

"Like what?"

"You—you went to bed with him, didn't you?"

"That's not your business one way or the other."

"But it screws everything up. Can't you see that?"

She drew him into the living room and sat him in one of the armchairs while she took the other. "Tell me what you mean."

"People sleeping together, without being married. If Dad hadn't started sleeping with…her…he'd still be here."

"Maybe. Sex certainly drives some people to make big mistakes."

"And you said yourself, you and Pete got in trouble back when you were in high school."

"Well, I had graduated, to be exact. But, yes, we slept

together that summer and I got pregnant and it was a very difficult time.''

''So why are you making the same mistake now?''

''I don't think I am, Trace.'' *I hope I'm not, anyway.* ''Pete and I are much older. We know what we want from our lives and where we're going. This time, we're not planning to take our relationship too seriously.'' Only after she'd said it did she realize how cheap the confession sounded.

Judging by his disgusted expression, Trace agreed with that assessment. ''You're just in it for fun? What happened to serious commitment? To being with the right person at the right time? To long-term, stable relationships?''

''You've listened pretty closely when people talked about this, haven't you?''

''I thought it was important. What is Kelsey supposed to think? If it's okay for you and Mr. Pete, then it's okay for her and Sal, right?''

''Not at all. Like I said, we're older.''

He went to the fireplace, where he began to fiddle with the teacups on the mantel. ''Maybe it doesn't matter what she thinks about you and Mr. Pete. She and Sal are probably already doing it, anyway.''

''What are you saying?'' Mary Rose got slowly to her feet.

''She spent all night with him last weekend. What else would they have been up to?''

''Kelsey was out all night? Which night?''

''Saturday. Didn't get in until the sun was coming up Sunday morning.''

Which would explain how tired she'd been. ''And you didn't tell Kate?''

"Kelse would have been pissed." He shrugged. "I guess she's gonna be now, anyway."

"A lot of people are going to be pissed." She rubbed her temples with her fingertips. "Go to bed, Trace. We'll talk some more tomorrow."

He didn't have to be told twice. Before she sat down again, Trace was upstairs.

Alone in the living room, Mary Rose propped her forehead against her fists. Her first inclination was to wake Kelsey up and thrash out the whole issue right this minute.

But a huge argument at two in the morning would only make everything worse. In any event, Kate needed to be told first. These were her children. She should be the one handling the discipline. Once Kate knew, she could decide how to confront Kelsey. And what to do.

How had all of this come to pass? How had the situation gotten so desperate? Kelsey had sneaked out of the house to be with Sal, had spent the whole night with him. As Trace said, it was very unlikely that they hadn't had sex. At fifteen, Kelsey was in serious emotional and physical jeopardy from engaging in a sexual relationship.

At fifteen, Kelsey was also a minor. That might even put Sal in the position of committing statutory rape.

Kate would be devastated. L.T. would be ready to kill. And Pete...he really counted on Sal. How hurt would he be to find himself so dreadfully betrayed?

Somewhere near dawn, Mary Rose finally went upstairs, past her niece's closed door, to the guest room. Standing in the doorway, though, she gave in to impulse and went back to Kelsey's room. The door swung in quietly and she peeked without remorse into the darkened space.

There was definitely a lump under the covers. She went to the head of the bed and pulled the coverlet down just enough to see the golden hair underneath. Just as she straightened up, the bundle on the bed stirred and turned; Kelsey rolled to her back and let the covers drift down a little bit. Tonight there really was no doubt that the girl had stayed home, in bed.

Which was more than Mary Rose could say for herself.

Burdened now by guilt, she pulled the door to Kelsey's room closed behind her and went wearily to her own. As she stripped off the wrinkled clothes, she wondered if Trace had noticed that she wasn't wearing a bra. Probably not. Thirteen-year-old boys just weren't that perceptive. Were they?

She decided she didn't want to know. With her night-gown on, she got into bed and lay flat on her back, staring up at the ceiling. A few hours ago she'd believed she would float into sleep thinking about her evening with Pete, about the slow glide of his hands over her skin, the sweet taste of his kisses.

Instead, she worried over Kelsey and Kate. And poor Trace, so confused. She visualized the confrontations yet to come.

And fell asleep with her hands clenched into fists.

THE PHONE RANG at seven Saturday morning. Pete swore and swiped at it with one hand. When it continued to ring, he managed to open his eyes enough to locate and actually lift the receiver. "'Lo."

"This is Mary Rose. You need to wake up."

Her voice was worth the effort. "Hey. How are you?"

"I am furious. I thought you were going to talk to Sal about Kelsey."

"I did."

"Well, whatever you said didn't do much good. Trace told me that Sal and Kelsey spent all of last Saturday night together. Got that, Pete? My fifteen-year-old niece spent the night with your protégé."

"Doing what?"

"What do you think?"

"Are you sure?"

"There aren't too many other conclusions to draw. She left the house about eleven-thirty and didn't come back until dawn. What does that sound like to you? It sounds like statutory rape to me."

"You're sure she was with Sal?"

"Trace was sure."

"But did he see them together?"

"Oh, for heaven's sake, are you looking for evidence? This isn't a police investigation."

"Well, yeah, it is, kinda. You need some proof that she was with Sal and not just out somewhere fooling around. Have you talked to Kelsey?"

"Not yet. I want to talk to Kate first."

"Good idea. And I'll talk with Sal this morning. We'll get to the truth of things. But right now, I'm not sure that's what you're seeing, Mary Rose. Trace and his buddies aren't fans of the Hispanic crowd. He could just be making trouble."

She was silent for a long time. "You know, you bend over backward to give Sal the benefit of the doubt. I sure do hope your confidence is justified. Because if it's not, my niece is the one who'll get hurt." Without a goodbye, the phone went dead.

Pete flopped back on his pillow. "Good morning to you, too, Ms. Mary Rose."

SAL WATCHED Pete yawn as he stumbled toward the high school's garage door on Saturday morning. "Late night?"

The trooper rubbed his hands over his face. "Yeah. Then I got up early to play ball this morning. Might as well have stayed in bed, for all the good I did." He unlocked the door and pushed the panel up. "A man can't shoot worth a damn on half a night's sleep."

Figuring out what Pete had done with the other half a night didn't take much imagination. But that was none of his business. "Well, we got one hell of a mess in here to deal with, that's for sure. Is there any part of the body we can salvage?"

Pete stood staring at the Camaro, yawning again. "The rear bumper?"

They spent the day taking the body parts off the roll-bar cage which made up the true frame of the car—a dirty, unpleasant job all the way around. They didn't talk much, never had, except about the work. Pete didn't pry into matters that didn't concern him, didn't mess with a guy's personal business. Sal appreciated the courtesy and tried to return the favor.

About six, he stepped back and wiped a hand over his sweaty face. "I gotta get out of here. Can we finish up tomorrow?"

"Hot date?" Pete grinned, making the question into a casual joke.

Sal smiled. "Something like that."

But then the trooper turned serious on him. "We talked a couple of times about Kelsey LaRue, what a mistake it would be for you to get involved with her. I assumed you took me seriously."

"So?"

"So I guess I'm asking you to tell me you're not seeing Kelsey for your hot date tonight."

Lying to Pete was a tough proposition. Sal usually got by with evasion, but he wasn't sure that was gonna work this time. He'd give it a shot, though. "The way I hear it, Kelsey has been grounded for the rest of her life."

"That's the story. But I doubt she's been chained to the wall in her room. I was fifteen once, and I know that a teenager who wants to get out of the house can manage without much trouble."

Sal shrugged. "I don't know anything about all that."

"You're not seeing Kelsey tonight?"

"I'm going to a party, man. I don't know everybody who'll be there."

"How about last weekend? Did you see Kelsey last weekend?"

This was gonna be tough. "None of your business, Pete. Back off."

"I can't do that. Did you spend the night with Kelsey on Saturday? And does that mean what it usually does these days?"

"Screw this. Screw you." Sal jerked his shirt on and started for the door.

"I want a straight answer, Sal."

"I'll give you something straight." He raised his fist with the third finger pointed at Pete in a universal gesture. *"Buenas noches."*

When he got to his car, he was still steaming mad. He peeled out of the school parking lot and nearly rear-ended a car leaving the diner. Sitting on the horn expressed his mood without improving it. He turned right at the light, took the highway out of town at a speed Trooper Pete would arrest him for. But he'd have to catch him first.

The fact that Pete was right only made the situation worse. Sal knew he had, in so many words, guaranteed the trooper that he wouldn't take advantage of Kelsey

LaRue. The girl was jailbait, a good enough reason to leave her alone, without all the bullshit rules and regulations.

Ah, but then there was Ke... with her pale skin and her blond hair and big brown eyes... ding him on like Eve in the Garden. Her courage, showing him on like at his house—the last place on earth she should that night just blown him away. He hadn't been able to resist had since. She made him feel like a hero.

So she was gonna sneak out tonight and they would go on a real date, just the two of them. He had it all planned—dinner at a Mexican place on the edge of town, then a midnight movie. He'd already met with Frank, the restaurant owner, and arranged for a special table, a nice meal. They would talk, he and Kelsey. He'd discovered this week at school, during lunch, that it could be fun to talk to a girl.

The tricky part would be getting her back home again without spending too much time alone. Because even better than talking to Kelsey was touching her, kissing her, teaching her how to kiss him back. Sal was smart enough to recognize the danger. If he took Kelsey too far, there would be hell to pay. For him. For her.

And, strange as it might seem to Pete and all the other stupid adults who couldn't mind their own business, his main concern was to keep Kelsey from getting hurt.

He pulled the Taurus to the curb where she'd told him to wait with about ten minutes before their ten o'clock meeting time. His car fit into this neighborhood about as well as a herd of sheep would. But it was late, and dark. With a little luck, nobody would notice.

At ten-fifteen, he was still waiting. By ten-thirty, he was getting mad. If she couldn't come, she was supposed to call him. Stuff got in the way, he understood that. But she could've called. When Kelsey hadn't shown by eleven, Sal gunned the gas and roared out of the neighborhood.

He didn't give a shit whether the neighbors noticed him or not.

KELSEY SAT the kitchen table and watched the hands creep past ten…ten-thirty…eleven. Somewhere outside the open windows, an engine sprang to life, roared down the street, faded into the distance. She knew it was Sal. She just knew it.

And here she was, trapped in hell. Kate had taken her phone out of her room, forbidden her to use any phone in the house unless she or Aunt M was in the room, listening. And she wasn't going to call Sal with someone listening. No way.

They didn't believe her. Didn't believe that all she'd done with him last week was dance and talk. And drink, but she hadn't told them that part. They thought she and Sal had had sex. They wouldn't take her word for it that nothing like that had happened. Nothing.

She wasn't allowed to be anywhere in the house by herself. Kate or Mary Rose expected to be able to see her at all times, which was why she sat here in the kitchen while Kate was in the laundry room loading the washer. The worst indignity of all was that Kate had nailed her window shut *and* taken her bedroom door off its hinges. For privacy, she could dress in the bathroom. But the bathroom didn't have a window. She couldn't get out the bedroom window now without making noise, and she couldn't do anything in her bedroom that anybody couldn't see. All the doors in the house had dead bolts, and Kate was keeping the key.

She put her head in her hands. Damn Trace and his

big mouth. She would get him for this, someday, somehow. He would pay big time for ratting on her.

~~Kate came into the kitchen~~ with a laundry basket. "Okay. Upstairs." Their stepmother had never been this terse, never this hard.

Kelsey pushed on the table and got to her feet. "Can't I watch some TV?"

"I've been working all day and I'm tired. I want to go to bed. Upstairs." She followed Kelsey through the dining room and up the steps. Kelsey turned left into her bedroom and Kate turned right into the room she had shared with Dad.

"Are you going to tell him?" Kelsey came back to stand in the doorway, watching Kate put neatly folded clothes into drawers.

"I'll let you know."

"He'll go after Sal with a gun. You know he will."

Kate stopped working for a minute. Her shoulders lifted on a deep breath. "I know."

Then Kelsey said for the hundredth time, "Nothing happened. You can take me to a doctor and they'll tell you. Sal and I didn't make love."

But she really wished they had. At least then this suffering would have been worth something.

MARY ROSE TALKED to Pete on the telephone late Saturday night.

"How's it going?" he asked.

She closed her eyes and blew out a deep breath. "Horrible."

"What did Kelsey say about that night?"

"She says nothing happened, that they spent the night dancing and talking at a party."

"You don't believe her?"

"I want to. But her credibility is somewhat questionable at this point. What did Sal say?"

Pete was quiet for a long moment. "I didn't get a lot of cooperation from Sal."

"Cooperation isn't the point."

"I couldn't torture the truth out of him, Mary Rose."

"What did he say?"

"He basically evaded telling me anything, then gave me the finger and walked out."

"A really great person for Kelsey to be involved with."

"He's a teenager, for God's sake. It's their job to resist authority."

"And it's our responsibility as adults to take care of them, make sure they don't ruin their lives."

"Like your parents did for you?"

The accusation stopped her breath in her chest. "That's...not fair."

"I think it's pretty accurate, myself."

"Our marriage wouldn't have lasted, Pete. We were too young."

"I'm not so sure. We were crazy for each other."

"So crazy that, at the first opportunity, you walked away."

"I didn't walk away until you were already gone."

"What does that mean?"

"You came home from the hospital, your parents swooped in, and I never really had another chance to talk to you. We never even tried to deal with what happened to us, Mary Rose. I recognized a losing proposition when I saw it. Your folks weren't going to let me get close enough to try to make you stay, and you let them run the show. So I did what had to be done, cut the strings and got the hell out of Dodge."

His version of those long-ago days fought violently with her own memories. Mary Rose realized she had a headache pounding in her temples, behind her eyes. "I think it's time to say good-night."

"What about lunch tomorrow?"

She took a deep breath against the pain. "Not a good idea. I—I'll call you."

"Mary Rose—"

"'Night, Pete."

She hung up and rolled onto the bed, drawing the covers up around her shoulders, pressing her head into Kate's soft, down-filled pillows. She'd suffered with migraines during her freshman year in college, and occasionally since. But not for several years. Between them, Pete and Kelsey had raised her stress level to epic proportions.

And now she had to pay the price.

CHAPTER TWELVE

KELSEY WAITED until she was sure Mary Rose and Kate were asleep. Then, wishing she had a weapon to take with her, she opened the door to Trace's room.

He sat at his computer, his face illuminated with the swirls of green, blue and black on the monitor. "What do you want?"

"To kill you, for starters." She shut the door behind her and leaned back against it. "What a shitty thing to do, giving me up to Mary Rose. What for, Trace? What did I ever do to you?"

His answer was a shrug. He turned back to the computer.

Kelsey took a step, grabbed his shoulder and turned him around on the swivel chair. "I'm not taking that crap. You're gonna tell me why you couldn't just keep your stupid mouth shut."

"Because I wanted them to know, okay? Because I think it's a really bad idea, you and that Spic."

"Who I date is none of your business."

"Yeah, just like Dad. What he did was none of my business, either. And look how that ended up."

"What are you talking about?"

"I would go with him to work, you know? And I saw him flirting with that secretary. But when I said something, he told me it was none of my business." Trace put his head in his hands. "So I just let him do his own thing. Couple of months later, he was outta here."

Some of her anger bled away. "You're not in control. Not of him, not of me."

"That's pretty obvious. But if Kate had known earlier, maybe she could have done something to stop him. And she can damn sure stop you from screwing that Mexican."

Before she realized what she was doing, she slapped him. "You're a racist and a bigot and you have a filthy mind. I don't want to talk to you anymore." As she left, Trace turned woodenly back to the computer, put his hand over the mouse.

In her room without a door, Kelsey threw herself on her bed and cried herself to sleep.

PETE'S MOTHER raised her eyebrows when he came into her kitchen after church on Sunday. "I thought you said you wouldn't be here for lunch." He'd called her Saturday morning to say he was having lunch somewhere else, and had known she wasn't happy about his defection. Now she let him kiss her cheek, but turned quickly away. Still miffed. "I didn't set you a place."

"We can probably change that, can't we?" He grabbed a cheese-stuffed celery stick from the relish tray and bit off a big, crunchy piece. Destroying something felt good.

"I suppose we can. Your brothers went to the store for ice cream to eat with the chocolate cake. So you have time to tell me what's wrong."

"Nothing."

"'Nothing' would be why you look like you haven't slept in two days."

That about covered it. "Nothing important?"

"I never knew you to lose sleep over the unimportant things. But if you don't want to tell me—"

Amazing, how his mother could convey hurt feelings with a lift of her shoulder. And how hurting her twisted him inside. "I had...an argument...with a friend. A woman."

Peeling potatoes, she nodded. "Someone you're dating?"

"Kinda."

"So apologize."

"Just like that? What if she's the one who's wrong?"

"What does that have to do with anything?"

"Well—"

"A gentleman takes responsibility for the disagreement with a lady, whether he was in the right or not."

"Maybe a century ago they did that."

His mother put down the potato peeler and set her hands on her hips. "Do you value this relationship or not?"

"I do." With those two words, he realized just how much.

"Then you'll shoulder the blame and do what's necessary to make things right. And then, together, you can work through the problem, figuring out how to keep it from happening again." She went back to the potatoes. "That's how I see it, anyway."

Pete munched on the celery stick, thinking about the argument with Mary Rose. It probably wouldn't have happened if he hadn't brought up that summer, and her parents. Not that he was wrong about what happened. But maybe inserting it into the situation with Sal and Kelsey was not a good idea.

"So is this woman someone I know?"

"I don't think you've ever met." Now he sounded like Sal, avoiding the truth.

"Is she someone you work with?"

Pete went to stand at the counter beside his mother. "Mom, to be honest, I've been seeing Mary Rose Bowdrey the last few weeks."

"Mary Rose..." She went still, and stared up at him with a furrow between her eyebrows. "*That* Mary Rose?"

"The one I married? Yes, ma'am. That one."

"I know her family still lives here, but I thought she had gone somewhere else. Charlotte?"

"Charleston."

"But she's come home?"

"Temporarily."

"Ah." Pulling the potato masher out of the drawer, she went to work. A little more aggressively than the recipe called for, Pete thought. "So this is a temporary...friendship."

The thought bothered him. "I don't know."

She mashed for a minute. Then the words seemed to burst out. "Why would you get involved with her at all? After that summer? You didn't say much, but I could see the hurt in you. Why do that again?"

"It doesn't have to end up that way this time, Mom."

"Yes, I can see you're having no trouble at all dealing with what's going on." Dumping the potatoes into a serving bowl, she stalked into the dining room. Pete heard the clink of china and silverware as she set another place. And then his brothers came through the back door.

"Hey, man." Rick clapped him on the back as he went toward the refrigerator. "Thought you had other plans."

"Plans change."

"You want to watch the race with us this afternoon?

After we get the kitchen cleaned up, of course,'' he added as their mom came back into the room.

"Good idea.'' Pete picked up the platter with the roast on it before she could and headed toward the dining-room door. "An afternoon with the guys sounds like just what I need.''

KELSEY WENT to the back of the gym at lunch on Monday. Sal wasn't there. She prowled the halls but couldn't find him, and had to go to algebra, finally, without lunch and without a chance to explain.

Then he didn't show up for the money class Monday night. Some of the other kids came, though not as many as the week before. Kelsey couldn't concentrate, couldn't have said what Aunt M talked about. During break time, she doodled on the worksheets, writing Sal's name over and over and over. He might be sick, taking the day off from school.

But she knew in her heart that he was mad because she hadn't met him on Friday night. Somehow, she had to reach him, had to explain.

In the midst of her own preoccupation, she noticed that Aunt M was in a real hurry to leave that night. She got her briefcase packed before all of the other kids had left the classroom. As soon as possible, she turned off the lights and locked the door. And then she was hurrying down the hallway toward the gym, fast enough that Kelsey had to skip to keep up. Trace, the jerk, didn't make the effort.

Inside the gym, Mary Rose skirted the basketball court without a glance to the left or the right. But Kelsey noticed Mr. Pete look over, noticed that he paused for a second in what he was saying to one of the kids. If he'd planned to catch Mary Rose in her exit, though, he changed his mind and went back to his teaching.

Kelsey used the ride home to work up her petition. In the house, she found Kate in the kitchen, on the phone with somebody about extra flowers for the Azalea Festival Street Fair. Not an encouraging situation. But she waited until that call ended, took a deep breath and jumped in before Kate could dial again.

"I need to ask a favor."

Her stepmother made notes on a legal pad, then put the pencil down. "What favor?"

"I—I need to call Sal."

Kate's sweet gaze turned hard. "No." She picked up her pencil again.

"Please. He wasn't at school today. And I need to talk to him."

"I don't want you to talk to him. I want you to stay away from that boy."

"But…" Maybe by admitting everything, she could earn a little sympathy. "But I was supposed to meet him the other night. Friday. And I didn't. He won't know why and he'll think I just stood him up."

"Kelsey, I don't understand why you believe I care what he thinks."

"*I* care. Doesn't that make a difference? It matters to me what he thinks."

For a minute, Kate just stared at her. "No, I'm afraid it doesn't make a difference that you care what he thinks. Because I truly believe that seeing him is wrong for you and I'll do whatever I can to keep you safe."

Something in the usually soft voice told Kelsey that her cause was hopeless. And she was too tired to throw another tantrum, even to protest. She didn't say anything, just got up from the table and went to her room. If she couldn't find Sal tomorrow, her only option would be to write him a letter.

But she always got her stamps from Kate.

With a moan, Kelsey put her head down on the desk.

PETE DISMISSED his Wednesday-night class fifteen minutes early so he could be at Mary Rose's door when her kids left the room. He waited outside until only Kelsey and Trace remained.

Then he stepped around the door frame and gave them a nod. "Would y'all excuse us a few minutes?"

Trace threw him a dirty look, but left without protest. Indulging in what appeared to be a first-class pout, Kelsey flung her purse over her shoulder and stomped out into the hallway. That left Mary Rose on one side of the teacher's desk and Pete on the other.

"Sal didn't come to class tonight or Monday," she said, keeping her eyes on the papers she was straightening into a perfect stack. "A lot of his friends stayed away as well. I guess that's my punishment."

"I haven't seen or heard from him since Saturday. That probably means he's done with both of us. And you've obviously got Kelsey corralled. So can we get back to where we were before all this hit the fan?" Reaching out, he ran a finger down her cheek. "I miss you, Mary Rose. I know…it's been all of five days. But I do."

Under his touch, her cheek flushed a pretty pink. "I'm not sure. Things are so complicated."

"Not between us."

She stepped back. "Is this just about sex, Pete? Because we did that before and it didn't work out very well."

"We did not do that before. I didn't, anyway. I loved

you from the very beginning and I was ready to spend my whole life with you. Sex was just part of the package.''

''Shh.'' Mary Rose held up her hand. ''I'm sorry. You're right. We did love each other. Then. But now…''

''Now we're older, more cautious.'' Pete took the hand she'd held up and captured the other one, too. ''We're not ready to risk everything quite so fast. But we'll never know what this could be if we don't let it breathe, give it a chance to grow. That's all I'm asking for.''

She stared up at him, worrying her lower lip with her teeth. ''You could talk a leopard out of his spots, I think. Okay, we can try.'' Then she smiled shyly. ''I've missed you, too.''

Pete wanted to make the risk worth her while. After she drove Trace and Kelsey home from REWARDS on Thursday, they went for coffee at one of the upscale shops where there was live music to listen to and foam to get through before you reached the real brew. And he drove her straight home, with a few heated kisses as their goodbye.

After work on Friday, he took her to dinner at New Skye's fanciest restaurant, then surprised her with tickets to a performance by the North Carolina Symphony in the local auditorium. Classical music wasn't Pete's first choice but, for Mary Rose, he'd make the sacrifice.

When the lights came up at halftime—uh, intermission—he looked over to find her checking her watch. ''Didn't seem like an hour, did it?'' he asked.

''Actually…'' She made a funny face. ''It seemed longer. I never have quite understood this kind of music.''

''No kidding? I thought you would like it. You should have said something.''

"You already had the tickets. I didn't want to disappoint you."

"Listen, Ms. Mary Rose." He turned in his seat and took her hands in his. "Just tell me the truth. Don't worry about my feelings—they're pretty tough by now. Let's just say what we think to each other and deal with the issues as they fall."

She looked almost as scared as when she'd agreed to start seeing him again. But then she swallowed hard and smiled. "Sounds good."

"So what do you want to do now?"

Leaning close, she whispered something in his ear that drove his blood pressure sky-high...and made him glad he was wearing a suit jacket.

Face flaming, Pete cleared his throat. "Let's get out of here."

With Miss Dixie shut outside the bedroom door, they spent several long, lazy hours in bed. It was after midnight when Mary Rose stretched and sighed. "I have to go home."

Pete's first impulse was to catch her back against him and forbid her to go anywhere. But he'd promised himself to give her as much freedom as she needed. "I guess you do."

He dragged on some jeans and a T-shirt, watching as Mary Rose replaced the pale purple lingerie he'd eased out of the way earlier, then the stockings and the deep purple dress, the high-heeled purple sandals.

"Whew." He wiped a hand across his face. "That was almost as sexy as taking it all off in the first place."

The smile she gave him in the mirror was sexier still.

"I think I'll go let Miss Dixie out." As he passed behind her, he put his hands on her shoulders and leaned in to set a kiss behind her ear. "Or else you're never getting out of this room at all."

Mary Rose watched him leave, closing the door behind him. Then she backed up, sat on the edge of the bed and put her head in her hands.

Oh, this was hard. Seeing Pete, being with him, making love with him…and not letting herself really care. Trying to take as little as possible from their time together, so there wouldn't be memories to sigh over. She couldn't afford to sigh over Pete—she'd done too much of that in her life already.

His footsteps approached from down the hallway, and she got to her feet, putting on a smile she hoped would hide her feelings.

He knocked, then came in. "Dixie's curled up on the couch again, headed back to sleep. Are you ready?"

"I am." She stepped close and put her arms around his neck. "It's been a wonderful night. Thank you." The kiss they shared nearly swept her good intentions away.

But Pete did the thinking for her. "I'd better get you home."

Too short a time later, she watched from the front window of Kate's living room as he drove away, and realized that she understood why Kelsey was in such despair.

TRACE AND KELSEY were scheduled to see their father for breakfast on Saturday morning, and then to spend the rest of the day with Pete, rebuilding the mailboxes they'd knocked down. Everyone was awake early, silently glancing at each other from their bedroom doorways, dreading the inevitable knock on the door.

L.T. arrived punctually at nine o'clock. Mary Rose just happened to be in the living room when Kate opened the door.

"Kids ready?" He strolled in with his hands in the pockets of his khaki slacks. "Melanie's waiting in the car."

"They're coming." Kate backed up against the fireplace. "Would you like to sit down?"

"No, thanks." He prowled the room, a handsome man with a winning smile. "Um...did you get the papers?"

"Papers?"

"From the lawyer. He said he'd sent out the separation papers."

"Oh." She clasped her hands together in front of her, pressed her lips together. "No, no, I haven't received them."

Mary Rose stirred in her chair. "Dad will bring them over, I'm sure."

"Well, just sign 'em and send 'em back." He turned and walked to the foot of the stairs. "C'mon, Trace, Kelsey. We don't have all day."

Trace came to the top of the stairs, with Kelsey behind him. They stood for a few seconds, then started slowly down the steps. When they reached the bottom, L.T. grabbed at Trace's neck with one hand and rubbed the top of his head with the other. "How you doin', boy?" His son staggered as he pulled free, but didn't answer.

L.T. looked at Kelsey. "You're looking pretty, princess. Let's go."

Like condemned prisoners, the kids followed their dad out the door. Kelsey looked in again as she turned to close the door behind her, and the desperation in her eyes was all too obvious.

Then the door closed, and Kate collapsed into a huddle on the hearth.

"Oh, honey." Mary Rose lifted her to her feet, got her to a chair. "I'm so sorry."

Kate curled over her folded arms, her head on her knees, as tremors passed through her slender body. "I knew it was coming. I shouldn't be surprised." After a long silence, she said, "Do you think the children heard him?"

"No." She wasn't really sure. She only hoped so. "I think they were still in their rooms."

"Kelsey doesn't have a door."

"She was probably in the bathroom finishing her makeup. Don't worry about them, Kate. Take care of yourself right now."

"There is no *me*, don't you see? If I was any sort of real person, he wouldn't treat me like this. If I were adequate as a mother, Trace and Kelsey wouldn't be disintegrating in front of my eyes."

"Kate, honey, stop." Mary Rose knelt in front of her sister. "This is not your fault. L.T. treats you this way because he's a loser. Why do you think his first wife left? She wasn't going to put up with his tyranny, not even to stay with her babies. And then he lucked out and found a girl who was always determined to please, to earn approval. You fit his needs perfectly. You've done everything he wanted you to—gave up law school to come back and raise his children, gave up hopes of having your own babies because two kids in the house was enough. You think I don't remember the things you've let slip all these years? And Mother and Daddy thought this was just great, mostly because Daddy liked the money L.T. earned for them and the lifestyle he bought 'for you.' And you wanted the parents to approve of you, so you just put up with being made a cipher in your own marriage."

She halted, panting with rage and sorrow over the mountain of insights she hadn't really registered until now. "I stood by and let this happen. I don't like that at all. But we can change things, Kate. You don't have to take this—this shit from L.T.''

''What am I supposed to do?''

Mary Rose sat down on the floor. ''Well…well, you can read those papers, for a start, and see if you like the terms. Chances are good that L.T. has set things up to benefit himself and not done anything for you or the kids. You can make a counterproposal with terms you like.''

''Daddy won't be happy with that.''

''Then we'll get another lawyer. There are plenty in this town.''

''How could we?''

She got to her feet, found Kate's hands and pulled her to a standing position, too. ''I don't know. But this can't go on. You've got to reclaim your independence. Make a life on your own terms.''

''Like you've done.''

Mary Rose thought of the years behind her, the way they looked so empty now. ''Sort of. But you've got Kelsey and Trace in your life. The three of you can build a team.''

Kate wilted again. ''If they ever speak to me.''

''They will. They just need to see that you're strong enough for them to depend on. You show them who's boss, and I really do think they'll be easier to deal with.''

''And just how am I supposed to demonstrate who's boss?''

''Let's have some tea and figure that out.''

THE DINER WAS PACKED with the usual breakfast suspects, Pete noticed, including L. T. LaRue, his girlfriend and his kids. Kelsey and Trace looked miserable, and the girlfriend wasn't smiling. But L.T. seemed unconscious of it all. The man was an—

"Earth to Trooper Mitchell. Come in, Mitchell. You with us?" Tommy Crawford elbowed him in the side. "You ain't worth a damn on the court or off these days, Pete. There must be a woman involved."

"D-definitely a woman," Adam DeVries confirmed. "Saw her with my own two eyes at the s-s-symphony last night."

"The symphony? Pete Mitchell at the symphony?" Rob Warren let his fork clatter to his plate, drawing the attention of the people at the tables around them. "This woman must be spectacular."

Adam nodded again. "M-Mary Rose B-Bowdrey."

The silence expanded. Pete rolled his eyes, sat forward and braced his fingers on the edge of the table. "Yeah, you jerks. I'm dating Mary Rose. You got a problem with that?"

The three guys at his table looked at each other, shrugged and shook their heads. "Nope, no problem." "N-not me." "No way, man."

"Good." He pushed to his feet. "Ready to go?"

They paid Charlie at the register and made their way to the door. Pete managed to catch Kelsey's eye and gave her a grin and a wink. She didn't smile back at him.

Outside, the other guys headed for their cars. Pete had parked on the edge of the lot, which gave him a chance to see Abby around the corner of the building, staring at that huge expanse of brick.

She had tears running down her face.

"Abby, you okay?" He jogged over, took hold of her shoulders. "Something I can do?"

"Just look." She shrugged off his hands and pointed, her voice quivering with rage. "Just look at what they've done to our wall!"

He didn't understand how he'd missed this earlier in

the morning. A new assault had been made on the wall, with scrawled insults and obscenities and vulgar drawings in glaring colors that made every word seem like a shout, or a scream. The gang marks tucked in between the nastinesses—Los Lobos, of course, and Los Presidentes—seemed almost polite in contrast.

"Damn, Abby. I'm sorry." Pete put his arm around her shoulders, turned her away. "You go inside and call the police. And don't come out and look at this anymore."

She followed his instructions without a fight, which told its own tale about her state of mind. DeVries, Warren and Crawford had noticed something was wrong, and came over to check out the damage. Between the four of them, they kept other sightseers at a distance until New Skye's finest arrived. They also developed a new plan for Pete's Saturday afternoon—a plan involving lots of paint and a really big brick wall. And a bunch of troublemaking kids.

They were still considering the damage when the LaRues left the diner. Of the four, only Trace glanced at the commotion around the side. He veered off the track toward LaRue's Yukon and came to get a better look. "Wow. Somebody really did a number on that wall."

Pete raised an eyebrow. "Somebody with a lousy sense of humor."

"Oh, I don't know." The boy's shoulders shook with a laugh. "Some of it's pretty funny."

"Then you have a lousy sense of humor, too. But that's okay, 'cause you're gonna be part of the solution to the problem. Step behind the yellow line." He lifted the crime-scene tape with one hand and put the other on Trace's shoulder to pull him under.

"Keep your hands off my boy." L. T. LaRue had joined them. "He's coming with me."

"Actually, the law says he's staying here with me to do some of the community service he owes."

"Big-deal state trooper." LaRue looked him up and down with contempt. "Sniffin' around my sister-in-law like some horny hound…for the second time, no less. You oughta learn to recognize women who're too good for you."

Even as Pete wrapped his fingers into fists, Adam's hand clamped hard on his shoulder. "G-get on with your d-day, LaRue."

Without acknowledging the other man, L.T. turned away. "C'mon, son."

Trace stood still, obviously uncertain of which way he should go. Seeing his conflict, Pete took pity on him. "Let your dad take you home," he told the boy. "Change into work clothes. Then Kate or Mary Rose can bring you and Kelsey back. The other kids will be here about noon."

After throwing Pete a surprised glance, Trace turned on his heel and ran across the parking lot to catch up with his dad. From the back, father and son looked almost identical as they walked toward the SUV.

"There are s-s-some men who truly d-deserve what's coming to them," Adam said. "I hope I'm there wh-when LaRue gets h-his."

"I hope I get to be the one who gives it to him." Pete finally relaxed his hands. "Meanwhile, we've got a wall to paint."

Most of the kids took the change in plans—from mailboxes to brick wall—with good spirits. Adam used his builder's discount to get the paint and equipment they needed, and Rob and Tommy stayed all afternoon to supervise. A couple of boom boxes supplied the music that adolescents seemed to need to accompany any meaningful effort, and Abby brought out drinks and snacks at regular intervals. They had themselves a real party going on.

Mary Rose drove Kelsey and Trace back a little after twelve o'clock. She stood for a minute staring at the wall. "That's disgusting. I can't imagine that kids even have those…those words in their minds." Then she shook her head. "The world is not as nice a place as I would like it to be."

"But we're trying, right?" Pete let his hand rest on her shoulder for just a second. No sense in giving the kids something to comment on.

"You definitely are." She recovered her smile. "Speaking of which, how's the fund-raising going?"

He shook his head. "Now I'm depressed. Even if I had the time to talk to people, I don't know who to start with."

"I talked to Kate about that. She said there are organizations that provide grants of money for programs like yours."

"How do you get a grant? Lots of forms to fill out, I suppose?"

"Not always. Basically, you write an application describing what you're doing and explaining why you deserve some of their money."

Pete groaned. "My many talents do not include writing up anything longer than a traffic violation. My chief will tell you—he hates to read my reports."

"Then you find someone to write the applications for you."

"And am I looking at just that person?"

"I—" She looked past him, and her eyes widened. "Oh. No."

At first all Pete saw, when he looked around, was a long splash of paint on the wall, obliterating some of the worst graffiti.

Then he realized that underneath part of that long splash of paint was a body. It took him a couple of seconds to recognize the boy standing with his hands clenched, his eyes and mouth squeezed shut.

Meanwhile, at the top of the tallest ladder stood the person who had been painting the upper edge of the wall. Pete had no trouble at all recognizing the one who had somehow managed to upset most of a gallon of bright yellow paint on the kid down below. And who now perched above them all, laughing.

Kelsey LaRue had spilled—dumped?—that can of paint on her brother Trace.

Pete looked at Mary Rose and grinned. "Revenge is sweet." He glanced beyond her to the parking lot and the car in which she'd brought the kids. "Good thing you didn't drive the Porsche. I'll wrap him up in a sheet so you can take him home."

CHAPTER THIRTEEN

MARY ROSE LISTENED to Trace swear all during the drive home, but didn't interrupt him. He deserved the privilege. At the house, they hosed him down in the grass before letting him inside to take a shower. Not surprisingly, once in his room, he didn't reappear, even when Kate called to him to come down for a late lunch.

"Plotting his own revenge, do you suppose?" Kate covered the plate of sandwiches with plastic wrap and set it aside. "Do I have a feud on my hands as well as everything else?"

Mary Rose was fast losing her optimism when it came to her niece and nephew. "I wouldn't be surprised."

In response to Kate's earlier phone call, their dad brought over the separation papers at about two-thirty that afternoon. He brought their mother, too.

"I've gone over them," he said, settling in his chair at the dining-room table. "I didn't see any glaring problems. I believe you could simply sign and let me get them back to L.T.'s attorney."

Kate took a copy from him. The paper shook a little as she held it between her fingers. "I—I think I should probably read them for myself."

"But it's a lot of legal wording." Their mother brought in a tray of glasses and a pitcher of tea. "You won't follow all of that, Kate. Let your father take care of it."

But as Frances poured the drinks, Kate started to study the agreement. The room became very quiet, except for the clink of ice.

"Page two, third paragraph," Kate said. "Am I reading this correctly? L.T. takes sole ownership of the house, but the kids and I can live here, rent free?"

Their father scanned the agreement. "Yes. That's correct."

"For how long?"

He pushed up his glasses and stared at her in surprise. "What do you mean?"

Mary Rose smiled to herself. *Way to go, Katie.*

"Without any time frame specified, he could throw us out of here next week."

"L.T. wouldn't do that," their mother assured her.

Kate gazed at her with a weary sort of patience in her face. "Six months ago, you would have said he would never leave me. I'm not sure you know L.T. as well as you think you do, Mama."

Frances raised her eyebrows as high as they would go. "I beg your pardon!"

Her daughter ignored her. "There must be some sort of time guarantee in that provision, Daddy, so the kids and I are sure we have someplace to live and a reasonable amount of time to find a new home when L.T. decides to throw us out."

"I suppose that makes sense." John Bowdrey took a silver pen out of his shirt pocket and made a note on the page.

Kate kept reading. After a minute, she dropped the papers on the table and slapped her hand on top of them. "He can't have my car. Here it says that he gets the title to both vehicles. But I can't take care of the children properly without a car. He'll have to give me the title to the Volvo. Unless…'' Her voice shook suddenly. ''Is he taking custody of Kelsey and Trace?''

She flipped several pages, then read intently. ''No, thank God. He's claiming joint custody but allowing them to live with me. He wouldn't want the responsibility, anyway. Back to the property.''

An hour later, Kate had examined and questioned a number of L.T.'s arrangements. ''The children must remain on his insurance until they can get their own,'' she insisted. ''Whether or not I get coverage on my own, whether or not I marry again. They are his responsibility, for heaven's sake.''

John Bowdrey shook his head. ''L.T. is going to throw a fit when his attorney gives him all these changes.''

Kate looked at him with her chin cocked. ''You think we should keep L.T. calm and just let him cheat me and his children out of what we deserve?''

Their father took out his handkerchief and polished his glasses. ''No, my dear, I don't suppose I do.''

Convinced that her sister was on her way to independence, Mary Rose helped her mother gather the glasses and take them to the kitchen.

''I can't believe Kate is behaving this way.'' Frances paced across the kitchen and back again.

Mary Rose was smiling as she put the glasses in the dishwasher. ''Isn't it great?''

''No, it is not. What hope do you think there will be that L.T. will come back once she insists on these excessive conditions? I can tell you, a man won't stay with a demanding woman.''

''She's not being demanding, Mother. She's protecting herself and Trace and Kelsey. Besides, she doesn't want L.T. back. He's not worth having.''

''He's her husband.''

"He's a liar, a cheat and abusive, to boot. The Bim—um, secretary is welcome to him. Kate's better off alone."

"No woman is better off alone." There was real fear in Frances's voice. Mary Rose saw that she truly believed what she said. "Who will take care of her?"

"Kate can take care of herself. I have, all these years. And I've done okay." Suddenly feeling sorry for her mother, she went over and put an arm around her shoulders. "You raised a couple of capable women. We can make it on our own."

Frances looked at her searchingly. "I wish I had your strength."

"You do. You just chose a different path."

And that path had turned out well enough, she thought, watching her parents walk to their car. Frances would have struggled as a single mother. Whatever sacrifices she had made to keep her husband at home must have been justified by the comfort of having him there.

"But you," she told Kate in the middle of a big hug, "were fantastic. Superwoman. I can't believe how you tore into that agreement and then put it back together again the way you wanted it."

Kate's smile was the most carefree she'd managed in months...maybe years. "I know. It got to be a game, looking for ways to jerk L.T.'s chain. I bet we hear him screaming all the way over here from his office when he sees what I've done."

Mary Rose grinned. "Won't that be fun?"

KATE WENT to pick up Kelsey at about 6:00 p.m. Judging from the girl's quick dash to her room when she arrived at the house, a lecture had been delivered on the drive home. After eating a peaceful supper with her sister,

Mary Rose went down to the diner to check on the day's progress. The kids had all gone home, but Pete was still working on the last third of the wall. The friends who had been there when she'd come earlier, but whom she hadn't had a chance to meet, had stayed with him until the bitter end.

"Adam DeVries," Pete said, indicating the lean, dark-haired man who, Abby had said, never ate at home. Tommy Crawford was short, blond, powerfully built. Rob Warren, also blond, was otherwise Tommy's exact opposite—very tall, lanky, wearing a mustache and saying his hello with a Southern accent as thick as blackstrap molasses.

Mary Rose nodded and smiled, but didn't shake their paint-coated hands. "More members of the class of '89, I presume?"

Tommy grinned. "You stick around the old hometown, you tend to keep running into the same people. At least you don't have to learn a lot of new names."

"You and the kids have done a fine job." The red bricks now glowed a sunny yellow. "Nobody's going to miss the diner in the dark, are they?"

She watched them paint for the last few minutes. The day had been a warm one, and the guys had shed their shirts during the afternoon. Presented with a view of four well-muscled backs, Mary Rose found her eyes irresistibly drawn to only one. Pete was simply more smoothly drawn, more beautifully shaped. Her imagination displayed an alarming tendency to remove the rest of his clothes and picture him as he'd been in her arms last night.

Not at all a comfortable train of thought. At least, not in public.

As the light began to soften, the four men finished up

the last corner. Abby and her dad came out to survey the work. "Well." Charlie stood with his hands in his pockets, his head tilted. "Looks like a damn nursery school."

"Dad." Abby linked her hands through his arm. "It's clean, in more ways than one. And we're very grateful," she told Pete and the others. "Except…"

Pete nodded. "Except it's a nice, big, blank surface for them to start over on."

"Well, yeah."

"The New Skye P.D. is going to increase their drive-by in this direction. Between the vandalism at the school and here, this is obviously a situation that needs to be handled. They'll do their best to spot the jerks who are causing the trouble."

Abby rested her head on Charlie's shoulder. "All these years, and nobody has caused us this much grief. Why now?" When no one could give her an answer, she sighed and shook her head. "Oh, well. You boys come on in and have some supper. It's been a long time since those sandwiches at lunch." She smiled at Mary Rose. "Have you eaten? You're welcome, too."

"I've had dinner, thanks."

"Well, have a glass of tea. And maybe one of those banana splits? You do have a weakness."

"A weakness for banana splits?" Pete pulled on his T-shirt and came up beside her. "You eat banana splits?"

"Once or twice a year." More often, of course, since coming home to New Skye.

"Wow. I wish I'd known."

"Why?"

"I could have bribed you into going out with me so much sooner."

She laughed, and kept on laughing throughout the meal at the easy banter between four men who had been friends since childhood. Adam's wit was dry, pointed; his construction company competed head-to-head with L.T. for contracts around the city. "N-needless to say, we aren't c-c-close f-friends."

"Is anybody close friends with L. T. LaRue?" Tommy polished off his second plate of meat loaf. "I never heard about it. Seems like he's cheated just about everybody in town."

Rob was the quiet one, with a twinkle in his eye. "He and the mayor share enemies. That must make them friends."

After the laughter, there were a few moments of altercation when Charlie refused to accept payment for the meals, including Mary Rose's banana split. Outside again, Pete and his friends collected the brushes and leftover paint from their job. They were loading their trucks with ladders when a convoy of cars screeched through the intersection and slid to a stop on the gravel of the diner parking lot. A variety of young men got out and swaggered—that really was the only word—over to look at the wall. Among them was Sal Torres.

This, Mary Rose surmised, was Los Lobos.

Pete stepped up to Sal. "Something we can do for you?"

There was an arrogance, a power, in the younger man's stance she hadn't seen before. "Just came to look, man. We heard about the artwork, wanted to see for ourselves. But I guess we're too late."

"You didn't get a good look during the process?"

Sal raised his hands and took a step back. "Hey, don't blame us. Wasn't anybody I know who did this job."

"I'm supposed to believe that?" Pete's stare was as hard as she'd ever seen it.

"Believe it or not. I'm telling the truth."

"Well, like you said, you're too late. Filth like that couldn't be allowed to stay in plain sight."

"*Yo comprendo.*" The younger man turned to walk away.

"You have any idea who might have been this stupid?" Pete called after him. "Los Presidentes, maybe?"

Sal stopped and appeared to consider for a minute. Then he pivoted to look at Pete again. "I told you before, I think you're looking for white kids trying to blame it on the gangs. I coulda told you better if I'd seen the wall. But that's my take."

As he walked back to his car, Mary Rose went after him. "Sal."

With the door open, he watched her warily.

"I missed you at class last week. Will you be coming back?"

"I don't think so."

"There's a lot more to know about financing a business."

"I'll figure it out on my own."

"But—"

He cut her off with a chop of his hand. "Look, stop bugging me. You don't think I'm good enough for Kelsey, but you want to keep me hanging around her. For torture, maybe? Sorry, I don't play that game. You got your sweet little girl back. Still innocent, in case you were wondering. Now…" He swallowed hard. "Leave me alone." Dropping into the driver's seat, he slammed the door and revved the engine.

Mary Rose caught the edge of the open window. "One more thing. It's not her fault she stood you up. Her brother told us she'd spent the night with you. She's been practically under house arrest ever since. She's not even allowed to use the phone in private. Just so you know."

Sal shook his head, not glancing her way. She stepped back, and the beat-up Taurus fishtailed out of the parking lot, with all the various other vehicles in its wake.

Pete came up beside her. "What did he say?"

"That he and Kelsey haven't had sex."

"You must be relieved."

"Yes." But Sal looked as miserable as Kelsey did these days. And Mary Rose remembered that kind of misery.

"So there's no real harm done."

"Except that there are two people who care about each other and can't be together."

Pete looked down at her, and she knew he understood her reference. "Sometimes, that's what has to happen."

"I suppose. But I wonder..."

"What?"

"I wonder if it's always for the best."

They were alone in the diner parking lot again, under a full moon in a clear sky. Pete backed her up against the side of the Porsche and braced his elbows on either side of her shoulders. "That's a very interesting point, Ms. Bowdrey."

Smiling, she rested her hands at his waist, tugged him closer against her. "You think so? Why?"

"Because it sounds like you're reconsidering this whole 'different lives' issue."

"And if I am?"

"Well...I am, too."

She caught her breath at the confession.

"You know, there are banks in New Skye." Pete grazed his lips along her jawline, the curve of her throat.

"I had noticed that."

"And we have more than our share of crotchety old ladies with money to invest."

"I'm prepared to believe it." She tugged his shirt out of his jeans, let her hands drift over the muscles she'd been admiring earlier.

"You did say you thought it might be time for you to move to a new job."

"I did."

"While I don't know that New Skye is a step up the ladder from Charleston..."

"Um, I think that's a negative."

Pete lifted his head and looked down at her with those wonderful dark-lashed eyes. "I do believe we can offer you some fringe benefits."

"Such as?"

He kissed her then, with an intensity and a demand that drove every thought, every feeling out of her. Except need. And a desperate desire to take and hold this moment forever.

"We could make it this time," he murmured in her ear a little later. "We could go all the way. Think about it, Mary Rose. You and I could be those crotchety old folks, giving the bankers and the troopers a hard time together. Wouldn't it be fun?"

Late that night, as she lay curled beside him in the warmth of his bed, Mary Rose admitted to herself that she wanted exactly what Pete offered. Passion, laughter, adventure. Family? Perhaps. All the things she'd denied herself during these ten years.

Because she couldn't have them with him.

Did she dare take hold of the dream again? Could she make it come true this time?

SUNDAY AFTERNOON, Mary Rose found Kelsey in her room. "I wanted to tell you that I talked to Sal last night."

The girl flipped over on her bed and sat up, her face lit with eagerness. "About me? Did he ask about me?"

"We did talk about you. He confirmed what you said about that night."

"And is he coming back to class tomorrow?"

"I don't think so." Kelsey's face fell. "From what he said, I think he finds it hard to be around you when we're all so set against you seeing each other."

"But—"

"We only had a couple of minutes. I just wanted to tell you that I think Sal does care about you. Even if you can't see him, I thought you'd like to know that."

"But why can't I see him? If people would just get rid of this ridiculous prejudice, they would see that he's a decent person. Half the boys in this neighborhood get into more trouble than Sal does. Including my own brother."

"It's more than just the legal trouble, Kelsey."

"Oh, go away." She threw herself facedown on the pillow. "I'm tired of hearing about 'same culture, same beliefs.' It's only an excuse for prejudice."

Mary Rose did as she was asked and stepped out into the hallway, just in time to look across into Kate's room and see Trace hanging up the phone.

"You're not supposed to be making calls."

"I needed to know about some homework." He gave her his father's charming grin as he slipped by. "That's all. I promise."

She didn't believe him. But where did she start looking for the truth?

TUESDAY WAS ONE of those nights when Pete wondered why he had ever started the REWARDS program in the first place. The kids were full of themselves, full of the unique craziness that always seemed to grab hold of them in the spring and turn reasonably tolerable teenagers into insufferable brats. Sal had stopped showing up to work on the car or to help out with the class, and Pete had his hands full trying to run herd on a garage full of smart-mouthed kids by himself.

When he stopped his lecture for the fourth time in fifteen minutes because the extraneous conversations around him were too loud to talk over, he even found himself thinking that maybe the budget crunch was a blessing in disguise. It would give him an excuse to give up on REWARDS, if only to avoid the dreaded fund-raising. He believed in the program, of course, but the thought of pestering people for money, trying to persuade them to do what was good for the community when they should be willing and eager to help, turned his stomach. He was a state trooper, dammit, not a door-to-door sales-man.

The kids finally noticed that he was waiting for their attention and quieted down. "Thank you very much," he said with a wide edge of sarcasm in his tone. "In the few minutes we have left, would one of you like to re-view the purpose of the catalytic converter and how it works?" He'd spent the first hour of class on a detailed explanation.

No one volunteered, and the whispers were starting up again. Pete leaned a hip against the bumper of the car. "Did a single, solitary piece of information stick in somebody's brain tonight? One little word?"

"Pollution," a voice volunteered from the back of the group.

"Very good. The converter reduces pollution. Any-body remember how?"

"Oxidation," the same voice answered after a pause. "Reduction."

The kids were quiet now, paying attention.

Pete nodded. "What kinds of pollution?"

"Nitrogen oxides, carbon monoxide, organic compounds." A shift in the crowd brought Trace into view. "The gases flow across these coated grids in the converter and get changed into less harmful chemicals—nitrogen, oxygen and stuff." He spoke without looking up, shoulders hunched and hands in his pockets as if he was ashamed to be revealing what he knew.

"That pretty much covers it." Pete kept his voice cool to avoid making too big a deal out of the contribution. "And we're done for the night. See you guys Thursday."

The crowd dispersed quickly, as usual. Kelsey and Trace were almost out the door when Pete casually glanced over. "Thanks for the input," he told the boy. "For a minute there, I was on the verge of telling jokes to try and get their attention. Believe me, you don't want to hear my stand-up routine. Seinfeld has no reason to fear."

Kelsey rolled her eyes and slipped away. A reluctant grin flashed across Trace's face. "I can imagine."

"I'm not sure you can. There's this alien monster, see, and it walks into a bar in a little town in Texas. But the bartender can't understand what the alien wants. 'Spit it out, stranger,' he says. 'Just—'"

Hands up in a gesture of surrender, Trace backed out the door. "That's okay," he said with a kind of panicked chuckle. "Honest. I get the point. Bad. Really, really bad." Before Pete could finish the joke, his victim had vanished down the hallway.

But Pete found himself grinning as he closed up the garage and shut down REWARDS for the night. Trace

LaRue was a far cry from the classic definition of a hardened juvenile offender. Still, he was a kid in trouble, a kid with a bad attitude…and tonight that attitude had changed for the better. A small step, but encouraging. And, fortunately or not, all it took to revive Pete's spirits was that one small step.

REWARDS would go on, he knew, if he had to stand on a downtown street corner with a dancing monkey and a music box, begging people for spare change!

L.T. CALLED ON Wednesday, about lunchtime. Kate held the phone away from her ear and, even across the kitchen, Mary Rose could hear him yelling about the separation agreement. She and Kate just smiled at each other, listening to him wear himself out.

When he took a breath, Kate brought the phone close again. "You're free to make counterproposals, L.T. And I'll consider them. But don't think you're going to give me and your children the shaft. Those days are gone." She hung up while he was still screaming.

The rest of the week passed in a flurry of preparations for the Azalea Festival Street Fair. Kate was constantly occupied with meetings and shopping expeditions. Mary Rose drove the kids to and from school and to the REWARDS program each night. She and Pete saw each other late in the evenings, and she usually got to bed sometime between one and two o'clock. Since school started at 8:00 a.m., it wasn't long before she began to feel sleep deprived.

In an attempt at self-preservation, she postponed Pete's Friday invitation to burgers and a movie to Saturday night, planning to stay home and get to bed early for once. The day was rainy and chilly—just the kind of weather they hoped not to have next weekend for the street fair—so she watched movies with Trace and Kelsey all afternoon and into the night. The last film ended just before the late news.

"Let's see if they have a long-range weather forecast." Mary Rose commandeered the remote control and turned up the volume. Trace groaned and stumbled up the stairs to his room. Kelsey, asleep in the other recliner, didn't notice one way or the other.

As the opening for the news program played, Kate came hurrying down the hallway. "Mary Rose, I just heard—"

"In an ongoing local story," the TV commentator said, "the state highway patrol has been involved in pursuit of a robbery suspect since midafternoon. Leaving a bank security guard and two state troopers injured in his wake, the suspect has stolen and discarded two different vehicles in a desperate effort to escape arrest. More after this commercial message."

Mary Rose sat without moving, or even breathing, through the endless commercial. Kate perched on the arm of her chair, holding her hand. "There are thousands of state troopers. Pete's probably at home watching a ball game."

"Can you hand me the phone?" She dialed his number and got his answering machine. "He's not there."

The news program returned. "The suspect approached a teller at the Main Street branch of Citizen's Bank about two o'clock this afternoon and demanded an undisclosed sum of money at gunpoint. When the security guard tried to stop him, the suspect fired. The guard is in critical condition at New Skye Hospital."

Told with the journalist's relish for a good story, the news only got worse. The robber had forcibly taken an older woman's car and left her lying in the street with a broken elbow. A state trooper had pursued him to the interstate but was seriously injured when he lost control of his patrol car during the chase, which had exceeded a hundred miles an hour.

"That wouldn't be Pete," Mary Rose told herself. "He wouldn't wreck the car."

The suspect left the interstate and drove through several small towns, discarding the first stolen car, and then a second, absconding with yet another. Another state trooper was shot when he tried to prevent the suspect from taking the third car; the trooper's condition was unknown but believed to be critical.

"At present, the highway patrol and local police have instituted a wide-scale search for the suspect and the car he is believed to be driving. We'll bring you more information as it becomes available."

After sending Kelsey to her room, Mary Rose and Kate sat up through the long night, but the news never changed. They called the hospitals in several counties, but even with Kate's contacts among the doctors, they couldn't get the names of the injured troopers or information on their respective conditions.

Pete didn't answer his telephone at 2:00 a.m. Or 4:00. Or 6:00. She was beginning to understand his second wife's perspective. Why take hold of the joy being with Pete offered, when it could be snatched away without warning?

The morning news rehashed the same version of events they'd heard all night long. Mary Rose drank two cups of strong coffee and decided she had to do something or go crazy. She changed into gardening clothes, gathered up the shovels and a hoe, and went to the very back of the garden, where Kate's tree-form wisteria had sent up shoots all over the place. Now was as good a time as any to clear away those suckers, before they took over the whole yard.

She worked hard, chopping at the underground runners and cutting back the beautiful but aggressive vine to its original trunk. The heavy bloom time had passed, but she could still catch a hint of the heavenly scent in the air. Whenever her mind started to wander, she visualized how thick the rich lavender blossoms would be next year and kept pruning.

"I didn't think proper Southern ladies ever worked up a sweat."

At the sound of his voice she jumped, and screeched, and whirled around, the hoe held like a battle sword before her.

Pete put his hands up in surrender. "Don't hurt me."

She stared for a second. He was alive, and whole. "Oh, Pete. I was so sure I'd lost you." Dropping the hoe, she threw herself into his arms.

"I know, I know." He murmured it against her hair, over her ear. "It's okay."

Mary Rose drew back. "Why didn't you let me know?"

"I came as soon as I could." He gestured to the uniform he still wore. "I haven't even gone home to change. Miss Dixie's sure to have wet the floor by now."

"You could have called."

"Well, no, I couldn't. I was in my car almost the whole time, and they don't like us using the equipment for personal calls."

"Did you chase that man?"

"Across four counties and back again, the bastard."

"And did you catch him?"

"Yeah, we finally cornered him on a farm up in Johnson County."

"What time was that?"

"About two or so this morning."

She drew a shocked breath. "It's almost ten. You couldn't find a single second in the last eight hours to let me know you weren't in the hospital? Or even dead? I've been terrified all this time."

"Well, no, I really couldn't. You see, the guy had an arsenal in his barn. Every time we thought he'd finally run out of ammo, he came up with a new weapon. And the only way we got hold of him in the end was to take him out."

Mary Rose stared at him with her mouth open, not sure she understood. Pete nodded. "Yeah, I had the pleasure of killing the guy. So in addition to writing up the usual reports, I was writing up a report on the death of the suspect. And then they like to talk to you about it, back at HQ, get their initial sounding on whether or not this was a necessary death or you just being macho. Oh, and they send a shrink in, to gauge your reaction. So I guess you could say I've been a little busy these last eight hours. Sorry I couldn't drop everything and rush to the phone. To tell the truth, I don't think I had the change on me to make a call, anyway." He turned and started back across the grass, toward the driveway.

"Pete—" She went after him, caught hold of his arm with both hands. "I'm sorry. It's just—"

"Yeah, now that you know all the facts, you're sorry." He swung around again, shrugging her off in the process. "But you know, I think it would have been really nice if you could have given me the benefit of the doubt. If you could have assumed that I was doing my best in the situation, that I would take care of you as soon as I was able, because I care about you and I wouldn't want you to worry any more than you had to."

She started to speak, but he shook his head. "It's just like you assumed that I left you when the baby died because I was so glad to be cut loose. You never looked at it from my perspective, never considered that I would have stayed if you had only said the word. You never even gave me a chance to tell you how sorry I was about our child, how sad it made me that he didn't survive. You just assumed I had no...no sensitivity. Because, after all, I was just a kid from the other side of the tracks, where we don't grow them with an appreciation for the finer things in life."

He came a step closer. "Here's the truth about that. I was torn up that our baby died. And I missed you like hell for the better part of two years, until I finally realized I had to do something with what was left of my life. I even tried building another family, although God knows that didn't work, either. I should have listened when my brain kept telling me not to try again. Not to believe the promise in those blue eyes of yours. But I convinced myself you were different now. I thought *we* were different.

"Well, third strike and you're out. So I'm finally listening to good sense. You stay on your side of the tracks from now on, Ms. Mary Rose Bowdrey. And I'll damn sure stay on mine."

CHAPTER FOURTEEN

NEEDLESS TO SAY, their Saturday-night date didn't happen. Hoping against hope, Mary Rose got dressed and waited at the time they'd set, but Pete didn't arrive. She could have felt angry at being stood up, but she knew the fault was her own. She hadn't trusted him. Hadn't believed in him. Why shouldn't he have walked away?

Only Trace and Kelsey came to the Making Money Work class on Monday night. When the same thing happened on Wednesday, she knew that the experiment had failed. Without Sal's support, which depended on Pete's influence, the kids just weren't going to show up.

She waited until she thought Pete would be home that night to call. "I think I'll cancel the rest of my classes. The course doesn't seem to be working."

"That's too bad." His voice was cool. "The kids could really have benefited from what you had to say."

"Perhaps you'll give the topic another try in the future. I'm sure one of your local bankers would be glad to help you out. And they would have more time. I'll be going back to Charleston next week, after the Azalea Festival."

"It's probably just as well. I talked to Principal Floyd yesterday. I'm going to have to cut REWARDS back to two nights anyway, because I can't afford the rent for four nights a week."

"Oh, Pete, I am sorry."

"Yeah. Me, too."

An uncomfortable silence stretched between them. Mary Rose forced herself to break it. "Listen, I really do apologize for my reaction on Saturday. I had no right to make demands of you, and even if I did have the right, the timing was absolutely wretched. I'm sure this has been a very difficult situation. I'm sorry I made things worse for you."

"Thanks. I probably reacted too strongly, myself." Those were the words she wanted to hear. But the warm, loving tone she'd come to expect was gone. He'd given her a formal agreement of cooperation between distant allies, not a resumption of friendship…let alone anything more intimate.

With tears burning her eyes and welling up in her throat, she fell back on time-honored formulas. "Well. I—I don't know if we'll run into each other before I go home. So take care of yourself. It's been good to see you again."

"Mary Rose—" Pete heard the phone cut off before he could go on. Then he clicked his own off and let it rest on his chest. What more did he want to say?

After Saturday morning, there shouldn't be anything left to talk about. The last thing he needed in his life was a woman who couldn't—wouldn't—understand the circumstances of his job. Most days were simple enough. Show up, keep the speeds down on the interstate, go home. But some days, the unpredictable happened. Some days, he was called on to use all the skills he'd trained to acquire. Some days, he actually got to protect the public welfare from the real bad guys.

He understood that those days were scary for the ones waiting at home. He'd done everything he could to reassure Sherrill. They'd even gone to counseling together, trying to make things easier for her. In the end, only a divorce had made things easier.

But this time the problem was even more basic than the job. With Mary Rose, the issue was a lack of trust. She didn't believe in him. Maybe because he was from the wrong side of town. Maybe because he just didn't understand what it would take to convince her that he cared.

And if he didn't understand now, what hope was there for the future?

None, he had decided over the weekend. The interlude with Mary Rose had been just that, and he'd always known it. They'd had a lot of laughs and some great sex. Not enough great sex…he would miss holding her for a long time to come. And maybe not enough laughs. Not enough chances just to talk, either, to trade their thoughts on the way the world worked.

Oh, hell. Just thinking about Mary Rose woke up all those aches he was determined to ignore. But they would pass, with time. They had to.

He couldn't live the rest of his life hurting like this.

KELSEY HAD GIVEN UP looking for Sal at school. She'd pretty much given up on ever being happy again, too. Her days passed in a Jack Black–induced haze, and she liked it that way.

So she was stunned speechless when she closed her locker door on Friday and turned around to find him standing behind her.

"Hey." He didn't smile. "How are you?"

She wanted to be cool, but there was no way. "Terrible."

Sal nodded. "I see that. Can we talk?"

"What's there to say?"

"Let's find out." He put his hand on her back and steered her down the hall. The combination of excitement and nerves that hit her was so strong she thought she might die. Or maybe throw up.

He didn't say anything until they'd walked all the way across the parking lot to the very limit of the school grounds, where a row of trees gave a little shade from the sun. And maybe some privacy, though there were people all around. But when Sal glanced their way, everybody seemed to back off.

Though she'd been wanting to talk to him for weeks, Kelsey suddenly couldn't think of a single thing to say. And even though she loved looking at him, she stared across the street at the diner, which was now completely yellow on all sides.

"They got a new awning," she said almost to herself. "Blue and white."

"Yeah, I guess they decided to dress the place up a little, to go with the new paint."

She gathered all her strength and turned to face him. "What do you want?"

He braced his shoulder against the trunk of the tree. "First, I want to warn you. I think your brother is headed for trouble."

"Trouble?"

"He's hanging with those two jerks, Eric and Bo. I'm hearing rumors that they've got something planned."

Kelsey shrugged. "They're thirteen years old. How bad could it be?"

"I'm just telling you what I hear. Nobody has any details. But Eric and Bo and Trace keep talking like they're gonna really do some damage."

"Trace wouldn't seriously hurt anybody."

"You're giving him more credit than he deserves."

"Did you drag me out here to rag on my brother? Because I have to tell you, I can do without more hassles in that direction." Kelsey turned, blinking away tears, hoping she could get back to the school building before anybody saw her cry.

But Sal held her back with a hand around her arm. "I think the three of them are marking up the walls, at school and across the street."

"Oh, right. Trace has been grounded for the last month, remember? How would he do that?"

"He's not the only one."

She saw his point. "What do you want me to do? Tell Kate?"

"That's up to you. I thought you would want to know."

Great. He'd asked her out here to talk about Trace. She felt like a deflated balloon. "Is that all?"

Sal turned her around to face him. "No, that's not all. I've been watching you. You're drinking in school."

"And?"

"And you don't look like you're sleeping or eating much." He flashed a grin. "Those curves I like aren't quite so curvy these days."

She fought down a surge of pleasure. "I needed to lose some weight."

"No, you didn't." He pulled her farther underneath the tree, to stand between his feet as he leaned back against the trunk. "And I'm not doing so good, either. I've tried to stay away, but it's taking all my willpower. I'm not good for much but trying not to think about you."

The idea made her dizzy. "Sal…"

"So I guess what I'm saying," he told her, drawing her even closer, "is that I miss you. And I'm tired of trying to play by stupid rules I don't believe in. I want to be with you. If that's what you want, too.''

There really wasn't a decision to make. ''That's all I've ever wanted.'' She waited to be kissed. Wanted to be kissed.

But he still held her away from him. ''You need to cut out the liquor during class.''

''Okay.'' Anything, if it meant having Sal back in her life.

''And start eating decent meals.''

''Sure. Whatever you say.''

''All right. That's what I like to hear.'' He slipped his arms around her waist. ''There's only one way to seal this bargain.''

Kissing on school property was strictly against the rules. Somehow, Kelsey couldn't bring herself to care.

THE PHONE RANG Friday afternoon as Mary Rose sat at the kitchen table with a cold cup of coffee, staring into space.

''Mary Rose?''

For an instant, hearing her name in a man's voice, her heart jumped into her throat.

Then she realized this was not Pete's deep tone. ''Marty?''

''Hello, darlin'. I finally got back to the good ol' U.S.A. How've you been?''

''O-okay.''

''How's your sister? Is she getting things straightened out with that husband of hers?''

''She's doing pretty well, actually.''

''And the kids? Are they settling down?''

''More or less.''

''Well, the folks at the office will be glad to hear that.

They're missing you down here, Mary Rose. You need to come back to work." He lowered his voice. "I'm missing you, too, darlin'. It's been forever. When are you coming home?"

Home. She tried to visualize Charleston as home, couldn't even quite picture the condo she'd so carefully decorated. "I—I'm not sure. Soon."

"Or I could hop in the BMW, be there in three hours or so. What do you think? You could show me around your hometown. I've never met your parents—it's about time, don't you think?"

Her mother would love him. "This isn't a really good time, Marty. My sister's in the middle of a big project. Let's wait until later in the summer. Maybe we can meet up with them at the beach."

"Whatever you say, darlin', long as you get yourself down here. When can we look for you to come back?"

She put him off with vague promises and said goodbye. Then she pushed her coffee out of the way and buried her head in her arms on the table.

A week without seeing Pete had drained her beyond belief. Every night she fought the urge to call him, just to hear his voice again. A couple of times during the day she had called and listened to his message. "This is Pete Mitchell's machine. You know what to do." How ridiculous was that, taking comfort from listening to an impersonal recording? Did she expect to call long distance from Charleston for the rest of her life?

And what would she do if one day the message was in a woman's voice?

She moaned and rolled her head back and forth. Now she was torturing herself with thoughts of Pete and another woman. Why had she stopped thinking of this as a temporary relationship? Why had she come to believe there was something more between them than just good times?

Why had she fallen in love with Pete Mitchell all over again?

Outside in the driveway, the slamming of car doors announced the arrival of Kate and the kids. Mary Rose sat up quickly, brushed at her hair and wiped her fingertips under her eyes. She was at the sink, pouring her coffee down the drain, when they all trooped in.

"Well, good afternoon." She turned to see Trace's back as he headed for the stairs. When she glanced at Kelsey, she did a double take; this was a different girl from the one she'd taken to school that morning. "You look like you had a really good day."

Kelsey smiled widely. "It was great. Are there any cookies? I'm going to watch a movie." She dived into the pantry and brought out a handful of Kate's thick chocolate chip creations, poured herself a glass of milk and then disappeared into the family room.

Mary Rose looked at Kate. "Sal must have talked to her."

Her sister nodded soberly. "That's all I can think of. But I don't know what to do about it. I can't very well follow her at school all day."

"No."

"You, on the other hand, have taken over as chief moper." Kate put her arm around Mary Rose's shoulders. "Why don't you talk to him? He's probably as miserable as you are."

"There's no use. I'm going back…home. He's staying here. We always knew that. I just let it slip my mind."

"It doesn't have to be that way."

"Oh, I think it does. Pete and I…there's no trust between us. How can we be together if we don't trust each other?''

"You don't trust him to be faithful?''

"Not in the way you mean. I guess I don't trust him to…to come through for me. To be there when I need him. I didn't trust his love enough when we were married, thought he'd be glad to escape.''

"You were eighteen years old. What did you know?''

"I should have known Pete. We were so close that summer… Then, last week, I expected him to prove he cared about me by putting me ahead of all his other responsibilities.'' She hung her head. "Or, at least, that's the way it sounded. And he jumped to that conclusion immediately, because that's the kind of woman he thinks I am. Demanding, self-absorbed.''

"Oh, honey, no.''

Mary Rose shrugged. "I don't know, he just may be right. I really was terrified I'd lost him.''

She turned her face into her sister's shoulder. "And I lost him anyway.''

KELSEY HAD AVOIDED saying anything more meaningful than "Pass the salt" to her brother since he'd ratted on her. And she thought she'd gotten her own back with the paint trick.

But if he was planning trouble, her life would get messed up, too, just when it looked as if there might actually be a reason to get up tomorrow morning.

So she knocked on his door late that night, after Kate and Mary Rose had gone to bed. Trace didn't answer. She knocked again, tried the doorknob and found it locked. He could be asleep. Or he could be gone.

A couple of minutes spent breaking and entering gave

her the answer she didn't want. Trace's room was empty. The little bastard had skipped out.

So did she give him up to Kate? That would definitely make all their lives miserable. And this last week before the Azalea Festival was already about as stressful as anybody could stand. One more problem and who knew what kind of meltdown would happen?

Kelsey sat on her bed for what seemed like hours, trying to decide what to do, waiting to hear Trace come home…only to wake up in the morning and find that she'd fallen asleep before doing either. When she checked this time, his door was unlocked. She gathered that meant he was in bed, asleep, and didn't care if somebody came in.

So he'd come back safe from wherever he'd gone. But really, a thirteen-year-old couldn't wander around in the middle of the night. Somebody had to stop him. And that somebody, evidently, was her.

When she got downstairs, Mary Rose was alone in the kitchen. Kelsey took that as a sign. "Aunt M, I have to talk to you."

"Okay." Her aunt turned from the window over the sink. "What's going on?"

"I think…" Kelsey swallowed hard. This was harder than she'd expected. "I think Trace is getting into trouble."

"What kind of trouble?"

"I'm not sure. But he wasn't in his room last night. And Sal told me—" Mary Rose raised an eyebrow in question. "I talked to him yesterday at school. He wanted me to know he'd heard that Trace and those guys he's been hanging with, Eric and Bo, were planning some kind of stunt. Sal didn't know the details, just that they'd been bragging about it around school."

"Trace has been sneaking phone calls, too. But you haven't talked to him?"

"We're not exactly on friendly terms."

"I guess not." She studied her hands for a minute. "And nothing your mother or I have said in the last month has made much of an impact. Do you suppose there's anybody Trace might listen to? Your dad?"

"That would be the last person on the list. Trace is so mad, he can barely sit still when we have to go out with him. If he'd just blow up about it, he might feel better. But he closes it all inside and just kind of shakes. It's weird, sitting next to him."

"Poor Trace."

"Do you think Mr. Pete would talk to him?"

Mary Rose looked startled. "Do you think it would make a difference?"

"Trace likes him, though you probably couldn't tell. But he listens in the auto shop class. And he laughs."

"Well, then." She took a deep breath. "I'll call Pete and see if he can come over to talk to Trace."

HEARING MARY ROSE'S VOICE on his answering machine was such a shock that Pete completely missed what she said the first time through. He had to rewind and listen to the message again to actually understand the words.

"Hi, Pete. This is…" She cleared her throat. "This is Mary Rose. I wondered if you would have a few minutes tomorrow to come by and talk with Trace. He's been sneaking out of his room at night and, according to rumors Sal has heard at school, he and his friends are planning some kind of mischief. Kelsey suggested that you might think of a way to—to put the fear of God into him. I'll be home tonight if you want to call. Thanks."

Pete dropped into the nearest chair. He didn't know

whether to be mad at Trace for causing trouble, or thankful that the boy had provided him with an excuse to see Mary Rose again. And he wasn't at all sure whether seeing her again was a blessing or a curse.

Nonetheless, he showed up at the LaRue house at three on Sunday afternoon, after dinner at his mom's house. Mary Rose answered the door. "Hi. Come in."

"Thanks." She looked tired, but that might be the trouble the kids had been causing. The afternoon was warm and sunny, and she'd done justice to it with a pair of khaki shorts and a white shirt that left her arms bare. All that smooth skin... "Have you talked to Trace, gotten any information at all about what's going on?"

"I was afraid that would just make him more resistant. We're depending on you to get the goods." Her smile was strained, a little sad. "Kate's downtown working on the festival arrangements, so I didn't even mention that you were coming. Maybe we can solve this problem without having to let her know?"

"I'll do my best. Where is he?"

"In his room. Upstairs, the last door on the right."

She'd been standing beside the newel post at the foot of the steps. As he started up, he put his hand on the rail without thinking...right on top of both of hers. Mary Rose jumped as his palm covered her fingers, but she didn't draw away, just gazed at him, her blue eyes wide. The experience of touching her again was startling, powerful. Pete wanted to take hold and never let go.

But he pulled in a deep breath and forced himself to look away, to lift his hand and climb the steps, to act as if nothing had happened. Disturbed, distracted, he went upstairs to see if he could keep Trace LaRue from making a big mistake.

Mary Rose held herself still though her heart was

pounding and she could hardly breathe. She stood there until she heard his knock, until she heard their voices—Pete's low, Trace's much lighter—and then the closing of the door. Finally, she walked on weak knees to a chair and collapsed into it.

Seeing him again was wonderful…and torture at the same time. She had never expected to touch him, and the longing for more of him was an ache in her chest that might never go away. But the hardest part was simply looking into his face, seeing the wariness there.

The man she loved expected her to hurt him. How could she live with that knowledge? But what other choice did she have?

He spent a long time in Trace's room; his footsteps were heavy as he finally came back down the stairs. When he saw her sitting in the living room, he crossed the hall to join her.

Before she could ask a question, Pete shook his head. "He wouldn't say beans about anything. I tried to be as friendly, as unthreatening as I know how. I didn't talk about punishment, but about options and opportunities and possibilities that start to disappear if a kid gets into too much trouble. Respect for the community, for Kate, for himself… I gave it my best shot. He may have heard me, but he wasn't about to give anything back."

"I can't say I'm surprised." Mary Rose sighed and rubbed her aching temples. "I guess we'll just have to wait and see what kind of bomb he drops on our heads. I'll try to keep an eye on him—perhaps he'll let something slip that'll give us a hint."

Pete braced his elbows on his knees and stared at his clasped hands. "Sal told Kelsey about this?"

"He talked to her Friday. She's been flying high ever since."

"I guess he had something else to say as well."

"Probably. I don't have the heart to start lecturing again. I don't know how she'll see much of him, between being grounded and having her windows nailed shut. Next we'll be putting up bars over all the glass, and they can call this the LaRue Detention Center."

He laughed, but only for a moment. "Sal told me, when the gym was vandalized, that he thought the trouble was being caused by white boys making it look like Hispanic gangs. If Trace has been sneaking out…"

"Oh, my God. He could have done that. And the diner, too." Tears pricked in her eyes. "How awful, hurting Abby and Charlie that way. It makes me furious to think somebody in my family could be so cruel."

"Yeah. But there's a lot of pain on Trace's side, too. I say we lay the blame where it truly belongs—L.T.'s shoulders."

"Which does no good, because he wouldn't accept the responsibility if it slapped him in the face. He only owns up to things he wants credit for."

"Great role model." With a deep breath, Pete got to his feet. "Well, I guess I'll get out of your way. Sorry I couldn't be more help."

She followed him to the door. "I can't tell you how much I appreciate the fact that you tried." Looking up at him, the realization of all they could have had swept over her. Ideas tried to form—apologies, persuasions, promises. If only she could take that first step, find that first vital word…

"Well, you take care, Ms. Mary Rose." He was opening the door, turning to the outside. Going away.

"Pete—"

"Yeah?" He turned back, and she read expectation in his gaze.

But then she saw his second thoughts gain hold, and caution replaced eagerness. She let her hand drop. "Thank you again."

"Sure."

Indulging herself one last time, she watched him as he went to the Jeep, tried to imprint his swift, clean stride into her memory, tried to capture the look of him in suit pants and a starched white shirt. She realized she'd never been to church with him—they hadn't thought such things important that summer they'd spent together. What she wouldn't give for the chance to sing hymns beside him, to hold his hand while they listened to a prayer.

Just one of a million experiences she would always regret not sharing with Pete Mitchell.

THE NEXT BAD NEWS of the week came on Tuesday, when the long-range weather forecast predicted rain for Saturday. "It can't," Kate insisted. "It simply can't."

Trace remained in his room, coming out only for food and school. Mary Rose and Kelsey fetched, sorted, arranged—whatever Kate needed to have done, they tried to help. And they kept a constant eye on the weather report.

The storm swept in Friday morning with heavy downpours that made setting up the street fair impossible. On the phone constantly, Kate postponed the event until Sunday, hoping the forecasters were again correct in their prediction for bright sun and warm temperatures.

Saturday was a grim, rainy day. Kelsey stayed in bed with a cough, sore throat and headache. Kate and Mary Rose moved around the house through a maze of festival accessories—baskets of flowers, boxes of programs, advertising flyers, maps, tabletop umbrellas and paper lanterns. The phone rang constantly.

Upstairs during a check on Kelsey, Mary Rose once again came upon Trace using Kate's telephone. He hung up as soon as he saw her standing in the doorway.

She crossed her arms and leaned against the door frame, blocking his way out. "More homework?"

Hands in his pockets, Trace looked down at the floor.

"Whatever you're planning, you know it's wrong. You're going to cause pain for people you care about—used to care about, anyway. Doesn't that matter at all to you?"

He answered with a shrug.

Her temper snapped. "You know, I could just shake you until your teeth fall out. What in the world are you thinking? Why can't you get out of yourself and see what you're doing to the rest of us?"

Trace looked at her then, his eyes burning with fury and hurt. "Like anybody gives a shit what matters to me? I'm supposed to shut up and take it, no matter how anybody screws with my life. Well, piss on that. I'm not taking it anymore."

He came to the door and pushed her aside, knocking her off balance so she fell into the edge of the nearby chest. By the time she recovered, he'd slammed his bedroom door. The lock clicked loudly in the silence.

Pete's approach had been less provocative but no more productive.

SUNDAY DAWNED CLEAR, and Mary Rose was up with Kate at first light, loading the Volvo with baskets and boxes for the first of several trips downtown. They hesitated to leave the kids at home alone, but when threatened with having her grandparents—or, worse, her father—called over to baby-sit, Kelsey had pleaded for mercy and promised to be on her best behavior. Neither she nor Trace would leave the house all day. She'd learned her lesson, she swore. No more troublemaking. Everything would be just fine.

Kate chose to believe her stepdaughter, and so she and Mary Rose headed down the hill to Main Street, where the vendors were out early, as well, setting up food carts and novelty stands on the wet pavement. Work crews hustled to erect the four different stages that would host performers throughout the afternoon, while police cordoned off the downtown area and designated parking areas.

By midmorning, with the sun shining bright and not a cloud to be seen, downtown New Skye had taken on a carnival atmosphere. The rain had freshened all the planters and trees along the streets, so the blossoms and leaves stood bright and alert. Balloons and banners floated on a light breeze, and music from a dozen different radios sweetened the air.

"It's going to work, isn't it?" Kate surveyed their progress from the courthouse steps. "It's really going to happen."

"You've done it." Mary Rose gave her a one-armed hug. "I've never seen this town look so pretty. The whole community is going to turn out to see what a great job you've done."

"I just hope they have a good time. And that nothing strange happens. You never know these days."

With a pang of guilt, Mary Rose thought about Trace. "Nothing's going to happen. This festival will go off without a hitch."

The crowds started to arrive around noon; by one, the streets were packed with people. There were kids of all kinds—babies in strollers, toddlers holding tight to grown-up hands or riding high on somebody's shoulders, little kids zipping in and out amongst the taller people, teenagers pretending to ignore other teenagers, usually of the opposite sex. Mary Rose didn't recognize many of the younger set, but it seemed she couldn't take five steps without running into friends of her parents, or someone she'd gone to high school with, or even the students and staff she'd come to know in the REWARDS program.

At the funnel-cake cart, she ran into Abby and Charlie Brannon. "There aren't too many days in the year we close the diner," Abby told her. "But this is one of them. I'm so glad the weather cleared up." She took a sugar-dusted treat from Charlie. "Thanks, Dad. I'll pretend I didn't see that you got yourself one, too. Is this sinful, or what?"

"I'm not sure it beats Charlie's SDTS." Mary Rose bit into her own cake and sighed blissfully. "But since the diner's closed, it'll have to do."

The three of them wandered to the stage at the north end of Main, where a Celtic trio kept the audience laughing with their high-spirited songs. After a short time, Mary Rose left the Brannons and went back to roaming the streets in her self-appointed role as watchdog, hoping to head off trouble before it could spoil the fair. Kate deserved to have her hard work rewarded with a spectacularly successful event. The people of New Skye deserved to enjoy this celebration of their town, their sense of fellowship, the lush wonders of spring.

At three o'clock she checked in via cell phone with Kate at the command post in the foyer of the courthouse. "People just keep arriving," she said. "You've got a real hit on your hands."

"Along with lost kids and dogs." Kate spoke for a few moments to somebody in the room with her. "Fortunately, everybody's been reunited so far."

"Have you talked with Kelsey?" Their sick girl had still been asleep when they left the house for the last time this morning.

"About an hour ago. She was feeling better, but not up to doing more than watching TV. Trace hadn't come out of his room."

Since his window was now nailed shut, as well, that must mean he was still at home. Mary Rose relaxed a little. "Okay, then. I'll just keep moving around. Call if you need something."

"Will do."

She continued her patrol along the length of Main Street toward the south stage, where a group of dancers wearing kilts were demonstrating the Highland fling, accompanied by the wail of bagpipes. She started to move on, but then stayed to watch the next group, members of the Mexican-American Society of New Skye, performing traditional Mexican country dances. The women were like butterflies in their bright, full skirts and low-shouldered blouses, the men powerful and dynamic in slim pants and short jackets or vests. The courageous spirit of their ancestral country lived in the quick moves of the dance, and the crowd responded with calls for an encore.

But in a moment of relative quiet, before the music started up again, the afternoon went to hell.

"Bomb!" a voice shouted from somewhere close by. "There's a bomb in the trash can!"

CHAPTER FIFTEEN

WITH MEMORIES of last year's terrorist attacks still fresh in their minds, the crowd went crazy. Screams and shrieks blotted out the music. Everyone started to run in a thousand different directions. And that meant disaster, because the streets were so crowded no one could really go anywhere.

Mary Rose got knocked down almost right away, had both hands stepped on before she could get to her feet again. She couldn't see or travel five feet in front of her, no matter which way she turned. Shoving, trampling, stampeding people blocked her way.

If there was a bomb, they were all going to be blown up.

"Outta my way. Outta my way." A big, burly man came stumbling through the mob, pushing people to one side or the other. "Outta my way." He caught Mary Rose with a swing of his arm and sent her crashing into a nearby lamppost. Completely off balance, she staggered against the nearby trash can and knocked it over, then fell on top of it.

When she opened her eyes, the "bomb" was right in front of her face.

The twelve-inch-square cardboard box had Warning: Explosives written in Magic Marker on the outside. Gray smoke seeped out between the flaps. From inside the box came an ominous ticking.

No one tried to help her up. They stumbled over her, kicked at her, went around her, but not a person bent to give her a hand. And as she lay there, Mary Rose decided her predicament was almost funny. She could muffle the bomb with her body, or she could lie there and wait for it to go off…whenever that might be. Either way meant death. Or she could get up and run, which probably wouldn't get her very far and she'd end up just as dead.

Or she could follow her instincts, which told her that this was Trace's trick, that the bomb was a total fake, that she was in more danger from the people around her than this stupid box with its clumsily lettered warning. If she was wrong, would she be any worse off?

As she struggled to her feet again, she could hear a voice on the loudspeaker. "Do not run. Please remain calm. Stay where you are. The police will evacuate the area. Do not run…"

Mary Rose did the only thing she could think of and caught the arm of the person next to her. "There's no bomb," she said, ignoring their stare of disbelief. "It was a joke. There's no bomb," she said to the person on her other side. "No bomb."

She thought she heard the message moving through the throng around her. Or maybe it was the work of the police, or the fact that as they all stood there trapped between the buildings along each side of Main Street, nothing exploded. But the shoving gradually subsided. People stopped trying to fight their way out, began slowly clearing the area. Eventually, there was room to move, to breathe, to see.

What Mary Rose saw was the wreck of Kate's beautiful street fair. Carts were turned over, broken, with glass and food and merchandise trampled across the sidewalks and in the street. Some of the huge flowerpots had been upended, even shattered, the dirt and flowers they'd contained strewn over the rest of the wreckage.

Much worse, though, were the human victims. Everywhere she looked, someone was injured. A few were receiving assistance; most sat or lay there alone, calling out in distress.

She knelt beside the nearest, an older man with skin as gray as his hair. "Can I help you, sir? What's wrong?"

He clutched her shirt. "Can't breathe." His other hand came to his chest. "Hurts. Bad."

Oh, God. A heart attack. "I'll get someone. Right away."

She drew out her cell phone and punched in 911. "I need paramedics immediately. In front of Drew's Coffee Shop. It's a heart attack. Yes, I know there's been a riot. But this man is having a heart attack. Please…"

He lost consciousness while she was on the phone. His pulse was weak, but at least he had one. Sitting beside him on the sidewalk, Mary Rose held a stranger's hand and prayed for him to hang on just a little bit longer.

PETE KEPT HIS EYES open as he walked around the street fair. He didn't want to run into Mary Rose—it would spoil her day, he thought. And it would make him pretty miserable, seeing her and not having her.

So he watched carefully, keeping his distance from any and all blondes. He ran into Charlie and Abby Brannon, even saw Kate for a second at the courthouse. Rob Warren was there with his daughter, Ginny, and Jacquie Archer and Erin waved from the other side of the barbecue tent. Having sampled most of the food and listened to the country band he'd wanted to see, Pete decided to head home before his luck ran out.

He'd left the Jeep in a bank parking lot near the south

end of Main. With less than two blocks to go before making a clean escape, he spotted that familiar silver-and-gold hair not twenty feet in front of him. Just the tilt of her head told him this was Mary Rose. Intending to cross the street, he made a sharp left turn just as three kids ran past him, headed north.

"Bomb!" one of them yelled. The other two joined in. "There's a bomb in the trash can!" "It's gonna blow!"

In the second before the crowd panicked, Pete whipped around and started after the boys. He recognized at least one voice, knew the athletic build of the kid with short blond hair. Trace LaRue was running for his life.

And Pete wasn't letting him get away.

They quickly left the street fair behind as Trace dodged down alleys, skipped across parking lots, hid behind Dumpsters and cars and piles of lumber on a construction site. He had several years' advantage, but he was bound to get cocky and expect to win. Pete figured experience gave him the edge.

When Trace ran into the New Skye cemetery, Pete grinned. Four years on the New Skye High track team, running hurdles, had left him with important instincts when it came to jumping obstacles. The kid would have to go around at least some of the gravestones. But Pete was sure he could go over most of them.

He caught up as they reached the center of the old graveyard. Under the Victorian statue of a weeping angel, Pete launched himself off a stone directly onto Trace's back. They hit the mossy dirt hard; he heard the boy cry out in pain.

Rearing back, Pete turned Trace over underneath him and straddled his legs. Both of them were breathing hard.

"What's the matter? Did you bump your head?"

Trace was holding one wrist in the other hand. "You broke my arm, you a—"

Pete clamped a hand over Trace's mouth. "I wouldn't use that word if I were you. You're not exactly in a position to back it up."

"You broke my arm!"

"Let me see." He moved the protective hand away. "Yeah, looks broken to me, too. How 'bout that." He backed off and stood up, then bent over and hauled Trace to his feet, being sure to use the unbroken arm. "We'll get it looked at sooner or later. Right now, you've got an appointment to keep."

"Where?"

"Oh, use your brain, why don't you? I'm fed up with this adolescent don't-expect-me-to-think crap. Making a bomb threat is a Class H felony. So you're under arrest, Mr. Almighty Trace LaRue. You have the right to remain silent. You have the right to an attorney..."

KELSEY SPENT a long time in the shower Sunday morning, and an even longer time getting her hair just right, putting her makeup on, choosing her outfit. Then she made sure the downstairs was neat, after having Kate's stuff sitting around all week. She wanted everything to be perfect this afternoon.

For that reason, she decided to warn Trace that Sal was coming over. No sense trying to hide the fact—if he came downstairs, he would know right away. So she'd just tell him to stay in his room.

But the damn door was locked. Her heart tripped—he wasn't supposed to go anywhere, and she was supposed to be sure he didn't.

"Trace?" She knocked, and knocked again. "C'mon,

Trace, open up. You have to be there.'' When he didn't answer, she picked the lock. And found his room empty.

"Damn it, Trace." He must've waited until she was in the shower and sneaked out. He could be anywhere, doing anything. And it was all her fault.

So she wasn't as calm as she'd planned to be when Sal rang the doorbell a few minutes later. "Come in." She pulled him inside and leaned back against the door as it shut. "What am I going to do? Trace is gone."

"When did he leave?"

"I was in the shower around noon. I would have heard him go, otherwise."

Sal shrugged. "There's nothing you can do, Kelsey. It's almost three o'clock. Whatever he's been planning is done." Smiling, he stepped closer and put his hands on her shoulders. "Aren't you a little bit glad to see me?"

"Oh, Sal." She yielded to his pressure and put her arms around his neck. "I haven't thought about anything else for two days. I worked so hard yesterday to convince them I was sick."

"Glad to hear it." He bent his head and set a kiss just under her ear. "Seems like forever since I've been able to hold you."

"I know. It's just that…" But then his lips were on hers and Kelsey stopped worrying, stopped thinking about anything beyond the glorious knowledge that Sal wanted her. What else in the world really mattered?

As soon as the EMTs arrived, Mary Rose relinquished her place and staggered to her feet. She felt for her cell phone and punched in Kate's number, but got a busy signal, of course. Dazed, a little dizzy, she stared at the disaster area around her, trying to get her bearings. Which way was north?

"Can you help me?" A tiny, white-haired woman put a shaking hand on her arm.

Mary Rose blinked hard and took a deep breath, trying to focus. The woman's pink polyester pantsuit was streaked with dirt, but she seemed to be unhurt. "I'll try. What's wrong?"

"It's my dog." The woman held up a gold lamé leash with a jeweled collar dangling from the end. Empty. "When everything went crazy, he slipped away. Can you help me find him?"

From heart attacks to lost dogs. "Of course. What's his name?"

"Fuzzy. He's all curly and white. About the size of a bread box." She held up her hands to demonstrate.

Mary Rose looked around and saw that most of the people who were injured now appeared to have someone attending them. "Let's see where Fuzzy has run to. Mrs...."

"Taylor. *Miss* LuAnne Taylor."

They walked slowly up and down Main Street, side-stepping the debris and calling Fuzzy's name constantly, but without results.

"What will I do without him? He's my best friend." Miss Taylor was becoming tearful. "He sleeps on my bed every night."

"We'll find him, I know we will." Mary Rose gently squeezed the fragile old hand. "He's probably at one of the food carts, eating spilled sausage."

Miss Taylor stared at her in horror. "Sausage is so bad for him!"

"We'll find him," she repeated, deciding to leave the sausage issue alone. "Let's try the side streets."

But if Fuzzy was hiding somewhere off the main route, he didn't come when called. They reached the library and had started back toward the courthouse when Mary Rose heard a sound on their right, something like a whimper.

"Wait," she said, and Miss Taylor stopped obediently. "Is that Fuzzy?"

The older woman shook her head. "I don't think so. It sounds more like a child."

Mary Rose gazed around them, frustrated by the lack of places to hide. "Hello? Is somebody here?" The crying stopped for a moment, then started again. With sirens wailing on all sides and people still shouting just a block away, she couldn't pinpoint the source of the sound. "Please come out. We won't hurt you."

Finally, after another silence, a curly blond head appeared from behind the book drop box, and then a little girl stepped out into the open. Her yellow sundress was filthy, her face and arms and legs scraped raw. She looked up at them and gulped. "Where's my mommy?"

Miss Taylor thrust the leash at Mary Rose, then bent down and scooped the child up into her arms. "We'll find her, dear. I'm certain she's looking for you, too."

Mary Rose put a hand on the older woman's arm. "Are you sure you want to carry her all that way? I can—"

But Miss Taylor shook her head. "Nonsense. I'm quite strong and it's only a block or so. Let's get moving."

At the courthouse, Kate was white-faced and completely calm. "We have about twenty children without parents right now." She sat next to Miss Taylor, who held the little girl on her lap. "What's your name, sweetheart?"

"Molly."

"Molly, do you know your last name?" The girl shook her head.

Mary Rose bent closer. "What do people call your mommy? Mrs...."

She wiggled and cuddled closer. "Mrs. Molly's mommy."

Kate smiled a little as she and Mary Rose straightened up. Miss Taylor waved them away. "Y'all go on, help some other people. I'll just sit here and hold her. Her parents will turn up eventually. And maybe someone will bring Fuzzy here, too." Her blue eyes bright with tears, she rested her cheek against Molly's bright curls.

Standing on the front steps of the courthouse, they surveyed the ruins of the street fair. "A bomb," Kate murmured. "And it didn't even go off. Who would be so cruel?"

Mary Rose couldn't bear to break the news just at this moment. "Let's get everything straightened out, everyone back with the people they belong to. Then we'll figure that out." She started down the steps, intent on finding Fuzzy and dealing with any other emergencies that came her way.

But Kate stopped her with a hold on her arm. "Wait a minute—are you okay? There's blood on your face, your legs...did you get hurt?"

Since everything seemed to be working, she hadn't thought about it. "I took a couple of falls, but nothing's broken. I just need to get cleaned up." She glanced at the wreck of Main Street and sighed. "Along with the rest of this place."

Darkness fell before all the children were reunited with their parents. Molly's mother was one of the last to come into the courthouse. "I got knocked out," she explained, cradling her daughter close against her breast. "I've been lying down in the hospital tent, out of my senses until just an hour or so ago. And they didn't want me to leave then, but I hopped off that table while their backs were turned and started looking.'' She put a hand on Miss Taylor's shoulder. ''Thank you so much for taking care of Molly. I wish there was something I could do for you.''

Miss Taylor shook her head. ''I've enjoyed every minute. My great-nieces and -nephews live in California, and I don't get to hold them very often.'' She looked around at the empty room and sighed. ''If only someone had found Fuzzy.''

''Fuzzy's your dog?''

''Yes. He slipped off his leash.''

''Well, there was this little white dog down the street as I came by, chowing down on stuff spilled out of the kabob wagon. Could that be your Fuzzy?''

Mary Rose smiled as Miss Taylor surged to her feet. ''Oh, it must be Fuzzy. Could you come with me, Ms. Bowdrey?''

''Of course.''

Sure enough, Fuzzy heard his name this time and wagged his tail furiously, though he wasn't at all interested in leaving the windfall of grilled meat he had stumbled into. Mary Rose made sure Miss Taylor and her best friend got to their car, saw them headed for home. Then she walked back, for what she hoped would be the last time that night, to the courthouse.

The wide steps seemed steeper than she remembered, but she climbed them, pulling hard on the handrail to get herself up to the top. Inside, Kate stood in the center of the empty foyer. The man with her turned around as Mary Rose came through the door.

She pushed her hair back, almost too tired to believe her eyes. ''Pete?''

He crossed to her and put his hands on her shoulders. "Dear God, are you okay? You look like hell."

She managed a laugh. "Thanks so much. It's been a rough afternoon."

"An understatement, to say the least. But I think y'all have earned a break. The cleanup crew can take care of the rest."

"That would be good. I just want to go home, take a bath and go to bed."

"I, uh, don't think that'll work."

Something in his voice alerted her. "What's wrong?" She followed as he went back to stand in front of Kate.

"I was just about to explain." He hesitated, cleared his throat. "Trace is in custody at the police station."

Kate gripped her hands together. "Why? What has he done?"

Mary Rose put an arm around her sister's waist, felt the slight weight sag against her.

"I hate to say this." Pete shoved his hands in his pockets, looked down at the floor. Then he lifted his gaze to meet Kate's. "But I was standing right there when the kid yelled out that there was a bomb in the trash.

"That kid was Trace. It was him and his friends who caused the riot."

Though Mary Rose had hold of her, it was Pete who caught Kate before she hit the marble floor in a dead faint.

"SAL? What is it?" Kelsey sat up on the couch, pushed her hair out of her eyes, tried to get her breath back. "What did I do wrong?"

Standing across the room, he kept his back to her. "Nothing. You didn't do anything wrong."

Her shirt was open and her jeans were unzipped. But

she left her clothes as they were and went to put her arms around him from behind. "Then come back and make love to me. It's okay, really. I'm ready."

Sal laughed, but it sounded more like a groan. "Kelsey, you're too much."

"What does that mean?"

"You are such an innocent. You don't have any idea what you're talking about."

"Of course I do. I'll show you." She walked around in front of him and started to slide her shirt off her shoulders. "I want you, Sal. And I want you to be the first."

"Dammit, Kelsey. No." He grabbed the edges of her shirt and pulled them together, started fastening buttons. His hands were shaking.

"Then what you mean is that I'm not experienced enough for you. You want somebody who knows what they're doing, right?"

Turning away from him, she zipped her jeans, blinking hard, trying not to cry.

"No, I don't." She heard his deep breath. "I just want you to be safe. And safe is not having sex when you're fifteen."

"How old were you your first time?"

He choked. "That doesn't matter."

"How old were you?"

"Thirteen."

"See?" She turned around again, put her hands on his chest. "I really do want to love you, Sal. Please show me what to do." Feeling for his hand, she brought it up and placed his palm on her breast. "Please."

"Ah, Kelsey." His fingers cupped her for a moment while he bent his head and kissed her. But then he stepped away. "Come sit down."

At the couch, he put her on one end and sat down on

the other. "You stay there," he ordered when she started to scoot over.

She dropped back against the cushions. "So now you're going to explain how it's for my own good. How I shouldn't make this kind of decision when I'm so young. How I'll be glad I waited when I find the guy who's really right for me."

He grinned. "Thanks. You saved me some words there." Then he sobered and sat for a while with his elbows on his knees, his hands clasped between them. Finally, he looked at her. "You're the most special girl I've ever known, Kelsey."

"Not special enough to make love to."

"That's exactly backward. If I didn't care about you, it wouldn't make any difference if we had sex. There're lots of girls I don't care about I could have sex with."

"Sal..." She closed her eyes and sighed. "Why do you have to be such a good guy? They're not going to give you any credit. They'll see what they want to—gang leader, troublemaker, defiler of young girls. And you won't get anything out of it."

He laughed, and the couch cushions dipped as he moved closer. "I get to keep my self-respect. And yours, I hope." His hand cupped her face, turned her toward him as she opened her eyes. "And you do have the sweetest kisses. A man could spend a lifetime just kissing you."

It wasn't the wild, reckless passion of a few minutes ago. But Sal was right—there was something special, something very intimate about just kissing. Lost in the pleasure of his mouth on hers, Kelsey heard nothing but her own sighs and his deep breaths...until the slam of the front door broke them apart.

Sal looked up sharply. "What the hell?"

Like a marionette, he was jerked away from her, sent flying across the room to crash into the floor lamp, which came down on top of him. In his place above her, she saw a crazy man with a red face and burning blue eyes.

"You little slut, I'm gonna tan your hide. And then," her dad said with a glance at Sal, "I'm gonna kill *him*."

TONIGHT'S EXPERIENCE in the police station was not nearly so easy as the last. The afternoon's demands had worn every officer's patience to a shred; they were working overtime and had no tolerance for the mother of the kid who had caused their problems in the first place. Mary Rose had a feeling that only Pete's presence ensured them even moderate courtesy.

They waited an hour to see Trace. In the interim, Mary Rose explained to first one and then several more officers that she had found the "bomb" in the trash can. "It wasn't real. Trace didn't intend to hurt anybody."

"Yeah, the EMTs turned the box in this afternoon. We'll put your report in the record."

"They weren't very impressed that he didn't mean harm," she commented when she sat down with Pete and Kate again.

Pete crossed his arms. "Neither am I."

When the time finally came, Trace wasn't brought out to meet them, as had happened before. Instead, they were taken to an interrogation room—a bare space furnished with a table and a few hard chairs, a two-way mirror and a video camera high on the wall.

Trace looked up as the door opened, and Mary Rose caught a glimpse of the young, vulnerable boy he might still be. But then his face closed and he went back to staring at the thick splint wrapping his left arm.

Kate sat down next to him, put a hand on his shoulder. "Are you all right? Does your arm hurt much?"

Trace shrugged. Mary Rose itched to slap him, just to see if she could get some reaction besides that sullen lift of the shoulders.

His stepmother was more tolerant. "I've called the lawyer your granddad recommended. He should be here very soon." Trace made no response. "I gather the charges against you are pretty serious. There were a number of people hurt today, and—and a bomb threat of any kind is a real problem, after what happened last fall."

Pete sat down in the chair next to Kate, across the table from Mary Rose. "Trace, my guess is that you and Bo and Eric were in this together. You might get off a little lighter if your statement implicates them in the crime."

"No way."

Mary Rose leaned forward. "This isn't a time for the honor code, Trace. Those guys are in this with you and they deserve the same punishment. They won't thank you for sparing them—they'll just laugh at what a sucker you are."

He shifted in his chair, wincing as he moved his broken arm.

The door at the end of the room opened and a police officer ushered in Thad Wilson, the criminal defense attorney John Bowdrey had recommended. He smiled as he opened his briefcase and took out a yellow legal pad. "'Evening, everybody. I understand there's some trouble afoot. What's going on?" He shrugged out of his pale blue jacket, hung it on the back of a chair and sat down.

Kate looked at Pete as if she wanted him to make the explanations. But to Mary Rose's surprise, he gazed back at her sister without saying anything at all.

After a moment, Kate drew a deep breath and sat up

straight. "There was a bomb scare at the street fair this afternoon, for which Trace is responsible."

Mr. Wilson scribbled furiously. "Anybody else involved?"

They all looked at Trace. After a long pause, he nodded. "Yeah, there were two other guys…"

The attorney's interview lasted for more than an hour. Then he called in the police, who spent another hour asking the same questions and taking Trace's statement, which was typed and presented to him for a signature. Then the police and the attorney disappeared together.

After another long, mostly silent wait, Mr. Wilson came back to the interrogation room. "Okay, we're done for tonight. Trace, you're going home with your mother, and you'd better stay where she puts you. The judge is not going to abide any more tricks. There'll be a hearing tomorrow afternoon. I'll see y'all at the courthouse at one o'clock sharp." He picked up his jacket and briefcase and started for the door.

Kate got to her feet. "But, Mr. Wilson—"

The attorney turned to face her. "Yes, ma'am?"

"What can we expect? What are the charges?"

"The D.A. and I are still working that out. Y'all just go home and get a good night's sleep. We'll worry about this tomorrow."

Wordlessly, they filed down the hall to the front room of the station. Kate looked ready to collapse.

"I'll get the car," Mary Rose told her, taking the purse off Kate's shoulder before she could protest. "You wait here with Trace."

Her sister nodded, but seemed too dazed to think of sitting down or even moving out of the center of the room. Finally, Pete put an arm around her waist and led her to a chair against the wall. "Take it easy for a few minutes. I'll walk Mary Rose to the car, be sure she's safe.''

"Thank you," Mary Rose said once they were outside. "She's at the very end of her endurance."

"It's no wonder. The afternoon has been a nightmare."

"This whole month has been a nightmare. I don't know how I can go back to Charleston and leave her to face this alone. But I don't think I've actually accomplished much by being here."

Pete didn't say anything in reply. They walked through the warm night like strangers, side by side, yet completely separate. Just one more aspect of the hurt, Mary Rose decided. They couldn't even be friends.

The Volvo was parked several blocks over from Main Street, so they quickly left the disaster area behind them. This part of town wasn't as well restored as the rest—they passed by several bars open for business, even on a Sunday night. Raucous voices and blaring music followed them down the street.

"I appreciate the escort," Mary Rose said when they could hear again. "This would have been a scary walk by myself. You've spent a lot of time recently rescuing members of my family from their foolishness."

"My pleasure."

The short response, so unlike him, defeated her. Obviously, Pete didn't want to talk anymore. She couldn't blame him, but she couldn't stand this kind of estrangement between them, either. Picking up her pace, she stepped ahead of him on the sidewalk. The parking lot where they'd left the Volvo was just around the corner. Another minute, two at the most, and this torture would end.

Pete let Mary Rose go on ahead of him, though he

lengthened his stride so she wouldn't get out of his sight. She needed comfort, he thought, and reassurance.

But the words were jammed in his throat. If he let himself say something real…if he told her how worried he'd been about her, how bad he felt for Trace and Kate, how much he wanted to be there with her as her family went through this trial…there wouldn't be an end until he said it all. Until he told her he'd come to love her all over again, until he begged her to think about staying with him, about making their life together. Hell, he'd even considered moving to Charleston, taking some safe, boring job so she wouldn't have to worry about him anymore. Anything, he thought, that would convince her to marry him.

And that would be wrong. Because who he was and what he wanted mattered. He might not be classy enough for a woman whose family lived on The Hill, might not make an income that would support her lifestyle, or even pay for repairs on her fancy sports car. He didn't have a college degree and he didn't spend his vacations in foreign countries. Or even California.

But his life had value just the way he lived it. If Mary Rose wanted something more than he chose to be—and it seemed to him that she did—then there was, indeed, no common ground between them.

And so he held back the words. He reached the Volvo as she unlocked the door, and waited on the driver's side until she got in and started the engine.

She rolled down the window a few inches. "That's it, then. Thanks for walking with me." Her smile was cool, dismissive, like the one she'd flashed on the interstate a few weeks ago.

Pete resisted the automatic impulse to shake her up. He stood straight and tapped his hand on the roof.

"You're welcome. Take care." Backing up, he shoved his hands in his pockets as he watched her drive away.

Have a great life, Ms. Mary Rose.

THE FRONT DOOR was standing wide-open when they reached Kate's house. L.T.'s Yukon was parked at the front curb. Even through the closed car windows, they could hear his raised voice.

Kate straightened up in her seat. "What in the world is going on?"

When they reached that yawning doorway, they saw Kelsey cowering on the sofa in the TV room. Her father stood over her with his hand drawn back, clearly intending to administer a slap. Across the room, Sal Torres was scrambling to his feet. Blood poured down one side of his face, but that didn't obscure the rage in his eyes.

"Get away from her, you bastard," the boy shouted. "You touch her and I swear I'll kill you."

But Kate got to L.T. first. She took hold of the wrist on that upraised hand and jerked hard, swinging L.T. around to face her.

"Don't touch her," she said, her quiet voice as menacing as it was cold. "Don't lay a single finger on her. Or I'll make sure everybody in this town knows just what a lying, cheating, abusive jackass you really are."

CHAPTER SIXTEEN

FROM THE CORNER of the couch, Kelsey stared up at her stepmother in total shock. This was a Kate LaRue she'd never seen before.

"He was raping my daughter," her dad sputtered. "I was trying to protect her."

"That's not true." Kelsey scrambled off the couch and went to stand behind Kate. "We weren't doing anything at all and he just busted in and started throwing Sal around."

Kate dropped L.T.'s arm as if she had touched something slimy under a rock. "Sit down, all of you. Mary Rose, would you get Sal a cloth for his face?"

Just as Aunt M left the room, Trace stepped into the house with his arm wrapped up in a thick bandage. He looked really, really bad. Their dad caught sight of him and got to his feet again. "What the hell happened to you?"

"His arm is broken," Kate said. "And that's the least of our problems. Both of you, sit down."

Kelsey couldn't believe it when they did as they were told.

Kate remained standing. "Kelsey, what is Sal doing here?"

She glanced at Sal, but he was having his face cleaned up. "He...I asked him over. We watched some movies." And they had, for a while.

"I thought you were sick. I take it that was a lie?"

"Um…yeah." Why didn't she ever think about having to face this part of things when she did something stupid?

"I believe you mean, 'Yes, ma'am.'"

She hadn't heard that line in months. "Yes, ma'am."

"How long has he been here?"

Sal cleared his throat. "I got here about four, Mrs. LaRue." The bleeding had stopped, but Kelsey could see the long gash across his temple where the lamp had cut him.

"You knew we wouldn't be home?" Kate's voice was so severe, it was as if she'd become a completely different person.

"Yes, ma'am."

"Did you think that was a good idea? Being alone in the house with a fifteen-year-old girl?"

"I knew I wasn't going to hurt her. That nothing would happen. And it didn't. We were just kissing when—when *he* crashed in."

Kelsey looked down at her hands so no one would see in her eyes the memory of those other moments, when Sal had lost control. Maybe it wasn't just because she was too young that he'd stopped. Maybe he'd stopped for his own sake, as well.

Kate gazed at him for a long moment. Sal, Kelsey was proud to see, met her stepmother's stare without flinching.

Then she nodded. "I believe you. So now it's time for you to go home. Say good-night, Kelsey, and go up to your room. We'll deal with the rest of your issues later."

As she walked with Sal to the front door, her dad stood up again. "You're just letting him walk out of here? That—that wetback had his hands all over your little girl and you're letting him go? What kind of mother are you?''

Sal clenched his hands into fists and turned to face her dad. Kelsey caught his arm. ''Please. He's—he's an idiot. Just go home for now.''

She felt the struggle within him, but finally his body relaxed. With the door open, he touched her cheek with his fingertips and smiled down at her. '''Night, *querida,*'' he said softly.

''What does that mean?''

''I'll tell you Monday.'' She watched him stride down the front walk, head high, shoulders square, a young man who would not apologize for who and what he was. Who wouldn't love him?

A hand reached over her shoulder and shut the door. Kelsey turned and got a good look at her aunt for the first time. There was dirt and blood streaked over her face. Her hair was tangled, her dress torn, her arms and legs were bruised and scraped. ''Oh, my God. What happened to you?''

Desperately needing to sit down out of the line of fire, Mary Rose tilted her head toward the staircase. ''Come on up. I'll tell you about the afternoon.''

As they talked in Kelsey's bedroom, they could hear the voices downstairs—Kate's cool and controlled, L.T.'s explosive, and Trace's infrequent and too quiet to hear.

Until, suddenly, he spoke from the bottom of the stairs. ''I don't care what this does to your business. I don't care what the neighbors think, or the people at church, or the guys you work with. Don't you get it? I just don't care. Just like you didn't care when you started cheating on Kate. And when you decided you'd rather be single and have playtime with your girlfriend than stay home and be with us. You didn't think about responsibilities and commitments. You didn't think about what you owed to your family."

"Listen here, son—"

"And now all you can do is talk about how to fix things—how much money it's gonna cost to clean up the streets, how many strings you'll have to pull to keep me out of trouble. You never talk about coming home. You don't talk about spending time with Kelse and me, on our own. You put in your two hours at breakfast every couple of weeks and think you can check another item off the to-do list.

"Well, I'm telling you this. From now on, don't bother. You don't want to be part of our lives, that's okay. I'm tired of hoping you'll change your mind, thinking that maybe, if it gets bad enough, you'll see that we need you and come back to try to help us out.

"Bottom line—we don't need you. We do okay on our own." Then he told his dad to leave, in language that was completely inappropriate but unmistakable in meaning. Before L.T. could respond, Trace bolted up the stairs and slammed the door to his room. Even though L.T. stormed after him and stood in the hallway blustering and bellowing, Trace's door remained locked.

Before he'd quite finished, Kate came up and stood immovably in Kelsey's doorway, her back straight and her arms crossed. When L.T. stopped for breath, she broke in. "That's more than enough. You're not going to get him to talk to you again. Just do what he suggested, L.T., and go home. We can talk tomorrow at the hearing."

L.T. stared at her for a minute, breathing hard like a bull in the arena. Finally, he stomped down the stairs and left the house, slamming the door behind him.

Kate sagged against the door frame. "It's over. At

last.'' She turned slowly to look at Kelsey and Mary Rose. ''I would never have imagined such a day, or dreamed it up in my worst nightmares.''

Mary Rose got up and went to give her a hug. ''You are magnificent. Do you see how strong you are? Did you know you could handle L.T. like that?''

She smiled wearily. ''I had no idea. But it's not over. I'm sure he'll come back with some new weapon.'' As she looked at Kelsey, the smile faded. ''There's a lot we haven't settled. You lied to me. Repeatedly. If you and Sal want to see each other, the lies have to stop. But...'' A yawn ambushed her. ''We'll deal with that after we see what happens to Trace. Right now, I don't think I can manage anything but sleep.''

As Kate turned from the doorway and crossed to her room, Kelsey jumped up from her bed and followed. ''I'm sorry, Kate.'' She put her arms around her step-mother, rested her head on the slender shoulder. ''I really am sorry. It'll get better, I promise.''

Kate put her arms around Kelsey and smiled at Mary Rose over the top of the girl's head. ''I know it will, honey. I know it will.''

As THE ARRESTING OFFICER, Pete got permission to attend Trace's hearing on Monday afternoon, even though juvenile proceedings were routinely closed to the public. Thad Wilson was one of the craftiest lawyers in town; no doubt he'd managed to wrangle the D.A. into filing the least damaging charges possible in the situation. And then there was L.T.'s influence to be considered. Trace could get out of this with nothing more than a slap on the wrist.

But Judge Taylor seemed to be in a peevish mood. ''Lucky for you nobody died,'' he told Trace. ''Though that fella with the heart attack came close. And lucky for you the district attorney decided to keep this case in juvenile court. We could've tried you as an adult, boy.'' He peered over the top of his glasses. "Then you'd be looking at a felony, and jail time, instead of a misdemeanor.''

Standing before the bench, Trace shifted his weight back and forth uneasily.

"But as it is, I'm confined to the punishments suitable to a misdemeanor charge of communicating a threat. I hope your parents make you an allowance, boy, 'cause you've got a hell of a fine to pay, plus the costs of cleaning up the mess you made and reimbursing the merchants for lost merchandise and damaged equipment. And I don't care what the law says, I'm assigning you community service anyway. Two hundred hours. Plus professional counseling. You need to talk to somebody about what's in your head. That oughta keep you out of trouble for the foreseeable future.'' He banged his gavel on the bench. "Case closed.''

But then, as the family and lawyers still stood at the front of the courtroom, Judge Taylor returned and climbed back into his chair. He used that gavel again. "Order in the court. I forgot something.''

He looked at Mary Rose. "Ms. Bowdrey, my sister LuAnne mentioned to me how much help you were to her on Sunday when that infernal dog of hers went missing. I can't say I'm all that glad you got the beast back, but I know she would miss him sorely. Your kindness is most appreciated. And my sister would like for you to call on her Tuesday afternoon for tea. Four o'clock.'' With a nod, he disappeared into his chambers.

Pete watched for a minute as Mary Rose explained to Kelsey about Miss Taylor and Fuzzy. He'd heard the story from Kate on Sunday while they waited for Mary Rose to get back from escorting Miss Taylor, but he enjoyed watching her laugh as she recounted finding the dog hip deep in kabobs. That was the image he wanted to keep—her smile wide, her blue eyes bright.

But he spent a second too long staring at her, because she caught him at it. "Pete!" She slipped past Kate and Kelsey and came toward him. "I didn't know you were here. Thanks for coming."

"I wanted to see how it all turned out. Looks like Trace is luckier than he maybe deserves."

"I think you're right. But I also have a feeling things have taken a turn for the better. Kate really laid into L.T. last night."

Pete grinned. "I notice he's quieter than usual today."

Mary Rose nodded. "Mr. Wilson threatened to put him in jail if he said so much as one word during the hearing. But Trace made it clear to his dad that a lot of what's been going on is a result of his own behavior. I don't know if that'll change much on L.T.'s part. But I think Trace is feeling more like his old self."

The courtroom emptied, and Pete motioned Mary Rose to exit ahead of him. He almost put his hand on her back, but stopped himself just in time. *Off-limits. Remember?*

"And come to find out," he commented as they crossed the parking lot, "that this little old lady of yours belongs to *the* Taylors. Not that the Bowdreys aren't high up on the list of who's who in New Skye, but the Taylors are right there at the top, with the Crawfords and the other 'first families.' Very impressive."

"As if that really mattered. She just wants to thank me for finding the dog." They reached the Volvo, where Kate and the kids were waiting. Mary Rose gazed up at him, her eyes narrowed against the bright sunshine.

"Well, thanks again for coming. And—and for everything. For helping with Trace and Kelsey and..." She blinked hard and looked away. "I'm going back to Charleston on Friday, so this really will be goodbye." Her hand came up, lighted for an instant on his arm.

Then she turned, opened the car door and dropped down on the seat with less grace than he'd ever seen her display. Pete closed the door for her, waved at Kate and Kelsey, then watched as the Volvo left the parking lot.

Friday.

He had a lot of thinking to do before Friday.

WEARING A SILK DRESS and high heels, Mary Rose arrived for tea promptly at four o'clock on Tuesday afternoon. The Taylor house was one of the oldest in town, but while many of the old homes had fallen into ruins, the broad columns of this one were smoothly painted, the wide porch solid underfoot, the gardens beautifully maintained. During their two hundred years in New Skye, the family had found various ways to preserve and even to increase their fortune, so there was always money to keep the house in good repair.

Miss Taylor smiled widely as she opened the door. "Come in, my dear, come in. I'm so glad you could join me."

The house was just as elegant inside as out and filled with antiques, all dusted to shining perfection. Miss Taylor must have quite a household staff. "I'm honored that you invited me, Miss Taylor." She only hoped her hostess would be as pleased to have her as a guest when she explained the idea that had occurred to her in the middle of last night.

"Well, it's the least I could do, after you found Fuzzy for me." She led the way into the parlor. The dog in question lay sound asleep on a red velvet love seat, once again wearing his jeweled collar. "He's been tired these last two days, the poor dear. His adventure Sunday just plain tuckered him out."

The afternoon passed easily enough as Mary Rose sat across the tea table from Miss LuAnne and listened to her ramblings about whatever came to mind, most of it having to do with family and friends from the past. The teapot and cups had a story behind them dating back to "The War," as did the cookies she had baked that morning from a recipe her grandmother used when there was still a wood-burning stove in the kitchen. "Such corn bread that stove would make," Miss LuAnne recalled. "Buttermilk and corn bread was an excellent breakfast."

Then she sighed. "These days it's granola and cranberry juice. Just not the same sensibility at all."

Mary Rose laughed. "No, ma'am. I don't imagine it is."

When their tea grew cold, Miss LuAnne invited her for a walk around the grounds. "I've taken some of my ideas from the Low Country landscapes. Charleston courtyards are renowned for their beautiful gardens. I understand you'll be returning soon?"

"Yes, ma'am, I think it's time for me to get back to my job there."

"You haven't thought of coming home to work? Our community needs bright young women like you."

Now was the time to make her move. If she thought too long, she'd be too scared to say anything. So she simply plunged in. "Miss LuAnne, I don't think I can stay and work here, much as I'd like to. But I do know of someone who makes really important contributions to New Skye. He works with kids who are in trouble, like my nephew." She winced as LuAnne frowned. There wasn't anyone in New Skye who didn't know by now what Trace and his friends had done.

Still, she had to try. "My friend—his name is Pete Mitchell and he's a state trooper—runs an excellent program teaching these kids skills they can use to get jobs and become productive members of the community. But the city has cut the police budget and the police have cut his budget and he's down to bare bones, when he should be able to expand and offer new courses and new options to his kids."

They had stopped beside a dogwood tree that was leafing out, its blossoms fading away. Miss LuAnne picked one of the shriveled blooms and held it in her hand. "And what is your suggestion for me?"

"I thought…you might consider supporting Pete's program. And perhaps you have friends who might contribute, as well. It's presumptuous and rude, probably, when you invited me for a lovely afternoon, but I'm leaving town and I really hate that he won't be able to continue helping his kids."

Miss LuAnne studied the wisp of flower on her palm for a moment, then looked up and smiled. "You tell your Pete to give me a call."

Mary Rose let out a relieved breath.

"And tell him that if he lets you go back to Charleston, he's too big a fool for me to give money to."

WELL, she wouldn't tell Pete that part, of course. But she did call him Tuesday night, only to reach his answering machine.

"Pete, it's Mary Rose. I don't know how long I've got on this message, so I'll talk fast. I went to tea with Miss Taylor this afternoon and I mentioned your REWARDS program to her and suggested that she might contribute, and that she might have friends who would contribute. I mean, everybody in town knows the Taylors have always been rich as Croesus. Anyway, I thought she might be offended, but she wasn't and she told me to tell you to call her. I think that's a really promising sign, because she can connect you with the people in town who have lots of time for fund-raising and who know the other people who are willing to donate.''

She took a deep breath. ''And I would be happy to write grant applications for you. I can research the foundations and I think I understand what you're doing well enough to represent the program favorably. I'd run the applications by you, of course, before I sent them anywhere.'' *And you wouldn't have to see me, or even talk to me. We could do it all by mail if that's what you want.* But she didn't say that, either.

''So let me know if you want me to get started. And let me know what Miss Taylor says.''

After hesitating for too long, she decided to finish with what was in her heart. ''I can't leave without letting you know that you're wrong about what I think of you. You're the finest, most honorable, most dependable man I've ever known. I would be proud to stand beside you in front of anybody, anywhere, anytime. This world needs more men and women like you—people who are willing to meet their responsibilities and make the extra effort to improve their neighborhood, their town, their country. You're a hero, Pete. You're my hero. I only hope that one day I can be half as brave and effective as you are.''

The beep sounded. She'd run out of time. Probably just as well, because the next sentence was ''I love you.'' And he didn't want to hear that.

So Mary Rose whispered the words to herself.

SCREENING HIS CALLS, because there really wasn't anybody he wanted to talk to these days, Pete sat by the answering machine in a state of suspended animation for what must have been hours.

Mary Rose's message was too monumental to take in. The part about Miss Taylor was great, of course. He'd give it his best shot.

But the rest…what did it mean?

He replayed the message a dozen times, and still wasn't sure. Was this just a farewell address designed to smooth troubled waters? Or the beginnings of a bridge built to cross those waters and bring two islands together?

And when had he started thinking in such highbrow metaphors?

He ate supper at the diner after work Wednesday night, with all the time in the world because he'd canceled the REWARDS classes on Mondays and Wednesdays.

The crowd was light, and Abby sat down with him to have a glass of tea. "My yellow wall is still yellow."

"I noticed that. I don't think you'll be having as much trouble from now on. The problem seems to have been dealt with."

"Some kids'll go pretty far to signal that they need help."

"Yeah. Remember that guy who burned the class records just before graduation? What was his name?"

She didn't hesitate with the answer. "Noah Blake."

"That's right. Noah was always in trouble, as far back as I remember. His dad abandoned the family, wasn't it something like that? Noah set fire to the principal's office and then disappeared. I always wondered what happened to him."

Abby stirred her tea with her straw. "Me, too."

Pete finished up half his burger, but the other half

seemed like too much to handle. He pushed the plate to the side. "Guess I'll wander home, let Miss Dixie out."

"You want some coconut pie? Dad's lost his twenty pounds and I made just one pie to celebrate."

He wasn't really hungry, but he wasn't ready to go home, either. The house seemed kind of empty these days. He felt guilty about that, because Miss Dixie was doing her best. But some roles a dog just couldn't fill. "Sure. I'll have a piece of pie."

Abby brought a plate for both of them. "I need this like I need a hole in the head," she said. And then took the first bite. "But maybe you do need a hole in your head."

Pete groaned. "Don't start."

"You're just going to let her go? Let her walk out of your life again? When it's so clear she's exactly what you need?"

He ran a hand over his face. "The woman has a choice, you know. I can't drag her by the hair back to my cave and keep her there. She has to want what I want."

"And you think she doesn't?"

"I—"

"All I can say is, I've never seen anybody as miserable over a Super Dooper Triple Scooper as Mary Rose Bowdrey was last night. And the night before that. And three nights last week." She got to her feet and stacked up the empty pie plates. "Amazing, she can eat all those banana splits and still look like she's losing weight."

PACKING HER SUITCASES was one of the hardest things Mary Rose had done in a long, long time. She'd come to think of Kate's lovely guest room as her own, had come to feel as if she was home.

But Marty had called again on Thursday morning, pressuring her to return to Charleston. Her boss had called, too, with a not-too-subtle inquiry as to whether she still wanted the job.

And Pete hadn't called. So the decision was pretty much cut-and-dried.

Her parents came to dinner Thursday night. There were the predictable exclamations from Frances about what Trace had done, and somehow the story of Sal's visit and L.T.'s reaction had reached her, too. "I hope you've put an end to that relationship," she told Kate. "Completely unsuitable, as I'm sure you agree."

"Kelsey has a right to choose her own friends," Kate said quietly. "I'm allowing her the chance to prove her judgment is sound in this particular situation."

"But as her parent—"

"As her parent, I'm capable of making these decisions on my own. And…" She drew a deep breath. "And while I appreciate your advice, Mama, I would be grateful if you left the discipline of my children to me."

Frances stared at her daughter with her mouth open for a few seconds, then snapped her jaw shut with an audible click. She didn't venture another criticism during the rest of the meal…which didn't leave her much to say.

Later, as Mary Rose stood alone with her mother in the kitchen making up dessert plates and pouring coffee, Frances suddenly came over, put her hands on Mary Rose's shoulders and looked into her face.

"I've only wanted what would be best for you," Frances said quietly. "Perhaps I haven't always known what that was. But it's what your father and I both wanted."

Mary Rose enfolded her with a hug. "I know, Mama.

I know. And when I figure out what it is, I'll be sure to tell you, too.''

Her mother leaned back and smiled. ''That would be a change for the better.''

Kelsey and Trace and Kate were waiting in the kitchen Friday morning when Mary Rose came into the house after loading the car. They'd made breakfast—blueberry pancakes and sausages and fresh-squeezed orange juice.

''This looks delicious,'' she said, sitting down at her regular place. But she couldn't seem to eat a bite. When she glanced around the table, she saw that none of the others were eating, either. Tears stung her eyes and she stood up again. ''You know, I think we'll do better if I just get on the road. No sense in dragging out goodbye.''

They all stood out by the Porsche and cried. Even Trace had tears on his cheeks as he gave her an awkward hug with his newly casted arm. ''I'm sorry,'' he whispered in her ear. ''If you'll come back, I'll do better. Really.''

She held his face in her hands. ''I know. And I will come back. I want to see you on the varsity soccer team.''

Kelsey embraced her tightly. ''Oh, Aunt M, what are we gonna do without you?'' Without warning, she started sobbing against Mary Rose's shoulder.

''You're gonna be okay, that's what.'' Mary Rose stroked the silky hair. ''We'll talk on the phone and e-mail and you'll come see me this summer. Maybe you can bring Sal with you to the beach.'' Kelsey drew back, smiling through her tears. ''He can sleep in Trace's room.''

Trace growled and started to stalk back toward the house. Halfway there, he turned and came back. ''You're teasing, right?''

Mary Rose laughed and went to Kate, taking her hands. "I know you're going to be okay. If you can beat up on L. T. LaRue, you can handle the rest of the world."

"I couldn't have survived without you." Kate blinked away tears, which just kept falling. "I'm still not sure…"

"Oh, yes, you are. You've got two great kids to help you. The three of you are a family and that's all you need." She took a deep breath. "And those two kids are late for school. So y'all go on. I'll wave goodbye to you before I take off."

They left, finally, with numerous backward glances and one final hug from Kelsey. Mary Rose leaned against the door of the Porsche as casually as she could, waving, smiling with her eyes almost shut against her own tears. The Volvo pulled slowly out of the driveway and went by her with Kelsey calling "Write me!" through the window. Then Kate turned the corner, and they were gone.

Mary Rose sat in the Porsche for a long, long time and cried.

But she shouldn't be there when Kate came back, so eventually she started the engine and pulled away from the curb. Driving slowly around Courthouse Circle and through downtown, she noted that the cleanup efforts were just about done. The broken planters had yet to be replaced—they had to be specially ordered and cast by a pottery in Ohio. But the shop owners along Main had done what they could to restore the peaceful, settled ambience. L.T. would be paying big bucks for the restoration. Mary Rose almost smiled at the thought. If anyone deserved to pay, it was surely L.T.

Once out of the business district, she drove without thinking, trying to block thoughts of what—and who— she was leaving behind, trying to generate some enthusiasm for what lay ahead. Maybe she would find a new place to live, an older house, even one of the historic residences. The newness of her condo suddenly bothered her. It seemed so cold. So lacking in personality.

Would Marty want to live in a two-hundred-year-old house?

How could she possibly marry Marty after loving Pete again?

A couple of miles short of the interstate, she heard a siren in the distance, realized it was coming in her direction. When she checked her mirrors, though, she didn't see the ambulance or fire engine she expected. A police car edged up behind her, blue lights flashing in her weary eyes.

Mary Rose glanced at the speedometer. Dammit, she wasn't speeding this time. She was barely going the limit. For once, she really did not deserve a ticket. And she was going to tell this guy what she thought of being pulled over for absolutely nothing at all.

She braked the Porsche to a sliding stop on the shoulder of the highway. Without bothering to pull out her license and registration, she shoved the door open and lunged out of the car.

The officer was walking toward her, his face shaded by his state trooper's hat. "Now look here," she started, "I was barely even going the speed limit. My inspections and registration are up to date and you...have absolutely no...business..." Her frustration sputtered its way to a shocked silence as Pete came closer, taking off his hat and his shades.

"Hey, Mary Rose."

She squared her shoulders, attempted to regain some dignity. "I wasn't speeding."

"I know."

"So why did you stop me?"

"I missed you at Kate's house. Short of an all-points bulletin, this was the only way I could think of to catch you before you left town."

"I—" She didn't have any more words.

He laid his hat and sunglasses on the roof of the Porsche. "I talked to Miss LuAnne for a long time yesterday."

Disappointment nearly crushed her, but she kept her head up, her eyes on his. "Is she going to help you out?"

"Well, there was one stipulation to her generosity."

"Which was?"

"She said she wouldn't give me the money if I was such a fool as to let you leave town."

"So this…traffic stop…is about getting money from Miss LuAnne?"

His big hands came down on her shoulders. "No, this is about me finally admitting that I can't go back to living without you. I love you, Mary Rose Bowdrey. Please don't go. Stay and marry me."

"Oh, Pete." She was crying again, and she hid her face in her hands. "I thought I'd ruined everything."

He put his arms around her gently. "I'm the one who did that, by dragging the past into the present. After insisting that we aren't the same people as we were back then, I got everything confused."

"I was so afraid that we'd end up hurting each other again. And it was the fear that hurt us."

"Fear is always the enemy." He tilted her head back, brushed her hair out of her face. "I'll try to be brave, if you will."

"I love you." She linked her arms around his neck and drew his head down. "I love you and I'm going to die if you don't kiss me."

"Wouldn't want that on my conscience." His lips covered hers, commanding, persuading, in control and yet completely vulnerable to her least desire.

When the nearby honk of car horns and the comments of spectators became too loud, Mary Rose pulled back. "Here we are, at it again. Public displays of affection for all the world to see."

But the horn and the cheers hadn't stopped when the kisses did. She looked around in annoyance…and saw Kate's Volvo parked behind the highway patrol cruiser. Kelsey and Trace were sitting in the open windows, cheering at the tops of their lungs. Kate was in the driver's seat—responsible for that annoying horn!

Mary Rose hid her face against Pete's shoulder for a moment. Then she grabbed his hand and marched over to scold her family.

"What do you think you're doing? Why aren't you in school?" But she couldn't keep up the angry pretense for long. "He came after me," she said softly to Kate.

Her sister smiled serenely. "I knew he would."

"I STILL HAVE to go back to Charleston."

Pete tightened his arm around Mary Rose's shoulders and placed a kiss on her hair. "I know. I'm thinking about taking some leave time and going with you. Just so this guy down there knows what the situation is."

With a push of his foot, he set the glider in motion again. The night was perfect—deep purple twilight, a little cool once the sun went down, so Miss Dixie's warmth, stretched across both their laps, felt good.

Mary Rose stroked the beagle's head. "That might be nice. I think I could enjoy having you get all possessive over me."

"I'm happy to oblige. 'Sorry, dude, but the lady is mine.'"

"Yours. Always."

He turned a little so he could face her, catch her mouth with his. Miss Dixie grumbled and readjusted her position.

"Mine," Pete repeated, pressing kisses on her eyes, her lips. "The first and third—"

Mary Rose held up a hand, the one with his ring on it—an emerald-cut diamond flanked by sapphires to match her eyes. "And final."

"The first, third and most definitely final Mrs. Mitchell. Has a nice sound to it, don't you think?"

Mary Rose snuggled into his hold with a soft, satisfied sigh. "Perfect."

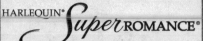

HARLEQUIN *Super*ROMANCE®

A Baby of Her Own
by Brenda Novak

She's pregnant. And she's on her own—or is she?

One night, one baby.
Delaney Lawson wants a baby more than anything in the world, but there are absolutely no prospects in her small Idaho town of Dundee. Then one night she meets a handsome stranger in Boise—a stranger who doesn't plan to stay a stranger long....

Another gripping and emotional story from this powerful writer.
Brenda Novak's "books are must-reads for the hopeless romantics among us."
—Bestselling author Merline Lovelace

Available in September wherever Harlequin books are sold.

HARLEQUIN®
Makes any time special ®

Visit us at www.eHarlequin.com

HSRBOHO

A
BETTY
NEELS
Christmas

What better way to celebrate the joyous
holiday season than with this special
anthology that celebrates the talent of
beloved author Betty Neels? Bringing to
readers two of Betty's trademark
tender romances, this volume will
make the perfect gift for
all romance readers.

*Available in October 2002
wherever paperbacks are sold.*

HARLEQUIN®
Makes any time special®

Visit us at www.eHarlequin.com

PHBNC

This is the family reunion you've been waiting for!

TRUEBLOOD
Christmas

JASMINE CRESSWELL
TARA TAYLOR QUINN
& KATE HOFFMANN

deliver three brand new Trueblood, Texas stories.

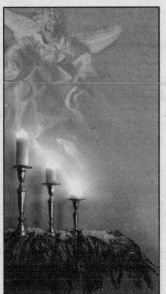

After many years, Major Brad Henderson is released from prison, exonerated after almost thirty years for a crime he didn't commit. His mission: to be reunited with his three daughters. How to find them? Contact Dylan Garrett of the Finders Keepers Detective Agency!

Look for it in November 2002.

HARLEQUIN®

Makes any time special ®

Visit us at www.eHarlequin.com

PHTBTCR

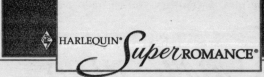

Montana Dreaming
by Nadia Nichols

Lack of money forces Jessie Weaver to sell the ranch her family has owned since the mid-1800s—and creates a rift between her and her boyfriend, Guthrie Sloane, that's as big as the Montana sky. But a grizzly on the loose, a crazy bear-hunting U.S. senator and a love that neither she nor Guthrie can deny soon make selling her Montana ranch the least of her worries!

Heartwarming stories with a sense of humor, genuine charm and emotion and lots of family!

On sale starting September 2002.

Available wherever Harlequin books are sold.

Visit us at www.eHarlequin.com

HSRMD

International bestselling author

SANDRA MARTON

invites you to attend the

WEDDING *of the* YEAR

Glitz and glamour prevail in this volume
containing a trio of stories in which
three couples meet at a
high society wedding—and
soon find themselves
walking down the aisle!

Look for it in November 2002.

Visit us at www.eHarlequin.com

BR3WOTY-R

eHARLEQUIN.com

community | membership
buy books | authors | online reads | magazine | learn to write

magazine

♥——————————————————— **quizzes**

Is he the one? What kind of lover are you? Visit the **Quizzes** area to find out!

♥——————————————————— **recipes for romance**

Get scrumptious meal ideas with our **Recipes for Romance**.

♥——————————————————— **romantic movies**

Peek at the **Romantic Movies** area to find Top 10 Flicks about First Love, ten Supersexy Movies, and more.

♥——————————————————— **royal romance**

Get the latest scoop on your favorite royals in **Royal Romance**.

♥——————————————————— **games**

Check out the **Games** pages to find a ton of interactive romantic fun!

♥——————————————————— **romantic travel**

In need of a romantic rendezvous? Visit the **Romantic Travel** section for articles and guides.

♥——————————————————— **lovescopes**

Are you two compatible? Click your way to the **Lovescopes** area to find out now!

HARLEQUIN® ♥♥

makes any time special—online...

Visit us online at
www.eHarlequin.com

HINTMAG